POLLY PILGRIM

Polly Pilgrim was a tall girl, a plumpish girl with a cloud of corn-coloured, wavy hair. Her mouth, though too wide for beauty, was normally set to smile, but that day it had a melancholy droop to it. At thirty-three, her face was unlined and had the open candour of a guileless child. She had borne a daughter, then a son with ease, and breast-fed them with pleasure. She cherished those she loved with a fierce and abiding protection. She loved children, dogs and old people, not with sentimentality, but with an all-embracing affection. Today she looked her age . . .

Polly Pilgrim

Marie Joseph

ARROW BOOKS

Arrow Books Limited
62–65 Chandos Place, London WC2N 4NW

An imprint of Century Hutchinson Ltd

London Melbourne Sydney Auckland
Johannesburg and agencies throughout
the world

First published 1984
Reprinted 1987
© Marie Joseph 1984

Phototypeset by Input Typesetting Ltd, London SW19 8DR
in Plantin
Printed and bound in Great Britain
by Anchor Brendon Ltd
Tiptree, Essex

ISBN 0 09 932920 4

For Tom Stevenson

— One —

Harry Pilgrim was a quiet man, a softly-spoken, reserved man who rarely lost his temper. But on that Sunday morning in September he stormed up the uncarpeted stairs in the cottage, leaving his wife, Polly, and his mother-in-law staring at each other in astonishment.

His voice, hoarse with uncontrolled rage, spiralled down to them: 'Out of bed this minute, Gatty! D'you hear me? If you're not up this minute, I'm coming in. You're not too old to have the blankets whipped off you, nor to feel the flat of my hand on your backside!'

'Your dad doesn't mean it, love.' Polly spoke quietly to her son standing at the foot of the stairs, his young face creased into lines of anxiety.

Then she turned to her mother. 'It's because he can't bear not having enough work to do. Harry doesn't feel right when he's not working. A man has to bring up his family with money earned from his own graft. You know that, Mam. It's been slowly killing him these past months hanging about with hardly anything to do.'

Polly's blue eyes were pleading as her husband clattered back down the stairs. 'Don't be too hard on Gatty, love. You know what long hours she has to put in at the shop, and last night she went dancing after finishing at eight o'clock. It's no wonder she wants to lie in.'

Harry Pilgrim held up his hands as if in supplication. 'That's right! Rub it in. Make it clear that my fifteen-year-old daughter is the bread-winner in this house. Show me up good and proper!'

His boots squeaked as he walked hump-shouldered towards the door. 'If you're coming with me, Martin, get a move on. If not, stop where you are.'

At a nod from Polly, the tall fair boy, thin wrists protruding from the sleeves of his grey pullover, followed his father outside. From the window Polly watched them go.

There was beauty all around, stretching as far as the eye could see. Over to the east the darkly smooth mass of Pendle Hill; to the west the long wooded valley, and beyond, far beyond, the Irish Sea. Already, in mid September, the thin sparse grass had died, and its faded colour was broken by rough, grey stones. The distant hills, covered by purple heather, drifted in mist, but on the lower slopes gorse blazed in sunburst clumps of glory.

Polly Pilgrim was a tall girl, a plumpish girl with a cloud of corn-coloured, wavy hair. Her mouth, though too wide for beauty, was normally set to smile, but that day it had a melancholy droop to it. At thirty-three, her face was unlined and had the open candour of a guileless child. She had borne a daughter, then a son with ease, and breast-fed them with pleasure. She cherished those she loved with a fierce and abiding protection. She loved children, dogs and old people, not with sentimentality, but with an all-embracing affection. Today she looked her age.

Her mother joined her at the window. 'Shine before

seven, rain before eleven, I always say.' She glared accusingly at the cloudless sky. 'Views are all right for folks who have the time to stand about gawping at them. If you want my opinion, when you've seen one you've seen the lot.'

Polly sighed heavily. She could do without her mother's gloomy predictions at the moment, but because loving came more naturally than exasperation, she merely shook her head in mock reproof.

'Oh, Mam . . . I know you hate it up here, but here's where I live and I'm happy enough. You know me.'

'Oh aye, I know you all right.'

Edna Myerscough sniffed. She wore her hat to protect the hard ridges of a recent perm, but had removed her coat so as to feel the benefit when she went back down the hill to catch her bus into town. If she lived to be a hundred, she often told herself, she'd never forgive her son-in-law for bringing her Polly to live up here in the back of beyond. Settling herself down on a chair as heavily as if she weighed fourteen stone instead of barely seven, she watched Polly take a roasting-tin from the fire oven.

'Rabbit again?' She chewed reflectively on nothing for a moment. 'Still, rabbit does come up like chicken if it's cooked slow.' She sniffed again as she stared round the untidy living-room. For by no means the first time, she told herself that if her only daughter could have bided her time instead of marrying the first man to come along, she could be living now in one of the new council houses on the Brownlow Estate on the outskirts of the nearby cotton town. She could have had a bathroom upstairs and a lavatory inside, instead of having to use that terrible hut where you sat on a plank with a hole in it, suspended over a bucket.

The cottage had been built in the first decade of the nineteenth century, and had a date stone over the door to prove it. The triple windows at the front bore evidence to the fact that it had once, long ago, been the family house of hand-loom weavers. The windows were made of small square panes, framed in lead, once protected by shutters. In the partitioned off, barely-used parlour next to the kitchen-cum-living-room, constant plastering of the walls had left the mortar soft. Harry had explained, with a kind of reverence, that in those far off days a water trough ran the length of the house to keep the air moist and prevent the cotton threads from snapping. Edna saw nothing to swank about in that. After all, it was 1933 now not the Dark Ages!

'I might put my coat on,' she said. 'It always smells damp in this place, and my rheumatism always plays me up at the back end.' She gave a cursory glance through the window at a towering oak tree, its flimsy leaves drifting down like red and gold pieces of tissue paper. 'It always strikes me when the leaves are on the turn.'

'Harry's going away tomorrow.'

Polly spoke quickly before her mother had time to reach for her coat. The sight of Edna sitting round the Sunday dinner table muffled to the eyeballs was one she could do without today. Already she felt bereft, anticipating the comfortless width of the feather mattress of their double bed without Harry's body warm beside her. He was her child, just as Gatty and Martin were her children. Her love for him was as much maternal as passionate, and his unhappiness reflected itself in Polly's own heart. One day, returning from an abortive search for work, he had stretched out his arms to her.

'I've nothing but what I've got in these hands,' he had shouted. 'Make them idle and I'm finished.'

The words had almost broken her heart.

'Going away? Where to? What do you mean, he's going away?' Polly saw her mother's pale blue eyes pop with surprise. 'Has he got another woman?'

Before she answered, Polly moved a pan of potatoes on its trivet nearer the fire. Then, turning round, she pushed a strand of hair away from her hot face.

'Harry's decided that as he can't find enough work round here to keep him going, he might as well go down south and try there.' She twisted a corner of her apron round and round in her fingers. 'He's had hardly any work at all for over a year now, and it's getting him down. You heard him shout at Gatty just now? That wasn't Harry talking, it was his frustration. He's desperate, Mam.'

'She's still up there, stopping in bed.'

Polly ignored her. Opening the drawer set in the side of the square table, she took out a handful of knives and forks.

'Nobody wants gardeners any more, not even special ones like Harry. The mills and factories are closing, so the bosses in the big houses have to cut back. They're managing with less servants, and the odd-job man does the garden. But Harry's a *specialist*, Mam. He's a landscape gardener; he's never been anything else.'

'Has he tried to get work down the town?'

'What as? There are skilled men being laid off every day. What chance would Harry have? Anyway, you know what the doctor said when he came back from the war. He will always have to work outside because of his chest.'

'And I suppose there's plenty of outdoor jobs going down London way?'

'We don't *know*, Mam. But the Depression hasn't hit

11

down south as much as it has up here. There's more money, bigger houses. They don't even understand what's going on up here.'

'Southerners think they're it. Always had it cushy that lot have.'

'Harry wrote to Kew Gardens and had a letter promising nothing but saying they'd see him. He'll be over the moon if he gets taken on there.'

Polly looked down at the knives and forks in her hands as if wondering what they were. 'The way things are, I can't bear to see Harry's self-respect seeping away. He's got to do *something* about it or die.'

'Now you're talking like an a'penny book.'

'No, I'm not, Mam! It was in the paper last week that there are over two-and-a-half million unemployed. That's a lot of men on the dole.' She frowned. 'Harry says that if *he* applied for the dole they would actually deduct his war disability pension from it.'

'So that would mean he went to France and got gassed by those Germans for nothing.' Edna spoke with a morbid satisfaction.

'Mam? Can't you see? He's *ashamed* of not getting steady work, and seeing Harry ashamed makes me want to cry. You know how proud he is.'

'His Romany blood,' Edna said at once. 'Gypsies are like that. And his grandfather was one, so don't go looking at me like that. I wouldn't be surprised if it didn't come out that his grandmother knocked on doors selling pegs and putting a curse on folks if they didn't buy a bundle. Bad blood will out. Nature always tells in the long run.'

Beneath the green hat, modelled like a flying helmet, Edna's mind was in a ferment. If her son-in-law got himself fixed up with a job down south, then his family

12

would follow on. The thought of the left-over years of her life lived without a weekly visit to Polly's house filled her with a dread that sharpened her features into a vixen-like mask of despair.

'He married you when you were seventeen,' she said bitterly. 'A girl hardly out of her gym-slip. Then he brought you to live at the top of a hill in a cottage with no emneties.' She frowned. Surely that word wasn't right? Still, *she* knew what she meant. 'You could have picked and choosed if you'd only waited. It's a wonder he didn't bring you to a caravan painted red and yellow, and sat you out on the steps with gold ear-rings dangling. When your Harry told me he could find his God in the hedgerows instead of in chapel, I had his measure straight off.'

A dog barked and Polly jumped up with relief. Harry was coming home. As she laid out the knives and forks she wondered what her mother's reaction would be if she suddenly said: 'But don't you see that I married Harry because I was drowning in love for him. I would have worn ear-rings as big as hoops and a red scarf round my hair at the time if that was what he'd wanted of me.'

She hurried to the door. Love was not a word bandied about loosely in her mother's vocabulary. Love, for Edna, was for soppy women who dyed their hair and read poetry in bed. In the whole of Polly's life, she realized with a pang, she could never remember her mother once holding her in her arms and speaking of love. And yet it was there, hidden inside Edna's unnecessarily corseted frame. She was sure of that. It was just not her way to speak of it.

They were coming up the cinder path now to the cottage – the dog called Jim, a mongrel bred from mong-rels, trotting to heel at Harry's side, and Martin, walking pigeon-toed, swishing a stick at nothing. Polly sighed as she saw the leaning stoop of her husband's thin shoulders. Harry was as dark as his wife was fair, a man with the shortish stature of one who comes from generations of cotton-mill workers. And gypsies, she reminded herself, her eyes twinkling.

The maternal, un-Romany side of Harry's family had been among the pioneers of the Industrial Revolution, forced from their hand-looms, he had told Polly, by the onset of machinery. Harry's grandmother had borne her children in a two-up, two-down terraced house in the very shadow of the tall mill chimneys. She had sent those children off, one after another, at the age of twelve, to stand at their looms on damp stone floors as half-timers. And she had buried two of them with rheumatic fever.

No wonder Harry had rebelled. No wonder he couldn't find his God in the ranting hell-fire sermons of the Wesleyans, seeking Him instead in the fields and hills and moors of his beloved Lancashire countryside.

'The dinner's nearly ready,' Polly told him, relieved to see his face was smoothed of its anger once again.

'It smells good.' Harry touched his wife's cheek gently with a finger.

As they went inside, Gatty appeared at the foot of the stairs, eyes puffed with the weeping that these days came as naturally to her as breathing.

Harry smiled at her, but looked away from the sight of his mother-in-law's pointed features set in lines of deep distrust between the false ear flaps of the atrocious hat.

When Polly climbed back up the hill after seeing her mother off on the bus back to her neat little house in

14

town, Gatty was standing at the mirror nailed over the slop-stone, gazing at herself, outlining her lips in Tangee lipstick.

'You're not going out on your dad's last night at home?'

Polly spoke without hope. Since turning fifteen, Gatty tended to treat her mother's every utterance with contempt, raising her eyebrows ceilingwards as if seeking the patience to tide her over to Polly's next stupid remark. Now she merely shrugged her shoulders, without turning round.

'I asked you a question, Gatty.' Polly fought down the exasperation rising in her throat. From the back Gatty looked like the good little girl she had been not all that long ago, thin legs protruding from beneath the gathered skirt of her striped cotton dress. Her hair, black like Harry's, hung like the hair on a Japanese doll, straight and shining almost to her shoulders. But when she turned round, Polly saw her cheeks had been dotted with rouge the same orange shade as the lipstick.

No longer able to keep her temper in check, Polly snatched up a flannel from the soap-dish and held it out.

'You can just wipe that muck off your face, Gatty. You don't need it, not at your age.' Reaching out she tried to draw Gatty towards her.

Immediately Gatty stepped back, eyes flashing. Grabbing the flannel from Polly's hand, she hurled it against the far wall.

'At my age!' she yelled. 'That's all I hear in this house! You were married at not much more than my age, remember? Why can't you leave me alone? Why can't you ever leave me ALONE?'

Polly leaned back against the table, feeling the need for support. 'Where are you going?' she asked quietly.

15

Again the dark eyes uplifted. 'To Winnie's house, if you must know.'

'Yes, I must.'

Gatty reached for her beige, swing-backed jacket, bought from C & A sales in the summer. 'Winnie doesn't have to account for her every movement. Her mother doesn't pry like you.'

Closing her eyes for a moment, Polly saw her daughter's bosom friend Winnie, red-haired, with freckles dotting her pale face like the surface of an unstirred glass of Horlicks malted milk. A small girl with pointed, foxy features and small eyes set slyly above a sharp nose.

'Was it Winnie you went dancing with last night after you'd both finished at the shop?'

Gatty dredged a sigh up from her chest, tiny bosoms sticking out like ice-cream cones in the new uplift bra. 'I know you don't like her. You don't like any of my friends.'

She moved towards the door, the coat swinging out as she turned. 'Winnie keeps asking me to stop the night at her house. She thinks it's daft me coming back on the bus to the village, then having to walk all the way up the hill.' She gave Polly a quick, underhand look. 'Mebbe when me dad's gone we'll get a house to rent down the town. We only live here because of him, anyroad.'

As this was a truth never openly acknowledged, Polly felt anger surface again. 'Don't you care about your dad going away, Gatty? Don't you know it's breaking his heart having to leave us?'

Slowly Gatty licked a finger and slowly drew it across first one dark winged eyebrow then the other. She shrugged, closing both eyes as her shoulders ascended almost to her ears.

16

'Does it matter?' she asked wearily, lifting the heavy sneck of the door, opening it just wide enough to slip through before closing it behind her.

'Gatty!'

Wrenching the door open so furiously it swung back against the plaster wall, Polly shouted at the top of her voice. What did it matter if she sounded like one of the common women her mother was always going on about. There was no one to hear; not for miles around was there anyone to hear. She could yell her head off and nobody would come running.

'You come back here, you cheeky young devil! I'll learn you to talk to me like that!'

In her rage she forgot her grammar. Hurt, mingled with anger, flushed the bright colour in her cheeks to an even deeper rose. If she hadn't seen the man plodding down towards the cottage from the hills, she would have chased after Gatty and landed her one as she'd often done when, as a rebellious child, her daughter had openly defied her. Without once making her cry, Polly remembered, going back wearily into the cottage.

And if Jack Thomson had seen her raising her arms and yelling like a fishwife, then he gave no sign. Polly watched him from the window, holding her hand over her breasts as if to still the pounding of her heart.

Jack Thomson walked on down the hill, treading softly with his soldier's steady plod a walk that ill-matched his big body. Polly leaned closer to the window. Jack was a handsome man, no doubt about that, with his thick brown curly hair and his strange, green eyes fringed with girlish lashes. Suddenly he began to run.

To catch Gatty up, Polly suspected. The thought made her bite her lips. There were things she'd heard about Jack and the pitiful women patients at the nearby mental

17

hospital where he worked as an orderly; always the young ones, it was rumoured. His wife would be waiting for him in their ramshackle cottage at the bottom of the hill. Bella Thomson was a tiny woman, built like a scribble, with a habit of blinking sandy eyelashes over pale eyes of an indeterminate shade. Polly had often asked herself how Bella had ever managed to produce even such a sickly baby as their seven-month-old son. Bella was all right though. Cowed and frightened of her husband as she was, she could hold her own when they were having one of their frequent shouting matches. There was still plenty of spirit in the untidy little body. And though Polly suspected that Jack knocked his wife about (finding it hard to believe that any woman could black her eye quite so often against a door, as Bella claimed), her little piping voice could often be heard intermingling with Jack's loud bellows.

'I've just seen Jack Thomson, but he was in too much of a hurry to stop. I'd have liked a word with him before tomorrow,' said Harry, as he came in with Martin, their arms loaded with logs.

'Jack told me he'll see you right for wood. He's a strange one all right is Jack, surly one minute then all over you the next.' Balling a fist, Harry cuffed his son affectionately on the shoulder. 'We've been watching a tree sparrow, this lad and me. He thought there was only one kind, didn't you, lad?'

Martin's voice was as chirpy as the little bird's he now described. 'It had a tiny black cap, like a skull-cap, our Mam. It was in a blackthorn bush.' He piled his logs in the large clothes basket set in the hearth. 'Did you know, Mam, that if a plant has four petals it's called a Latin name?' He hesitated, then at a nod from Harry went on. 'A *cruciferae*. You know, like a cross with four bits to it.

18

They won't need to teach me Latin when I start at the grammar school next week. I'll be able to tell them me dad's learned it me already.'

'*Taught* you already.' Harry winked at his wife. 'I'd best go up and put a few more things together if I'm to be off at first light in the morning.'

Bending his head as if he needed to shield it from the height of the low ceiling, he disappeared from view up the narrow winding staircase leading to the three rooms upstairs.

'Why does me dad have to go away?'

At the hoarse sound of her son's voice Polly turned round quickly, dismayed to see tears glistening on the stubbly eyelashes framing eyes as blue as her own. Martin was rocking his father's chair backwards and forwards as if the rhythmic movement gave him comfort.

'It's spoilin' everything me dad going away. If he goes and gets a job down south I'll have to leave me new school, won't I?' His voice quavered. 'An' I might have been picked for the cricket team. Besides, Arnold's going – you know Arnold Bolton – an' he says we can be mates, with him and me being the only ones from the bottom school to pass the scholarship.'

Polly knew her son. She knew the way his orderly mind worked. The phrase 'a place for everything and everything in its place' might have been written by Martin. His room upstairs was as neat as a captain's cabin, with his Meccano set pigeon-holed into little drawers, his comics arranged in two piles, one for *Wizard* and one for *Adventure*. His father going away interrupted the pattern. The tears were running unheeded now into the rolled collar of his grey pullover.

'Anyroad, me dad doesn't want to go. He's only reck-

19

oning on he does. An' Jim doesn't like it neither. He's only a dog, but dogs *know*.'

As if understanding, the dog raised its nose, whimpered, then settled down again into an uneasy, twitching sleep.

'Maybe it'll only be for a little while. Things are bound to buck up soon, then he'll be back. There's a lot of water to go under the bridge before we think of moving to another place.'

Polly lifted her chin to stare through the window. In the last rays of the dying sun the hills blazed as if on fire. When she went to kneel beside the rocking-chair, Martin was sobbing quietly, his tears seeming as constant and inevitable as the flow of a river.

Harry walked the dog down the hill later that night, ostensibly to give Jim his run out, but in reality to meet Gatty off the last bus back from town. When they came in Gatty went straight to bed, turning back at the foot of the stairs to kiss Harry on his cheek.

'Hope you go on all right, Dad,' she mumbled.

'Good night, lass.'

Harry exchanged a smile with his wife as the disconsolate figure plodded upstairs. 'Does she have to behave like a tragedy queen?' he whispered. 'Mebbe she thinks her face'll crack if she smiles.'

It had been a long day and Polly wasn't going to spoil what was left of it by discussing Gatty. Harry's eyes were telling her that he wanted to make love to her, and even after almost seventeen years of marriage the excitement was still there. There was the trick he had of slightly closing his eyes and gazing at her steadily, the way he was doing now. It was all there in his expression – his love for her, his thinking she was beautiful, his tenderness and his passion.

'We'll give Gatty a chance to get off to sleep, then we'll go up.'

Harry nodded. Oh, what was he going to do without her, his lovely Polly? From the minute he'd set eyes on her, he'd loved her. She was warmth, she was light, she was sunshine in a dark room.

When she took the torch and went outside he stood up, kicked the smouldering logs and sent a shower of sparks up the chimney. He put the guard round the fire, unlaced his boots and wound the clock on the mantelpiece. His nightly ritual, as safe and reassuring as the sound of the wind sighing now in the branches of the oak tree.

Never, never would he see her dragged down into real poverty like the wives of the unemployed men down the town. He'd seen them, faces bleak with the worry of penny-pinching, shouting at their husbands for no other reason than that they were there, idling their lives away, till it was time to go out and stand in line at the Labour Exchange, answering personal questions put to them by some chit of a clerk who'd sat out the war on his backside.

He'd calculated they could last four months, maybe six, on the savings accumulated over the years. And by then he'd have got settled; by then they could all be together again. He glanced round the room. What was a house but sticks and stones? To leave the cottage would half destroy him, but to stay would be infinitely worse.

He made love to his wife that night as though for the first time, passion unleashed and uncontrolled, then he slept, sinking deep into the feather mattress, his hand on Polly's rounded thigh.

And lying awake, staring up into the darkness, Polly saw the light on the ceiling and felt a finger of terror touch her heart.

It was a strange, shifting, fluid shape, as if from a lamp held aloft in a wavering hand. Polly had seen it only twice before. Once towards the end of the war when Harry was serving in France, coinciding, she discovered later, with the very day he had breathed in poisonous gas on the Somme, and been carried choking and yellow into the field hospital.

The second time the light appeared was on the night her father died, sighing softly in his sleep, leaving hold of his life as unobtrusively as he had lived it.

Sheer horror held Polly still. Eyes wide, she willed the pulsing light to disappear. The cottage might have stood for three hundred years and more, but there was no such thing as ghosts. They were figments of the imagination, tricks of light and shade; it could even be the moon forming shadows through the thin flowered curtains.

But when she slipped trembling from bed and went over to the window, the darkness outside was absolute, without a single star to pinprick the inky blackness of the sky. Leaving Harry sleeping, Polly crept down the stairs and crouched shivering on the rug by the pale grey ashes of the fire. Soon winter would come; there would be few hikers and picnickers walking down the hill past the cottage on their way to the banks of the river. At the moment the River Ribble meandered peacefully on its way, but winter rains could swell it to a raging torrent and, it was said, that on dark nights a young girl could be heard crying and wailing for her mother.

Superstition. Like the light on the bedroom ceiling, ignorant superstition. Polly felt her scalp crawl with the cold whisper of fear. The story went that a servant girl from one of the big houses spilt water and was cursed by her mistress, who was reputed to be a witch. 'I hope you break your neck!' the poor girl was told, and the curse was effective, because that same day she slipped down the icy bank into the river and was drowned.

The cottage was held in the grip of silence. Polly swayed to and fro with cold, telling herself that the creeping light in the bedroom was just her silly fancy – but not really believing it.

When Harry padded downstairs and knelt beside her, Polly leaned against him, feeling the terror slip away as his arms came round her. When he led her gently back to bed and snuffed out the candle, Polly squeezed her eyes tight shut before daring to open them again.

And the light on the ceiling, along with her dread and the premonition of unhappiness, had gone.

Sighing with relief and shaking her head at her own foolishness, Polly turned into her husband's arms and slept, held fast in his love.

— Two —

It was a bad time for the first few weeks after Harry's going, but somehow Polly managed to make ends meet.

In spite of the depressing state of the economy, the country was also managing to get by, and MPs' salaries were cut drastically.

'And about time,' said Polly's mother. 'I've heard tell them MPs don't get to work till dinner time. Other folks have put in a good half day by then.'

When Harry wrote to say he had been taken on at Kew Polly was thrilled even though he explained that it was only for the time being and then only as a casual labourer, sweeping leaves from the lawns and paths of the big gardens. He was having to pay ten shillings a week for a bed in an attic, he wrote, but he said nothing about the inadequate meals of watery soup and dry bread, or that he was sharing his room with an elderly tramp.

Meanwhile, Polly fed her family on the little she dared to take from their savings, but there was nothing left over for anything else. She kept the savings book behind the clock on the mantelpiece, and took it down often to stare at the balance with growing dismay.

'Reckoning your money up, pretty Polly?'

As startled as if she'd been prodded in the back, Polly whipped round to see Jack Thomson standing in the doorway. He was holding an armful of logs, and the rubber soles of his gumboots made no sound as he padded towards the basket in the hearth.

'I've put the rest outside, love,' he grinned, showing teeth so white and even they didn't look real, 'on the left. My, but it's parky out this morning.'

Quickly Polly replaced the bank book behind the clock.

'I didn't hear you knock, Jack,' she said deliberately. His familiarity was making her feel uneasy. With green eyes narrowed insolently, he was staring at her as if he could see right through her knitted jumper. Polly was aware that it had shrunk in the wash, and that it was straining over her breasts. Instinctively she folded her arms. 'Thanks for the wood and for sawing the logs. I really appreciate that.'

He laughed out loud as if she had said something witty. 'You're a good-looking lass, Polly Pilgrim. I like to see a woman with a bit of meat on her bones. Not like my missus. She looks as if she's been spoke-shaved since she had the nipper.' Pursing his lips he made a kissing noise. 'You know where to come if you get stuck for a bit of that there.'

'Don't say things like that!' Polly heard her voice rise, then became even more rattled as she wondered if he'd been teasing. She thought about his wife – thin, pale and anguished, trying to cope with a baby who vomited most of his feeds back down the front of his flannelette nighties. 'Bella's ill,' she reminded him. 'She's not been well since she had the baby. You know that without me telling you, Jack.'

25

Grinning, he took a step towards her. 'I like it when you lose your temper. I saw you t'other day shouting your head off at your Gatty.' His eyes narrowed. 'You want to watch her,' he said slyly. 'You know what young lasses get up to these days.'

'Do I?' Polly turned her head away from the smell of whisky on his breath. She felt confused and slightly hysterical. If she told him to keep away from Gatty, she could be putting ideas in his head. If they weren't there already, that is. She didn't understand him. One minute he was being kind bringing in the logs, and the next minute he was almost insultingly personal. She wasn't sure how to deal with him, and she knew that if Harry hadn't gone away, he wouldn't dare to speak to her like that.

'Give us a kiss and bit of a cuddle, Polly,' he said thickly. 'Just one friend to another. You'd enjoy it, lass. You're not as straight-laced as you make out. I've met your sort many a time.'

His handsome face was inches from her own. Although Polly was tall he seemed to tower over her, overwhelming her with the strength and animal violence of his big body. His mouth was red, his unshaven chin firm, and his green eyes glittered with excitement.

Polly stepped backwards but, with the table behind her, knew she was trapped. If she screamed no one would hear. As strong as she was, she knew she was no match for this man. She could feel the violence emanating from him, and his hot breath on her face. A shudder ran over her as she remembered the tales she had heard about him, and in that moment she knew them to be true.

He came closer. 'Come on, Polly. Don't hold back. There's nobody looking.'

26

Groping with a hand behind her, Polly opened the table drawer and closed her fingers round the bread knife. She wasn't sure whether she would have the nerve to use it, but with the blood pounding in her ears she knew she would fight if necessary. She wasn't some poor demented woman at the place where he worked, too doped and crazy to stand up for herself. Just let him lay one finger on her and he'd regret it!

When he pushed her away she was so surprised she almost fell. The hard edge of the table caught her in the small of her back as she stumbled, and made her cry out in pain. She had barely regained her balance when she saw with amazement the sudden change in his expression.

The excitement, the wild frustration had disappeared as if someone had taken a sponge and wiped them clean away. The green eyes were indolent now, teasing, unbelievably filled with laughter.

'Thought I was up to summat, didn't you, Polly Pilgrim?'

With a flick of a hairy wrist he took the knife from her, sending it clattering and skidding across the floor. 'I was having you on, you daft pie-can!' He turned and spat into the fire. 'You're too old for me, Mrs Pilgrim! Too old and too clever Dick for me. I wouldn't touch you with a barge pole. Not even if you was to go begging for it on your bended knees!'

Light-footed, with his soldier's tread he walked to the door. As he opened it the dog edged in, jumping up, barking with short staccato barks, tiny paws scrabbling at Jack's faded corduroy trousers, then whimpering with fright as a heavy gumboot sent him skidding across the floor.

'Bloody dog!' he said as he flicked at his trouser leg

as though removing a clinging thread. 'I'll have him one of these days, see if I don't!' Then, as if they'd been having a normal conversation, he said: 'There's two letters for you down at the cottage. I'd have fetched them if I hadn't forgot.'

Raising a hand in a casual farewell salute, he stepped outside, loping away down the path with his hands deep in his pockets.

'Poor old Jim.' Polly went to kneel by the basket where the dog cowered, his whole body panting with distress. She stroked the quivering black coat, and at once a pink tongue came out and licked her hand. Soft brown eyes looked into her face, seeking an explanation.

'You're as flummoxed as me,' Polly whispered, standing up and staring at the door, her face puckered into worry lines. She was sure of one thing – she'd be even more wary of Jack Thomson now. Harry might have tolerated him, but she wasn't going to try to. There was something evil about the big man, something that disturbed her. Sighing heavily she picked up the knife and replaced it in the table drawer. And remembered that Jack had said there were two letters waiting for her down at his cottage.

Pulling on her gumboots at the door, Polly stepped out into the splendour of an autumn morning. Mist seemed to move in harmony with the pearl-grey clouds drifting across the hills, but down in the valley she knew that the sun would be shining. Walking quickly down the steep and rocky slope, she was in shadow one minute and out of it the next. The drystone wall, almost two hundred years old, bisected the hill like a zip down the back of a dress. Polly smiled at the unpoetical way her mind ran on sometimes. Fancy likening an ancient wall to a zip! Harry would have laughed at that. Practical

Polly, he called her sometimes, feet on the ground, unflappable Polly. She pulled a face at a ring of sheep, standing immobile as at a prayer meeting. What would Harry have thought if he'd seen her brandishing a knife at Jack Thomson? Polly tugged at her scarf as a sudden gust of wind blew it back from her head. Of one thing she was certain, Jack Thomson would think twice before having a go at her again.

She could see the cottage now, a grey, tumbledown shack, with the skeleton of what had once been a barn tacked on to one side. The grass and weeds surrounding it were so tall it looked as if the building had subsided down into them. It was said that the cottage was four hundred years old, and Polly doubted if much had been done to it since then. When the snow came, it drifted beneath the ill-fitting door like the tide coming in across a beach. Polly had seen Bella sweeping it out, her hands and face purple with cold.

The door was on the latch as usual, and even before Polly had knocked and stepped inside, Bella's high-pitched voice called out: 'Come in, Polly. I know it's you.'

She was sitting by the fire, sandy hair falling forward like a curtain skimped of material over her face. On her lap, the baby lay wrapped in a grey fringed shawl, as still and floppy as a rag doll.

'He's asleep now.' Bella looked down at his little face. 'He's been crying all night with the colic. Jack said he'd throw him through the window if he didn't hush up.'

Gently Polly pulled the shawl away from the tiny mauve face, trying to conceal her dismay. Neither of her children as babies had looked like this one lying so still on his mother's knee. Both Gatty and Martin had been rosy, chunky babies, with rounded cheeks and dimpled limbs. Bella's baby had a look about him as if he should be lying in a shroud in a little white coffin, the purple-veined eyelids closed for ever. Suppressing a shudder, she laid a hand on his forehead.

'He's not hot,' she said, her voice warm and comforting. 'He hasn't got a fever.'

When Bella raised her head, Polly saw the bruise running from her chin to her ear. There were dull red marks on her neck, spaced like finger marks, and her whole face was blotched with weeping.

'He must've had the stomach-ache bad to cry all night,' she said in a dull and listless voice. 'He kept drawing his legs up and screaming. I were at me wits' end what to do, Polly.'

Polly's active mind was in a ferment. 'Never interfere between husband and wife', was an old northern saying, but surely to stand by and do nothing was worse? And yet she'd experienced at first hand that very morning Jack's violent nature. He was dangerous. He ought to be locked away.

'Jack's been knocking you about, hasn't he?'

There. The words were said straight out, no taking them back now. Polly held her breath.

Bella was staring into the fire, unblinking, her chin uplifted, her whole body as still as if she was sitting there having her portrait painted. There was a dignity in the way one hand clutched at the buttoned-up neck-line of her blouse, and a pride in the way she was obviously not going to answer.

'Your letters are there, on the mantelpiece,' she said at last. 'There's two, just the two. The postman fetched them this morning.'

'It's good of you to let him drop them here.' After a small hesitation Polly spoke evenly, taking her cue from

30

Bella. 'By rights I think he should bring them up to the cottage.'

'What are neighbours for?' Bella's mouth twisted into a semblance of a smile. 'You'd do the same for me.'

'I'd do *anything* to help you, love.'

'If there's anything I ever need, I'll ask.' To show that all was forgiven, Bella smiled her lopsided smile again.

'Oh, Bella.' Polly took the letters down from the high mantelpiece. 'This one's from Harry, so I'll save that.' She pushed it into her pocket. 'This one – well, I think I can guess what this one's about.' Carefully she opened it, drew out a sheet of headed notepaper and began to read.

When she looked up, her blue eyes were sparkling. 'I've done it, Bella! I've got an interview! At the first try!' The baby stirred, and she clapped a hand to her mouth. 'Sorry, love, but I can't help feeling a bit chuffed. The advertisement was only in the paper last week.' She studied the letter again. 'It says I've been short-listed. For a secretary, Bella. In an office down the town.'

It was no good. She couldn't take it calmly, not good news like that. Striking a pose, Polly put on what she called her posh voice: 'Take a letter, Mrs Pilgrim.' Imaginary spectacles were adjusted on the bridge of her nose. 'With reference to yours of the fifteenth instant, we have to inform you that your tender for the job in question is far too high. Even taking into account the cost of materials, we consider there is no justification for such an unacceptable price . . . etcetera . . . etcetera. . . .'

'Oh, Polly.' Bella's tired eyes lit up. 'You are a caution! You never told me you were going in for a job.'

'I never told nobody.' Polly folded the letter and

replaced it in the envelope. 'I only wrote off for a bit of a lark. You know me.'

'You've told Harry though?'

'No, I've not.' Polly shook her head. 'Oh, I'll tell him if I get it, but Harry's narrow-minded about married women working. He reckons women get themselves a meal ticket when they get married. My mother's the same.' She laughed. 'I suppose you could say that's the only thing they agree about.'

The baby began to whimper, and Bella lifted him against her shoulder, rubbing his back with little circular movements. 'I never knew you could do shorthand and typing.' She adjusted the shawl to cover the baby's tiny purple feet. 'I knew you were a lot cleverer than me, but shorthand and typing. . . .'

'Certificates to prove it.' Polly's tone was lofty. 'Stuck in a drawer somewhere. Mind you, it's a long while back. I got married when I was seventeen, you know, but it's like riding a bicycle or swimming – once you've done it you never forget the knack. Anyway, it'll likely be filing and answering the telephone at first.' She grinned. 'Bella, it's fifteen shillings a week! Just imagine what I could do with fifteen shillings coming in regularly every Friday! I'll be home before Gatty, and not long after Martin. He's old enough at eleven to let himself in after school. You know how sensible he is.'

For a moment, a disturbing picture of Martin taking the key from beneath the big stone outside the door and letting himself into a cold room with a firelighter and a heap of coal and logs in an empty grate, dampened her spirits. But only for a moment. 'I'll tack a white collar on to the neck of my best navy-blue dress,' she said, 'an' cut my hair with the nail scissors.' She held out her hands, roughened and red from years of washing with

32

nothing but a washboard to help her. 'I might even start putting polish on my nails.' She grinned mischievously, 'Pink to make the boys wink.'

The expression on Bella's thin face was wise and knowing. 'You've missed all that, haven't you, Polly? You're always laughing and joking, but underneath what you've really wanted to be is a secretary with a white collar on your frock and finger nails painted pink.'

Polly blinked in surprise. She'd only known Bella for a year, since she'd appeared one day pregnant and subdued as Jack Thomson's wife. And yet beneath that drab downtrodden exterior was an awareness that startled her sometimes. Guilt flooded Polly's heart.

'What about you, love?' she asked quietly. 'Isn't there something you'd rather be doing than living out here in this crumbling ruin of a house?'

Tact had never been Polly's strong point. In fact, her mother had often said that when tact had been given out, their Polly must have been on the back row and got missed. So when Bella's face crumpled and her eyes swam with tears, Polly was all contrition.

'Here, give me the baby.' She held out her arms, then sighed as the weightless little body was handed over. 'I didn't mean to upset you, love. You know me, always putting me big feet in it.'

'How old do you think I am, Polly?' Tears as thick as glycerine ran down Bella's bruised face.

Jiggling the baby up and down, Polly determined this time to be careful. 'Twenty?' she ventured. 'Maybe twenty-one. No more than that, definitely.'

'I'm not sixteen yet.' Putting her head down, Bella allowed her anguish to take over. 'I've only been left school two years.' Her mouth dropped open, showing decayed, uneven teeth. 'An' I'm not married neither.

Jack has a wife somewhere. He's supposed to send her money regular, but he never does.' Her tinny little voice rose in a wail. 'God knows how she's managing, but she's stopped bothering him. If the courts can't make him pay up, then I suppose she thinks she's flogging a dead horse.'

Polly pushed the letter deep inside the pocket of her coat. She felt as if she could have been felled with a feather. Bella fifteen! Oh, my God! She stared transfixed at the wizened little face. Bella must have looked middle-aged from the day she was born.

'But your mother?' Polly sat down on the horse-hair sofa drawn up at right angles to the fire. 'What does she have to say to all this?'

'My mother, whoever she were, left me. Dumped me on the doorstep of an orphanage when I was a baby.' Lifting the edge of her skirt, Bella wiped her eyes. 'I ran away, an' if the police ever started looking for me they soon stopped. I got work on a farm across t'other side.' She jerked her head in the direction of Pendle Hill. 'Across the moor. All found and no questions asked. That's where Jack found me.' Her voice rose in a kind of triumph. 'He used to walk across the moors to see me, an' oh, I thought he was lovely. I used to sneak out to meet him, then when I told him about the baby I thought he would never come again.' Her chin lifted. 'But he just picked me up and carried me all through that deep snow last winter. The road was blocked, but he carried me through the drifts till we got to where the snow-plough had reached, then it was all downhill past your cottage to here, an' he put a poker to the fire making it blaze up, an' I saw the pots on the dresser an' the rug on the floor, an' it was like heaven, Polly.'

She held out her arms for the baby. 'They're my *family*, Polly, like Harry and Gatty and Martin are your family, an' this is my house. So don't belittle Jack, Polly, 'cos I won't listen.' Her tears had dried now as she rocked backwards and forwards. 'He took the place of God for me that day he fetched me here, an' he's done more than what God's ever done for me, 'cos Him up there's done nowt!'

But all that didn't give Jack Thomson the right to knock his wife about, Polly muttered to herself as she climbed back up the hill. No more than it gave him the right to mess about with the young half-witted girls at his place of work.

Her fingers curled round the letters in her pocket, and she ran the last stretch to the cottage, arriving breathless and panting with a stitch in her side.

Harry wasn't much of a letter writer, but she read the two sheets of lined paper three times before she was satisfied.

Kew Gardens was a revelation to him. There was a pagoda, and a Palm House built like a glass palace, with palm trees from all over the world growing inside. And some day, when he got a step up, he might be allowed to work inside. In the meantime, he was happy to be sweeping leaves, trundling his wheelbarrow along the miles of paths. *Honoured* to be working there, his words implied. Polly folded the letter and replaced it in its envelope. No more mention of the 'digs' he'd found, but then, wasn't that Harry all over? A bite to eat and a place to get his head down at nights and he was satisfied. Sighing, Polly turned her attention to the second letter.

Tracing her finger round the signature, she felt her spirits rise again. Manny Goldberg. . . .

Manny Goldberg lifted his head as the last of the three interviewees was ushered into his office. It was raining outside, soot-laden rain falling from a leaden sky, and yet this girl, this young woman coming towards his desk was all bright colour, from her corn-gold hair to her scarlet coat. When she smiled, Manny had the fanciful thought that she had brought sunshine in with her.

He looked down at her letter, open on his blotter. Older than the two other girls he'd seen, and married. Vague about her speeds, but definite about her willingness to work hard. Promising him her undivided loyalty if only he'd employ her. Swearing he'd never regret it, in fact. Manny smiled. This was no stereotyped letter drafted as part of a commercial course at the Technical College. Maybe that was why he'd disobeyed his instincts and offered her an interview. Maybe this was why he needed now to be on his guard.

Emmanuel Goldberg had seen the cotton mill as a going proposition. Its fairly recent closure had left its interior free from the attentions of vandals, and once the looms had gone and his sewing machines installed in their place he'd known he'd be ready for business.

Raincoats were what Manny intended to produce. Drab, lined, utilitarian coats: functional, necessary, heavy and drab. Facings, linings, buttonholes and pockets all individually sewn so that only one machinist ever handled the finished article.

Motioning Polly to a chair, Manny folded his hands together on his blotting pad. 'You know we make raincoats, Mrs Pilgrim?'

'Oh yes.' Polly gave him a dazzling smile. 'You should be on to a good thing hereabouts, Mr Goldberg.'

Manny blinked. She had a dark brown, husky voice, this Polly Pilgrim, and her skin had a bloom on it like a peach. Just for a fraction of a second he let his thoughts wander to his own daughter, Miriam, insisting on staying in Germany to be near to her sweetheart even though the Nazis had been in power for almost a year now. Given differing circumstances, this girl would have stayed too; this girl, like his Miriam, would take her freedom completely for granted.

He controlled his thoughts, getting back to the business in hand. 'I don't believe in wasting time, so we'll leave the interview until I've seen you turn out a letter.' He glanced at his watch. 'I've an appointment in ten minutes which should take me till lunchtime, so I'll dictate the letter then you can come back at let's say two o'clock and type it.' His smile was fleshy and kind. 'Can you get yourself a bite to eat before then, Mrs Pilgrim?'

Polly nodded. 'There's no problem there, Mr Goldberg.' Taking out the lined notepad specially bought for the purpose, she unfastened her coat, licked the end of a pencil and assumed what she hoped was an expression of impressive intelligence.

'Dear Sirs.' That was easy. Polly's pencil skimmed over the familiar outline. 'With reference to yours of the twenty-fifth inst. . . .' That wasn't much of a hardship, either. Mr Goldberg seemed to be taking it slowly, then abruptly he gathered steam.

Gripping the pencil hard, Polly battled on. When he dictated a longish word she wrote it in longhand to make sure, then found she was lagging behind. Feverishly she tried to catch up, flipped over a page and felt the sweat begin to trickle down her sides as she realized she was getting hopelessly behind.

Thank God she had a freak memory, she told herself. If he didn't ask her any more questions when the dictating was finished, she could go somewhere quiet and sort it all out before she came back at two o'clock to type it.

'Yours etcetera.' At last Manny stopped. 'Got all that down, Mrs Pilgrim?'

'Yes, Mr Goldberg.'

Manny started to doodle on his blotting pad. 'That's the typewriter you'll be using, over there in the corner. Two carbons and a top copy. If I'm not here when you come back, just carry on.' He glanced through the window. 'Well, at least it's stopped raining, and I do believe the sun's coming out.' He spread podgy hands wide. 'Bad for my business but I ask you, what can you do?'

It was a joke, Polly supposed, but she daren't risk even a smile. She knew she couldn't let her concentration slip even for a second. She had to get out of the room before he said another word. Standing up, she closed her notebook and went to get her coat.

Manny stared at her in surprise. One of the first things he'd noticed about this bright faced and quite beautiful young woman had been the serenity of her expression. Now the vivid blue eyes were glazed as she gathered up her handbag, pushed the notepad inside and began to back away from his desk.

'Back at two o'clock, Mr Goldberg.'

The husky voice was high with what sounded like hysteria, and before Manny could blink twice she had gone, almost running from the room.

Manny shrugged wide shoulders and reached for the telephone. 'Now what brought that on?' he asked himself, dialling with a podgy finger.

Robert Dennis saw the young woman before she saw him. She was sitting on a bench overlooking the Garden of Remembrance, just inside the park gates, bending her head over a notepad balanced on her handbag, scribbling furiously. Her coat was as scarlet as the poppy wreaths that would be piled beneath the memorial in a few weeks' time and, framed by a backdrop of darkly glossy rhododendron bushes, she made a picture that gladdened the eye.

As drawn to her as if she'd been magnetized, Robert sat down at the far end of the bench. Taking off his brown trilby he closed his eyes, lifting his face to the watery sun.

At the age of forty-nine, Robert Dennis's hair was liberally streaked with silver. It had started to go that way in the mud of the trenches of Flanders Fields, but his face had stayed smooth, so that a second glance showed him to be a man barely into middle age. There was no corrosion of bitterness in his heart, in spite of the fact that the left sleeve of his coat hung loosely over an arm severed just below the elbow. The same philosophy had kept him on an even keel since the death of his wife four months ago. If anyone had told Robert Dennis he was a counter of blessings, he would have laughed in their faces; if they had said he was a brave man, he would have walked away in disgust. At a time when so many of his contemporaries were lying dead in well-tended graves over in France, at a time when so many who had returned were now searching for work, Robert Dennis told himself he was a lucky man. His job in local government, in the Education Offices opposite the Library, was secure. He had a house, small but big enough for his needs, and if at nights he sometimes awoke shouting in the darkness, from a nightmare in which he heard again the screams and moans of his wounded comrades, for the past few months at least there had been no one to hear him.

Opening his eyes, he stared at the frantic expression on the face of the young woman as she looked up from her notebook for a brief moment. Putting his hat back on his head again, Robert raised it an inch and smiled.

'A nice afternoon. For the time of the year,' he said, in his pleasantly deep voice.

'Hush!'

His pale grey eyes flew open in astonishment as he stared into Polly's furious face. 'I beg your pardon?'

'Don't speak! Not a word or I'm sunk!' Polly flipped over a page, gazed in mute horror at what she saw written, and groaned aloud. 'Does deliverance of our *retinue* make any sense to you?'

Robert blinked. Her eyes were the deep vivid blue of bluebells drenched with dew, and surely those weren't tears sparkling in their depths? He slid along the bench and saw a page of shorthand. 'Having difficulty transcribing your notes?' He rubbed his chin reflectively. 'I can't say I've ever exactly heard of anyone delivering a retinue. Not exactly put like that.'

'Retinue *could* be a collective noun for raincoats. You know. A gaggle of geese, a shoal of fish, a *retinue* of raincoats?' Polly gripped her pencil hard so that her knuckles gleamed white. 'Oh, flamin' 'enery, it's no good. I can't remember what he said.'

'He?'

'Mr Goldberg, the boss of the new raincoat factory. He's just interviewed me for the job as his secretary.' She flipped the notebook closed. 'I was that busy putting pink polish on my nails and sewing a lace collar into the neck of my frock, I never thought to practise my shorthand. And to think I was top of the class in it seventeen years ago!' She tapped her handbag with a finger and he saw that her nails were indeed varnished a rather pleasing shade of pink.

'*And* they clash with my coat,' Polly said, following his glance. 'The letter I've got to type'll look like the Chinese alphabet when I've finished with it.'

'Ara chickara, chickara, roony . . .' Robert said at once. 'My father used to recite it to me when I was small.'

Surprised, Polly burst out laughing. 'Mine too. And I'll tell you something else. I believed it *was* the Chinese alphabet till I was about twelve.' She made a wry face. 'If I type this out as it stands and someone from Scotland Yard reads it, I'll never be able to prove it isn't a list of military secrets.' Opening her bag she took out the notebook again. 'What do you make of "we must fraternize the heinekalls", for example?'

All at once she got up to go. 'Sorry I was rude to you, hushing you up. And yes, it is a nice afternoon, especially for the time of the year.' She smiled her wide smile. 'And please don't look so worried. I wasn't banking on getting the job.' She corrected herself. 'Well, at least, if I was, I'm not now. You can't win 'em all.'

He watched her go, long red coat flying open, small heels tapping on the gravel path, the sun making a glory of her corn-coloured hair. Before she turned the corner she looked back, raised a hand to wave, and was gone.

And immediately he felt a tiny *frisson* of excitement low down in his stomach, an almost forgotten sensation, catching him unawares.

Later that evening he sat alone in his quiet house, a glass of beer on the arm of his chair, remembering her.

Robert Dennis was no defeatist, shrinking into a shell

of solitude of his own making. His war service and the death of his wife had matured him to a state of mind where he believed that what would be would be.

Far from a recluse, he accepted that loneliness and being alone were two different states of mind. He liked his own company, he told himself, and self-pity nauseated him. Just being alive after coming back from France had taught him a sort of contentment, but in every man there dwells a sense of looking out for happiness, and not for a long, long time had he felt so attracted to a woman.

He found himself wondering just how much the girl in the red coat had needed that job. He wasn't fooled by her nonchalance, and without even knowing her name he felt a tender protectiveness towards her.

For the first time since his wife had died, just four months before, he accepted the fact that he was a man without a cause, a man so used to cherishing that, without a woman to cherish, he was in effect merely existing.

The thought was new and disturbing and he tried to reject it by putting a record on the turntable of his cabinet gramophone. Beethoven had always had the power to soothe, but tonight even the soaring music couldn't calm him. Tonight he felt his age.

'So what can you do?' Manny Goldberg asked himself, reading through the typed letter placed in front of him by a very subdued Mrs Pilgrim.

Strange how he'd found himself almost willing this lovely young woman to succeed. But watching her struggling to type out her notes, sighing when the keys of the typewriter came up bunched together, rubbing furiously

42

with an eraser, forgetful of the carbon underneath, tongue protruding slightly, face flushed, Manny had known she wasn't equal to the job. He passed a hand wearily across his eyes.

It would have to be the first girl he'd interviewed that morning. In his mind's eye he conjured her up. So thin that she'd need extensive padding even to look flat-chested; so keen and efficient, her fingers had flown over the keys like one-day butterflies. Physically so very unlike his Miriam back there in Germany, believing her youth and her beauty would save her from the terrors Manny was sure would come. His Miriam was all rounded curves, like the fine young woman standing at the other side of his desk, cushiony, womanly, her eyes fixed on him with a resigned expression in their deep blue depths.

'I've made a right mess of it, haven't I, Mr Goldberg?' Polly lifted her shoulders in a gesture of resignation. 'Ah, well, I suppose it's back to the salt mines.' She reached for the red coat hung on the peg next to his black Homburg. 'I'm sorry to have wasted your time.'

'So who said anything about wasting my time?' Manny came to one of his quick intuitive decisions. 'Can you use a sewing machine, Mrs Pilgrim?'

Polly nodded. 'I can *use* one all right, but I have to be honest. Granted we only had one sewing lesson a week at school, but it took me two years to make a pinny, and when I got it home it took my mother an hour to decide what it was. My daughter says she'd rather die a painful and lingering death than wear anything I've made for her.

Behind a well-manicured hand, Manny hid a smile. 'Which school did you go to, Mrs Pilgrim?'

'The High School.' Polly snrugged. 'But I left after

43

I'd got my School Certificate when I was sixteen. They didn't teach commercial subjects, and all I wanted to be was a secretary, so I went full time to the Technical College for a year. I was good at book-keeping. Double entry, you know? You won't believe it, but I got good speeds in shorthand and typing, then I got married. Not because I had to,' she added quickly, 'but I had a baby in the first year and that put paid to my career.' She stared straight into Manny's eyes. 'Married women up here don't have careers, Mr Goldberg. Not many of them try to do well at school really, not with knowing they'll finish up cooking and cleaning anyway.'

'And you say your husband has gone south to look for work?' Manny pulled Polly's letter towards him. 'Has he had any success yet?'

'Not in the way he wanted.' Polly lowered her voice confidentially. 'He's a clever man, Mr Goldberg. A landscape gardener, a landscape *architect* really, but he hasn't got the certificates to prove it. He's been taken on at Kew Gardens. Kew *Botanical* Gardens down London way. It'll only be a matter of time before they see his real worth. He can grow a seedling from a lump of granite, my Harry can.'

Manny was surprised to feel his eyes grow misty. He only hoped this gardener fellow deserved this lovely, frank, open-hearted young woman. For a moment he was tempted to take a chance, then the sight of the letter she'd typed hardened his resolve. Manny Goldberg hadn't pulled up his roots, started from scratch again, by being a soft touch. He fiddled with a fountain pen, taking off the cap then screwing it back on again.

'There is a little job I think you could do,' he said at last. 'Come with me down the yard into the mill and I'll show you. It only pays eight shillings a week, but it's

44

important. In some ways it's the most important job in the factory. Want to take a look-see?'

On the way home Polly called in to see her mother. Because it was a Monday afternoon Edna's washing was piled up ready for ironing, and while the last few things were steaming gently on a clothes horse in front of the fire, she was cleaning her windows with a wash-leather, rubbing them afterwards with one of her old vests to bring up the shine.

She was wearing a flowered cross-over pinafore topped by a black fent apron used for housework, which in its turn was topped by a sacking one when she mopped her step and her kitchen floor. Edna's floors were too clean even to eat off, and come the spring Polly knew her mother would lift the linoleum to scrub underneath. On the day she had seen her poking down the spout of a teapot with a little brush to clean it, Polly had given up.

When they were nicely settled with a cup of tea, she gave her news.

'I've got a job,' she announced, 'at the new raincoat factory in Holden's Mill.'

'I hope you haven't gone and kidded them you can sew?' Edna's face was wrenched out of shape as she struggled not to let her daughter see what it meant to her to have Polly dropping in unexpectedly on a Monday afternoon. 'It's God help anybody who has to wear any raincoat you've made. I remember you twice shortening the same sleeve of a new coat for your Gatty not all that long ago.' She sniffed. 'Your father would have taken on two jobs rather than let *me* go out to work. Bringing you up was my job.'

'And a right mess I made of that,' her expression said.

'Have another biscuit,' she said aloud. 'And take what's left home for your Martin. He loves custard creams.'

'Folding raincoats,' Polly told her. 'They come off the machines finished, buttonholes and everything, then I examine them for faults or loose threads, match the right shade belts to the right shade coats, button them up, lay them flat on a big table, face down, tuck the sleeves over, lop the bottom bit up, then the top, turn them face up, smooth the revers, and bob's your uncle!'

'And to end up clever enough to do that, you won a scholarship to the High School, learned how to sound your aitches, got certificates in shorthand and typing, and could have gone to the University if you hadn't gone and got married straight out of your gym-slip.' Edna reached for a biscuit, then drew back her hand as she remembered they were wrapped up for Martin. 'He's brought you down properly in the world, that Harry Pilgrim, and I just hope he's satisfied.' She narrowed her eyes into suspicious slits. 'And who's going to get your Martin his tea when he gets home from school? He's that thin now he could drop down a grate without barking his shins on the grids.'

'We need the money, Mam!' Polly stood up. 'And anyway a job will get me out of the cottage. I'd go mental this winter up there on me own without Harry popping in and out.' She smiled mischievously. 'I'm thinking of going to night school one or two nights a week to brush up my shorthand and typing. Then when Harry sends for us I'll be a qualified secretary.' She spread her arms wide. 'Life isn't meant to be all scrimping and scraping, Mam. There's a whole lot more to it than that. An' doing something off my own bat today has made me feel different already. I'm ready to try my wings, Mam, and if folding raincoats is a start then that's okay with me. Just now I have the feeling there's nothing in the world I can't do if I set my mind to it.' Devilment shone from her eyes. 'And do you know what? I got chatted up by a man at dinnertime, on a bench in the park. He had lovely hair with silver streaks in it, and a wavy smile to match, and he talked daft like me. I think he had a secret sorrow in his life, probably a wife who nags and makes him go to church on Sundays instead of having a round of golf. But he was lovely, Mam. Reely luvelly. . . .'

'Oh, our Polly. . . .' For an unguarded moment the affection was there on Edna's face. Then the shutter came down, changing her expression completely.

'You'd best be going if you want to be back for your Martin,' she said. 'And it would have served you right if you'd got yourself dragged into the rhododendron bushes and ravaged. Silvery hair, did you say? They're always the worst when they think they're getting past it. There's no fool like an old fool, I've always said that.'

When Polly let herself into the cottage, the bright promise of the afternoon had gone. Through the window she stared out at the hills, shadowed by billowing clouds. Soon Martin would be home, then later Gatty. There were potatoes to peel, and the oxtail simmering in the fire oven to thicken with cornflour. There was wood to bring in and water to boil, and the ashes to scatter on the cinder path at the back. Her expression grew pensive.

But from today things were going to be different. From next Monday she'd be catching the bus into town, leaving behind the windswept cottage. There'd be the company she'd craved, the laughter she needed, the escape from a loneliness never before acknowledged.

From next week she'd be reborn.

Putting out her tongue at the view and the great oak tree, its topmost branches stirred by a sighing wind, Polly turned her back and lifted a sack of potatoes from beneath the sink.

Frowning she stared at her pink finger nails. 'I might even start wearing rubber gloves to peel you,' she told a potato. 'And that would make your eyes pop out, wouldn't it?'

— Three —

In Kew Gardens in the soft sunlight of an October morning, Harry Pilgrim trundled a wheelbarrow along a winding path. There was a rhythm in the way he stopped, bent down and gathered up a pile of leaves between two boards. There was a definite grace in his movements, the slow concentration of a dedicated gardener at one with his surroundings.

The Royal Botanical Gardens on that mellow misty day was indeed a wondrous place to be.

Harry had worked since first light, sweeping the fallen leaves into orderly piles with a long birch broom, and now – if a wind didn't make a nonsense of his toil – he'd be finished before going home at six o'clock.

Home! What a travesty of the word. Home for Harry during the past month had been an attic room shared with a sick man, a down-and-out, who spent his days in bed, shambling downstairs for the evening meal of watery soup and dry bread, swilled down with a mug of hot tea.

Harry, his chest tightening with the pain that had bothered him since mustard gas had choked his lungs on the Somme, strangled a cough. He stared for a moment across an enormous lawn patterned in regular stripes, a tribute to the precision by which an under-gardener had guided and turned his mowing machine.

Once, a long time ago it seemed, Harry had been famed for his lawns back in his beloved Lancashire village. Now his status in the vast organization at Kew was far less than that of a student gardener.

Straight from school or college they came, walking the paths in groups, smoking – though smoking was forbidden – treating the labourers as less than the dirt clinging to the soles of their swanky knee-length boots. Only that morning one of them had spoken harshly to Harry for daring to approach a visitor.

'I was only putting him right,' Harry had said inno-cently. 'The man was obviously a foreigner wondering why a lilac bush was labelled *syringa* when what *he* had thought was *syringa* is called *philadelphus* here. And he went on to say that his journey had been well worth the while just to see the *sophoria* in the Palm House. He was right chuffed with himself about that.'

The student had scratched his head, bewildered by a labourer with a Lancashire accent who talked like a textbook. One of those working-class amateur botanists he'd read about, he'd decided, kicking out at a pile of leaves, scattering them across the gravelled path.

'You know the rules,' he'd said, walking away.

Harry bent down to his task again, muttering to himself. If Polly could write and tell him she was enjoying standing at a table in a factory folding raincoats all day, then he could surely follow her example and make the best of things. It was just that some people were *born* willing to make the best of things, while others flaked themselves out fighting against injustice, trying to beat the system. With as much chance of succeeding as

Nelson would've had trying to get his eye back, he told himself wryly.

At least he had a job. At least he was outside in God's good fresh air working in what was recognized as one of the most beautiful gardens in the world. Harry moved on down the path, the sun on the back of his neck like a blessing. He'd find the sort of work he wanted, a proper gardening job, given time. Even if he had to knock on all the doors of the big houses in Richmond and plead with some posh-spoken woman just to give him a chance to show what he could do. There was money down here, right enough.

Wielding his two boards with dexterity, he scraped up yet another pile of damp leaves, remembering for some reason a potting shed in a garden where he'd worked for years, before the family business went bust and they'd emigrated to Canada. Funny how he could recall every detail of that old shed. . . . Harry wheeled the barrow further down the path, walking with measured tread, soothed for the moment by memories.

There'd been a high bench under the window with seed boxes set out on it. He'd fixed a cupboard for small tools, balls of twine and catalogues. Even in that harsher climate he'd grown plums and cherries, training them against a south-facing wall. Harry rubbed his chin. Peaches now, they were another thing, but he'd grown them too, as big as apples, in a far from adequate greenhouse heated by a rusty coke stove. He stopped by yet another pile of rotting leaves.

Grapes had been what he'd enjoyed growing most. Narrowing his eyes, he remembered the bloom on them as he'd snipped a bunch off with his special scissors. He patted his top pocket as if the scissors were still there. His favourites had been the black Madresfield Court variety with their purple flesh, and not far behind the sharp-tasting white Muscats, brought to perfection in time for the lady of the house to present them to her church's harvest festival.

'Grapes for me?'

The man lying in the bed beneath the sloping roof of the attic room raised his head a few inches from his pillow, then let it drop back, closing his eyes as if the small effort had been too much for him.

'The smallest bunch I could buy.' Harry dangled them between his fingers. 'You know how it is. You go for weeks debating every blessed penny you part with, then what the heck?' He smiled. 'I remember my mother going out and buying a bag of coloured sugar when we were down to our last lump of coal for the fire. Coloured sugar! Can you believe that?'

Harry was talking for talking's sake, and he knew it. The face on the pillow was thin and drawn, his skin shades whiter than the grubby flannelette sheet pulled up to his chin. His lips were parted slightly, dry and caked with the scum of high fever, and his bony fingers scrabbled at the bedclothes like spiders scampering into a dark place to hide.

Drawing up a rickety chair to the bedside, Harry laid a hand on the burning forehead. 'Have you had plenty to drink today?' His voice was a concerned whisper, but tight with suppressed rage. 'Has she been up to see you, the old faggot?'

Wearily the head on the pillow moved in negation. 'I didn't want anything. Nothing. . . .'

'She hasn't been near you, has she?'

Taking a grape, Harry split it, took out the pips, then gently squeezed the juice into the parched mouth.

'I can taste the sun on that. Thank you, Harry.' Heavy eyelids lifted over bloodshot eyes, reminding Harry for a second of the way his dog's eyes had mutely expressed their thanks the day his paw had been released from a sprung-trap in the wood.

Tenderly he did the same with a second grape, then another, until the juice dribbling down the unshaven chin told him his friend could swallow no more.

And, oh yes, Roger Craven *was* his friend. Even with their short acquaintance it was as though he had always been a friend. Sometimes they had talked far into the night, whispering, because the wall dividing their room from the next was made of plywood. So that now Roger knew all about Polly laughing with the sunlight in her hair; about the cottage on its bleak and windy hill; about Harry's dream of making a better life for her and his children.

And he had heard about the job Harry would find some day, working as head gardener in a big country house. With his keenly perceptive mind he had noticed Harry's hands, the thumbs bearing the ingrained imprint of the soil as if from pressing seedlings down into plant-pots. He had listened to Harry talking about soil as if it was gold dust from heaven. And had marvelled at his dedication.

Just as Harry knew that Roger Craven had been a university man before the war, brought up in the country in a house with stables and resident maids. He knew how the drink had alienated him from his family when the problem turned into an obsession, *shaming* them when he'd taken to the road and rebelled against conformity. He'd ended up literally in the gutter, he'd

53

confessed, until some Salvation Army do-gooder had taken him to be dried out in hospital before setting him on his feet again.

'What is the purpose behind our time on this earth?' he had demanded one night. 'And don't go quoting Jesus! Apply His truths and where do they get you? Take me, now. I was self-indulgent to think I could shrug off my privileged background and find His kingdom and with it the truth. But what *is* truth, Harry? You try and explain that to me.'

'Go back home, Harry,' he said now, his normally deep voice high with fever. 'Draw the bloody dole. Starve. Live off your wife's earnings, idle your days away sitting in a chair in that cottage of yours, but go home.'

Raising his head with an immense effort of will, Roger Craven, MA peered through the mist clouding his eyes. His swollen, sore tongue cleaved to the roof of his mouth, so that his words came out as jumbled and thick as in the old days of his drinking. Groping, he reached for his friend's hand and felt it grasped firmly.

'Pride,' he whispered. 'Sod pride! I spit on pride! Go back and tell them you've failed down here. Admit it isn't the Utopia you dreamed about. Get back to where you're loved. Family, Harry. Exasperating, bloody awful family – even that mother-in-law with the serpent's tongue.' His head fell back, but his fingers clung to Harry's wrist as if he were drowning. 'You're not weak like me. You've got strength, integrity. Be the man I know you to be, and go home. Now, tomorrow. . . .'

On a rasping breath his voice petered out, and his fingers loosened their hold. Terrified, Harry bent over him, pulling back the flannel sheet with its bobbles as black as a sprinkling of soot. The heartbeat was there, faint and sporadic, but now the breath was coming laboured, heavy and choked with a mucus dribbling from the sick man's mouth.

'Mrs Cook!' Feet pounding on the uncarpeted stairs, Harry raced down three flights to the basement kitchen where his landlady lived. 'Mrs Cook! Can you tell me where I can find a doctor? It's Mr Craven. He needs help badly. I think he's dying.'

The thick-set woman standing by the gas cooker went on ladling soup into bowls set out on a tray. 'A doctor?' She spoke over her shoulder to the young girl slicing bread at a table covered with newspaper and a conglomeration of dirty dishes. 'Take these up, Maureen, and if Mr Craven won't be coming down, then cut two slices less.' She turned round, wiping hands on a filthy apron. 'So Mr Craven needs a doctor, does he?' A wisp of hair was tucked into an untidy bun. 'And where might I ask is the money coming from for a doctor's visit? Where is the money coming from for Mr Craven's board and lodging? That's more to the point.' Waddling flat-footed over to a massive brown teapot, she lifted it and slopped tea into five mugs. 'I don't suppose he's told you that since he stopped going down to the post office for his pension I've never seen as much as a penny piece.'

Harry stared at her in disbelief. She sickened him with her greasy apron and her small mean eyes set close over a sharp beak of a nose. Mrs Cook had sickened him ever since he first set eyes on her, but after a fruitless search for lodgings at the price he could afford he had decided that beggars couldn't be choosers.

Taking a mug of hot tea from the table and pouring milk into it from a bottle, he backed towards the door.

'All day he's been without a drink. All day long up there with his tongue hanging out from thirst. I'm taking this up to him, Mrs Cook, then I'm going out to find a doctor, and if it's a question of payment then I'll pay. You'll not be involved. An' if his money doesn't come through, then I'll pay you his lodgings too. I'm not skint. Not yet.'

Quite unperturbed, his landlady watched him disappear through the door, bending his head as if he were tall enough to knock himself senseless on the lintel.

'Suit yourself, Mr Pilgrim,' she muttered, dipping into a blue bag of sugar and measuring a spoonful into each cup. 'Be a bloody Good Samaritan if you want to and see where that'll get you. Bloody nowhere, that's where!'

Balancing the tray on an ample hip, she kicked open the door and started up the stairs, down-at-heel bedroom slippers slipping from bare heels as red and shiny as tomatoes.

When Harry carried the mug of tea over to the bed set beneath the sloping ceiling of the attic room, he saw at once that his friend was dead. That in the short time it had taken him to go downstairs Roger Craven, scholar, gentleman of the road, self-professed heathen, had gently solved the mystery of his own existence, his questioning mind silenced for ever.

With reverence Harry pulled the grubby sheet up over his friend's face.

'But I'm not going home,' he whispered. 'That's not my way, Roger, no more than it were yours.'

Harry's letter telling Polly about the death of his friend was, as usual, short and to the point, and apart from the obvious underlying sadness, as interesting as a flamin' seed catalogue, she thought. Harry might be good at communicating with Mother Nature, none better, but when it came to putting pen to paper he was hopeless.

'It seems to me,' he wrote, 'that an ordinary working-class man has a much better chance of being happy than an educated one. A trained mind dwells too much on things not always meant to be understood.'

'That last bit's not meant for you,' Polly told Martin. 'Your dad wouldn't be sweeping leaves now if he'd gone to an agricultural college and got some fancy letters behind his name, proving he knew the difference between a blade of grass and a clump of lilies-of-the-valley.'

At eleven years of age, Martin was going through the stage of taking every utterance quite seriously. Looking up from his books he pushed his Latin primer to one side. 'My dad didn't need any old teacher telling him about gardening. He knows the names of every plant in the whole of Lancashire. He could leave that lot down at Kew standing.' For a moment his blue eyes were wise beyond their years. 'I got a book called *Mary Barton* from the school library, Mum, and in it Mrs Gaskell writes about men like my dad. It's men like him who are the real botanists. Men like my dad don't think soil's mucky; they rub it through their fingers, knowing how precious it is.' Suddenly he grinned, looking like a mischievous schoolboy again. 'He was thinking about you, more likely. You wouldn't be folding raincoats if you'd stopped on at college and learned how to be a proper secretary.'

Polly ruffled his hair, her expression soft with love. 'Gatty will be home soon, so why don't you go up to my room and finish your homework? I've lit the oil stove so it's nice and warm.'

'I don't like your room.' Bending his head over his books, Martin began to write.

Polly drew in a sharp breath. 'What d'you mean?

What's wrong with my room?' Taking a textbook from Martin's hand she flipped it over, face downwards. 'Come on, you can't come out with something like that and then not explain it.'

'Ask Gatty. She's coming in now.' His head lowered, Martin refused to meet his mother's gaze. '*She* knows. Jack Thomson told her about it. She told me last week when you were at night school. She says she wouldn't go in your room after dark, not for anything. Just you ask our Gatty.'

'I only told him for a laugh, for goodness sake!' Pulling off her coat and beret as she came into the warmth of the cottage, Gatty flung herself down on the chair nearest the fire. She held out her hands to the blaze. 'He's such a softy-baby. He'd believe anything.'

'Well, if it's that funny, tell me.' Polly faced her daughter squarely. 'See if you can make *me* laugh.'

The dislike on Gatty's face was like a blow. If she hadn't known different, if she hadn't *hoped* different, Polly would have sworn hatred stared at her from the dark eyes. Crossing both arms over her chest she rocked backwards and forwards, needing and seeking comfort. 'I'm waiting,' she said, forcing her voice into calmness.

Gatty sighed, hunching her shoulders. 'Well, this cottage is haunted, isn't it? You've only lived here since you got married, but Jack's lived down at the bottom all his life. It was empty for a year before you came, that's why it was going cheap. Jack says there was a man living alone before we came, a poacher who was in and out of prison, always drunk.' She looked towards the table. 'I'm hungry. Me and Winnie were so busy at the shop, we only had time for a sandwich in the back. It's half-term school holiday so we had hundreds of mothers in buying gumboots for their kids before the bad weather comes. They buy them because they're cheaper than shoes, Mr Arnold says. He says the way things are going it'll soon be like Victorian times with kids running around in their bare feet.'

'Gatty!' Polly's voice was sharp. 'You can have your tea as soon as you tell me what you know. I want this thing settled here and now.' She gave a meaningful glance towards Martin who listened in silence, his eyes wide with apprehension. 'Let's have this ghost business over and done with right now.'

A familiar whine crept into Gatty's voice. Her dark eyes once again slewed ceilingwards. 'Well, if you *must* know, this poacher man woke up in the night, thought he saw something, rushed out of the cottage and was buried in a snowdrift. They found him frozen to death five days later when the thaw came.' She nodded towards the pan on the fire. 'Now can I have my tea?'

Before she had finished speaking, Polly was ready for her. 'So tell me how, if this man rushed out of the cottage to his death – how did anyone know that he'd seen something? Did his lips unfreeze for long enough to explain?'

The faint suspicion of a smile on Martin's lips was enough to urge Polly on. This wasn't something she could let go. It was only two years since Martin had stopped wanting a night-light burning by his bed, and she knew the way his over-imaginative mind worked. *Grimm's Fairy Tales* had scared him stiff as a child, and even now when he went out in the dark to the lavatory at the end of the flagged path, Polly would obligingly stand at the cottage door with the light streaming out. No, for Martin's sake this ghost business had to be denied once and for all. What she had seen, what she had *thought* she had seen, had also to be pushed to the back of *her* mind for the sake of them all.

'So that scotches Jack Thomson's ghost, doesn't it?' Taking up the pan she took it to the slop-stone and drained the potatoes to a fluffy dryness. Cutting a slice from a slab of margarine she mashed them up, with quick-tempered jabs of a fork. 'The sausages will be ready now. Get them out of the oven, will you please, Gatty?'

'You see,' Polly told Martin when they were sitting round the table, 'superstition is based on ignorance. I'd heard about the old man who lived here in the cottage before us. He was a hermit, living on scraps not fit for the pigs. The people in the village were afraid of him because he wore ragged clothes and never spoke to anyone. When they found him lying dead, they had to make something up to ease their consciences, because not one of them had ever stretched out a hand to help him. They didn't understand how anyone could choose to live in such squalor, so they made the ghost up instead of admitting that he died of malnutrition. Lancashire folk pride themselves on taking care of their own, and when the old man died, a bag of bones, they were uneasy, and it was more comfortable to blame the supernatural than admit their own guilt.'

'And Jack Thomson tells lies, anyway.' Spearing a sausage on his fork, Martin bit into it. 'He told our Gatty she was pretty, and that's a big laugh for a start.'

The blush, rising like a scald from Gatty's throat, filled Polly's heart with dismay. As soon as Martin had been sent to bed, fighting a rearguard action on every step of the winding staircase, Polly sat down facing her daughter, ready to do battle yet once again.

'Put that magazine down, Gatty. You and me have things to say to each other.'

It was a cosy scene in the big living kitchen, with the curtains drawn against the windows, the fire burning steadily in the grate, and the clock ticking away on the mantelpiece. True, Harry was away, but his being away should have brought mother and daughter closer together. She had given Gatty Harry's letter to read, but after a cursory glance it had been passed back as if it held nothing of interest.

Polly wished she could find the words to tell Gatty how Jack Thomson had deliberately let her think he was going to force himself on her that morning in the cottage. And how he'd backed away when he saw the knife. How she had known in that instant the kind of man he was. She shuddered as the memory of his glittering green eyes came back to her. She remembered the wild animal strength coming from his big body.

'Some men . . .' she began, then stopped, the words choked in her throat. Sex was a word having no part in Polly's vocabulary. Her mother would have blanched at the very sound of it. At seventeen, Polly had married knowing only vaguely what to expect on her marriage night, and to ask her mother would have been unthinkable. Women put up with their husbands' disgusting habits, then bore children as a result. That much Polly had gleaned from conversations overheard, but to talk about what went on between a man and a woman would have been worse than saying aloud the word beginning with 'f' that you sometimes saw written on walls.

Years of believing that her own body had rude places never to be touched had taken all of Harry's patience and tenderness on that first night, and even now after his love-making had been accepted, he had still to see his wife's naked body. On the rare occasions he had pulled Polly's nightdress over her head, dropping it over the side of the bed, she had always managed to retrieve it before she went to sleep.

'Yes?' Gatty kept a finger on the article she was reading.

Polly clenched her fist to prevent herself from snatching the magazine away. 'I've asked you to keep away from Jack Thomson,' she said, keeping her voice low. 'There are some men who like touching young girls,' she went on, despising herself for not being able to put it more clearly. 'You may not know this, but he got his wife into trouble when she was only fourteen. And there was talk about him going with a girl at the Home where he works. A poor girl not quite right in her mind.'

Polly's heart turned over as she saw the colour drain from Gatty's face. She wanted to reach out and draw Gatty into her arms, explain to her that she believed Jack had a sexual leaning towards girls young enough to be his daughter, but before she could speak Gatty was on her feet, dark eyes blazing in the pallor of her small face.

'You're always right, our Mam. You think you know everything! Well, if you must know, I've decided I don't like Jack Thomson any more than you do. I won't be speaking to him again if I can help it.' Her voice broke with emotion. 'So what are you going to say now you've won? Aren't you going to say you told me so? Because that's all I need!'

Stark fear, like an icy finger, trailed itself down Polly's spine. Grabbing Gatty by an arm she forced her to turn round. 'Tell me! Has he ever tried anything on with you? *Has* he? You have to tell me, Gatty. No matter how hard it is, you have to say!'

'No!' The harsh denial came swiftly. 'No, and no, and no!'

'You're sure?' Polly tightened her grip. 'You tell me now and I promise I'll never mention it again. Never. I promise.'

Something in Gatty's expression made her draw back. An adult awareness, a daring her to persist. Suddenly the fight went out of Polly.

'All right, then, love.' Releasing her hold she took a step backwards to slump down on to her chair. 'I'm sorry I misjudged you. It's just that loving you I worry, and not having your dad here makes me fuss even more.' She tried to smile. 'But I'll tell you something. If I thought Jack Thomson had laid a finger on you, I'd kill him. As big as he is I'd mash him up finer than those potatoes we had for our tea tonight.'

'Oh, Mam. . . .' Tears sprang to Gatty's eyes, but dashing them angrily away she made swiftly for the foot of the stairs. 'I'm going to bed.' Her small face worked convulsively. 'My head aches. Maybe I've got a cold coming on.' When Polly started to get up from her chair, she waved an arm, as if warding her off. 'Please, Mam. Leave me be. I'm all right. Honest.'

There was no settling Polly when the small woebegone figure had disappeared out of sight up the winding staircase. There were brasses to polish, jobs to be done, but she sat quite still, staring into the fire, hands idle in her lap. If Harry had been there opposite to her, smoking his pipe, reaching out now and again to place another log on the fire, she could have talked her anxiety out to him. He would have listened, quietly, the way he always did, then put her mind at rest with a softly spoken assurance. Polly shook her head slowly from side to side. No, she could never have told Harry about her

63

conversation with Gatty. What had been said was women's talk, too subtle for a mere man to understand. Given even the merest inkling of suspicion, Harry would have been haring down the hill to confront Jack Thomson, stirring up trouble, forcing issues when it was wiser to let be.

Gatty had to grow up in her own way, and if the growing up was painful then that was the way it had to be. Polly raised her eyes. But there was still the business of the ghost to face.

Running light-footed up the stairs, she pushed open the door to her room, closed it behind her and forced herself to look up at the ceiling. Nothing. Just velvety black darkness, and the sound of the wind sighing in the branches of the tall tree outside. Then on to Martin's room, hearing the rhythmic put-put of snoring, and telling herself that if his adenoids and tonsils had needed seeing to, it would have been diagnosed at the medical examination he'd had before starting at the Grammar School.

'I'm going out for a little while,' she whispered, standing on the threshold of Gatty's room. 'Down to see Bella. I won't be long.'

'You're not. . . ?' Panic rose in Gatty's voice as she lifted herself up on one elbow.

'Of course not.' Polly moved forward to sit on the narrow bed. 'I promised, didn't I? We've talked about it and now it's over.' Gently she touched the hunched shoulder, trying not to mind as Gatty winced away, burying her head beneath the sheet again. 'I *understand*, love. I wouldn't want to humiliate you, not for the world. I was once fifteen myself, believe it or not. I suppose my mother used to get fearful for me, and it must have been much worse for her because I could never talk to her like you talk to me.'

And *that* was wishful thinking, Polly told herself, as she went back downstairs after dropping a goodnight kiss on the tiny part of Gatty visible above the piled-up blankets. On a sudden impulse she went back.

'Why don't you bring Winnie out to Sunday dinner at the weekend? It seems silly that I hardly know her when you talk about her all the time.'

'I don't talk about her all the time. It's you that's always going on about her.'

Polly almost sagged against the door with relief. That was better. The exasperating, contradictory Gatty she could deal with; the one a little while ago with terror staring from her eyes, she'd rather forget.

'Well, ask Winnie anyway. Okay?'

'I might.'

Polly opened the front door of the cottage on to a vista of moonlight. To the east the stark mass of Pendle Hill was etched in cold-blue against a silver sky. On either side of the stony path, grass grew as grey as cobwebs, and the wall was a twisting serpent of black iron.

Jim trotted along by her side, too cold to be bothered barking at a ring of motionless silent sheep, anxious only to get where he was going then back to his basket and the glowing fire.

'It's bright enough to read a book by the moonlight,' Polly told Bella, as she stepped inside the tiny cottage. 'It would've been a waste of a battery to have my torch on. Moonlight in the country gives me the creeps somehow. It's all right in the town where buildings can throw shadows, but coming down the hill I was as exposed as a nit on a head of black hair.'

Bella's laugh startled Polly until she realized it was the first time she had heard her laugh out loud. Bella looked different, sounded different even discounting the laugh. Instead of her usual shrunken jumper and pinned together skirt, she was wearing a dress, black and sleeveless with a scooped-out neckline. Going further into the room, Polly could see where the sleeves had been cut out and the neckline lowered. A rim of grey shrunken vest showed like an obscene modesty vest, and two uneven protuberances stuck out where Bella had made an attempt to pad her inadequate chest into a more socially acceptable shape.

'It's the dance!' Polly clapped a hand to her mouth. 'Oh, love, I forgot. For weeks you've been telling me about the Staff Dance at the Institution, and here I am interrupting you when you're getting ready.' She glanced round the room. 'Where's the baby?'

Bella's pale eyelids were blinking so rapidly Polly felt she would start doing the same if she didn't look away. Bella had tried to put her sandy hair up on top of her head, and the resultant floret on top reminded Polly of a radish curled and peeled back to embellish a party salad. Her twig-like arms emerged from the fluted edges of the badly altered sleeves, and as she adjusted the belt of her dress Polly saw her hands tremble.

'I'm not in the middle of getting ready,' she burst out. 'The dance started at seven o'clock and it's nearly nine now. I've been ready since half-past six, and I put half a Cephos powder in the baby's bottle so he wouldn't wake up, and if Jack doesn't come for me soon the dance will be over and the baby'll be yelling his head off.' She lifted her head then dropped it to one side as if she could hear music. 'They'd got a band, Polly. We wasn't going to dance to records. We was having a band, and all the nurses and orderlies were going and some of the Grade A patients. Jack was on duty working the lights – for the spot prizes you know – but he said he'd get away and come and fetch me, and it's over at ten because of the nurses going back on duty and getting the patients to bed, so if he does come now it's too late.' The sandy eyelashes flickered rapidly up and down, up and down. 'I'd have walked through the woods on me own if I'd had a ticket, but Jack has the tickets and they won't let you in without one.'

'Oh, but they would.' Polly nodded towards Bella's coat draped over a chair. 'You go off now, and I'll stop with the baby. You won't need a ticket being Jack's wife. Go on. Off you go. I'll give the baby a bottle if he wakes up. I know where the things are.'

The sparse, sandy eyelashes were fluttering feverishly now. Bella's small face twisted with the force of her emotions. Deciding what to do for the best made her pulse race. It was all right Polly Pilgrim telling her what to do. She was always telling folks what to do, come to think of it. Bossy, Jack said she was, always bossing Gatty something shocking. Bella closed her eyes, the better to think. Jack had said she must wait. 'Stop there till I come for you,' he'd said. 'Think on, now.'

'I'm a good dancer,' she said slowly, seeing herself keeping up with the twiddly bits in a quickstep. 'It's ages since I went dancing.' Her thin mouth set in a stubborn line. 'But Jack said to wait. And, besides, he's got the tickets,' she added. 'There was a lot of bother last time with gatecrashers trying to get in without.' Averting her eyes from her coat, she slumped down into a chair. 'I'd best wait.'

'Well!' Polly stared at her in disbelief. 'It's nothing to do with me, but I think you're wrong. Obeying your husband is one thing, kowtowing to him is another.' She unfastened her coat. 'Well, I'll wait with you, love. If he comes in the next quarter of an hour you might be in time for the last waltz.'

Again the dignity was there, the determined withdrawal. Bella stared hard into the fire. She liked Polly well enough. In fact, she supposed Polly was the nearest thing she'd ever had to a best friend, but even Polly wasn't going to set her against Jack. Nobody could do that. 'Would you like a cup of cocoa?' she asked in a brittle, hostessy kind of voice.

In a strange way, as they sipped the cocoa in a companionable silence, it was Bella who was the calmer. Now that all hopes of going to the dance had gone, she accepted the inevitable as someone of her temperament would always accept the inevitable. She hadn't been sure her dress looked right anyway, and her hair hadn't looked a bit like the picture in the magazine she'd copied it from. An' suppose Jack had been busy with the lights and she'd sat there like a wallflower with nobody asking her to dance? Or worse than that. Suppose one of the patients had asked her and leered at her with a silly vacant face, stepping on her toes and breathing hard down her neck? And suppose the baby had wakened up, in spite of the half of a Cephos powder, and cried till he choked?

'I never really wanted to go,' she said, putting up a hand to the rubber band and releasing her hair from its unlikely top-knot.

'Can I ask you something, Bella?' Putting her mug down, Polly leaned forward, as if she too had come to a decision. 'Has Jack ever mentioned anything to you about my cottage being haunted?'

The sudden, unexpected question took Bella by surprise. 'Haunted? You mean by a ghost?'

Polly nodded. 'Gatty's heard some tale or other. About an old man who lived in the cottage before we came. She was told this man died of shock on account of something he'd seen. Or *thought* he'd seen. Jack would know, Bella. He's lived here all his life. He was born here in this house, so if there were tales he'd be bound to have heard them. Has he ever said anything to you?'

Bella considered. Jack had told her not to tell. He had said that Harry Pilgrim was his friend, and that with new folks coming all the time to the village the story would have died out anyway. But since Harry had gone away, Jack had changed. He'd started criticizing Polly, saying she was bossy, and he'd started trying to set Gatty against her too. Bella had heard him. She'd seen the way Gatty looked at him as well, seeing him as she herself saw him, big and handsome, with his thick curly hair and his eyes the colour of green glass bottles.

Jack had stopped telling her stories lately. Bella sighed. Nobody could tell a tale like Jack. In his good moods, after they'd made love, he used to whisper stories to her, making them up as he went along, doing the accents, acting the parts. Tickling her till she squealed for mercy, frightening her till she begged him to stop. But lately. . . . She frowned. Moody, that's what he was. Staring at her as if he didn't like what he saw, then going off walking in the woods, not telling her what shift he was on at work and yelling at her when his meals weren't ready on time.

'I forget the details,' she said, 'but something happened a long time ago.' Her untutored mind struggled with the effort of remembering. 'But it were more than a hundred years ago, I know that.'

'Go on.' Polly was on the edge of her chair. 'It's important, Bella. Go on. I'm listening.'

'There was a family living in your cottage what earned their living by weaving. On hand-looms.' Bella's mouth chewed on nothing for a while. 'Then when the mills got going with machinery it meant one man could do the work of five. Jack said a gang burned down a mill at Westhoughton, and another mob destroyed every single loom in the Blackburn mills. There were a name for them, but I can't think what it was.'

'Luddites,' Polly said at once.

'That's right. Fancy you knowing that. Yes, that were the name. Luddites. There were a mill in Clitheroe what had a moat round it to keep the gangs from getting in, but one night the man what lived in your cottage got some mates together and broke into the mill. They smashed up the looms and nearly got away, but their leader got shot in the back.'

'The man from my cottage?'

Bella nodded. 'Somehow his friends got him home and carried him upstairs to his bed. The local animal doctor took the bullet out with a knife, and they left him sleeping.' Bella's thin little voice sank to a whisper. 'When they'd gone, the man's wife went upstairs and stood by the bed holding the lamp high.'

'And?' Polly almost shouted the word.

'He was dead. Bled to death, lying there in blood-soaked sheets. An' from that day to this when something awful is going to happen, something shows itself in that room.' Bella's mouth clamped tight shut. 'But I don't know what it is. Nobody does, because nobody tells.' She sat back. 'An' that's all I know. God's honour.'

70

Polly sat as still as a waxwork, her mind going round in frantic reasoning. As if she was sitting on the front row at the pictures, she saw the woman standing by the bed, the lamp held high in her hand as she gazed down at her husband's face, candle-pale, with his blood drained away into the mattress. The horror of it froze her rigid, so that when the baby began to cry and Bella went upstairs she scarcely noticed her going.

She had seen that eerie ring of light on the ceiling three times now. When Harry was gassed in the war, when her father died, and on the night before Harry went away. And nothing bad had happened to Harry. He wasn't doing the work he wanted, but he was optimistically hoping for better things. Martin was settling down well at his new school, and Gatty . . . Polly hesitated. Well, Gatty had obviously had some sort of a scare. Maybe Jack Thomson had asked her for a kiss. But that was all, Polly was sure of it. Gatty was very naïve, in spite of the rouge on her cheeks and the packet of cigarettes hidden in her handbag. Polly nodded to herself. She didn't believe in ghosts, never had, but she *did* believe that a deep sense of unhappiness could perhaps linger in a room, manifesting itself years afterwards when the person presently occupying that same room was unhappy herself.

As she had been unhappy the night before Harry went away. . . . Yes, that was the explanation. It was her own thoughts put the light there. That was the explanation.

When Polly climbed back up the hill, the dog bounding ahead, her composure was restored. She had rationalized her ghost and come to terms with it. Not even the sight of Jack Thomson weaving his drunken way home on the other side of the wall had the power to scare. Waving his arms about he yelled something at her, but

Polly ignored him. At every step, she told herself that better things would come. Harry would find what he wanted, and Gatty's friend would come to Sunday dinner along with Polly's mother, and she would beam on them all. Compared to poor little Bella at the bottom of the hill, her life was rich was blessings.

As she reached the top of the hill, the light of the moon seemed even more white and incandescent. By the time Polly reached the cottage, her normal sense of well-being was complete. She knew, she just knew that something good was going to happen. The effort of climbing had sent the blood pounding through her veins, carrying away with it her former feeling of depression.

Life was too short to spend wallowing in misery, looking for trouble, anticipating disasters. The swift climb in the moonlight had revitalized her. Tomorrow was another day, full of exciting possibilities. She had never stayed 'down' for long. She just wasn't made that way.

Nothing had changed for the bad with Harry going away. He was all right, and she was all right. Their separation was a temporary thing. The whole Depression choking the life out of the north was a temporary thing. Soon smoke would belch forth from the tall mill chimneys again.

And even if she was wrong, then it would all be the same a hundred years from now. That great blue cold sweep of Pendle Hill would be there, that much was sure. She trudged on, the certainty of her optimism like a singing in her heart.

The next day, walking down the street in the late afternoon, after her day's stint at the factory, Polly saw a tall man wearing a brown trilby hat walking towards her. When he stopped and raised the hat and she saw the light from a standard lamp shine on his thick, silver-streaked hair, she remembered him at once.

— Four —

Polly's mother's reaction to the news that a strange man was coming to dinner evoked the response Polly could have anticipated, word for word.

'What did you say his name was?'

Polly told her.

'Robert Dennis?' Edna chewed it over as if it had rude connotations. 'I've never heard you mention him before.'

'He's a friend.'

Edna made a sound half-way between a sneer and a Victorian pshaw. 'Married women don't have men as *friends*. I wasn't born yesterday. Your Harry would have something to say if he knew you'd taken up with a *man* as a friend.'

Polly opened the door of the fire oven and stared hard at the hotpot in its brown dish. She'd saved the rounded ends of the potatoes till the last, layering them like fish-scales on the top. Already they were taking on the shiny brown crispness absolutely necessary to a real Lancashire hotpot. She slammed the door shut and got on with peeling the carrots.

To tell the truth, she was regretting her impulsive invitation herself. What on earth had made her ask the tall man to share their Sunday dinner? She frowned. Was it because he had so obviously wanted to keep her talking there on the windy corner of the street? Almost as if he'd had no home to go to. Or was it because it had registered for the first time that his left sleeve hung loose; that in spite of his cleanliness there had been about him an air of neglect, from the soft collar of his shirt in need of turning to a button hanging by a thread from his coat?

'He lost his wife recently,' she told Edna. 'With pneumonia. I don't think he looks after himself properly.' She nodded at the oven. 'Men don't make hotpots, not for themselves, and one more doesn't make any difference to me. Winnie's coming too,' she added. 'Gatty's friend from the shop, so we'll be six.'

'He's only got one arm, Gran.' Martin looked up from his book. 'Was it shot off by the Germans, Mam, or did he have it cut off because he got gangrene?' The blue eyes glittered. 'Has it got a hook on the end?'

'No staring now!' Polly began to slice the carrots, seeing, out of the corner of her eye, Martin holding an arm straight out in front of him.

'Is it off there?' Martin pointed with a forefinger above his pullover. 'Or there?' The finger moved down to below his elbow. 'I wonder how he knots his tie?'

Edna, at the window, nodded twice, moving her small head up and down. 'Well, he's coming, so you can ask him.' She stood up in order to see better. 'By the gum, but he's tall! You wouldn't get many like him in a packet of crisps!'

To Polly's dismay she felt her face flame. For the umpteenth time she asked herself, why? Why? What on earth had possessed her to ask this man to dinner? Even in the middle of the night she'd woken up searching her mind for the answer. He'd made her laugh. And she'd made him laugh, telling him about missing the job and having to fold raincoats all day. They'd exchanged names, family details, and she'd missed first one bus then another. People had walked past, hurrying home. It had begun to rain and still they'd talked, words bubbling out of them as if everything had to be told in a great hurry. He was like no man she'd ever known before. Softly spoken like Harry, yet with more of an air of authority about him. Robert Dennis wouldn't suffer fools gladly – that much she'd realized even as they talked. Her mother was wrong. It *was* possible for a woman to have a friend who just happened to be a man. And, oh God, how she needed a friend. Someone without the air of defeat about them. Not Bella with her servile attitude to her cruel husband; not Gatty who treated her mother as if she'd come out of the Ark; certainly not Edna with her preformed ideas and deep distrust of men in general; and heaven knows, though she wasn't a snob, not the young girls at the factory with their everlasting talk about film stars and crooners.

Polly wiped her hands on her apron and went to answer the door, her smile as welcoming as the noonday sun bathing the hills in soft diffused light.

'How d'you do?' Robert Dennis held Edna's hand for a long moment, his pale grey eyes steady and kind. 'So you're Polly's mother?' He gave a small bow. 'It's so kind of your daughter to include me in your family lunch. It's a long time since I walked in the country on a Sunday. I'd forgotten just how desolate it can be at this time of year.'

Polly held her breath, waiting for her mother's sniff of disapproval, the cutting remark. Edna was a past master at putting people down, withering them with a

76

glance, embarrassing them with some outspoken comment. She blinked in disbelief. Edna was simpering up at the tall man, a coquettish expression on her small wrinkled face.

'Not at all, Mr Dennis,' she was saying in an accent Polly recognized as the one she used when talking to the minister's wife. 'We always have a good lunch of a Sunday. One extra makes no difference. My mother had seven girls and two boys, but she could always make room for another pair of feet under the table. "Just chuck another few spuds in the pan and set an extra knife and fork", she'd say.'

'Ah, big families,' Robert handed his overcoat over and sat down in the chair pointed out to him. 'My ancestors were Irish Catholics, so I know quite a lot about big families, *and* extra tatties in the pot.'

Polly closed her eyes as well as holding her breath, then opened them in time to hear her mother say in that strangely clipped accent: 'I've known a lot of quite naice Catholics in my time, Mr Dennis.'

And that was that. Panic over, order restored. When the meal was ready, Polly sat at the head of the table, cheeks flushed, eyes bright, heaping plates, passing them round, listening with half an ear to her mother telling Robert what a good job she was sure he was doing with education. Boasting about Martin's winning of the scholarship, bemoaning the fact that *she'd* had to go in the mill as a half-timer at twelve.

Gatty and her friend Winnie seemed to be sharing some secret joke, shaking with giggles, spluttering into their glasses of water, digging each other in the ribs and snorting down their noses when spoken to.

Martin, as usual, was quiet, spellbound with fascination as he saw the way the one-armed man coped with

77

his food. His eyes narrowed as he stared at Robert's neatly knotted tie. Hotpot followed by rice pudding wasn't really much of a test, unfortunately. . . . He glanced round the table. Gatty and her friend Winnie were whispering together, planning a quick get-away, he guessed. His gran was all right though. Old, of course, probably coming up to dying one of these days. And his mother . . . *she* was looking quite pretty for someone of her age. He hoped she wouldn't die for a long time yet. Accepting a second helping, he surreptitiously dropped a morsel of food on to the floor for the dog waiting with longing eyes and slavering jaws.

'No, I honestly don't mind,' Edna told them. 'Off you go for a nice walk with Mr Dennis and Martin, dear, and leave me to do the washing-up. The fresh air will do you good.'

'Why is Gran talking funny?' Martin whispered as they left the cottage. Before Polly could answer he was off, streaking down the hill at breakneck speed, the dog lolloping along at his side, running pigeon-toed, throwing his cap in the air and whooping when he caught it again.

Now and again he tripped, lunged forward, caught his balance and hurtled forward again. 'I swear he could trip over the pattern on the oilcloth.' Polly said. 'He's dying to ask you how you fasten your tie.'

'By anchoring one end in a drawer,' Robert said at once. 'I'll show him when we get back.'

'That'll make his day.'

They walked on, climbing a stile, through a stubble field. Now and then Polly stole a glance at the man striding along by her side. He dressed to please himself, she guessed, and she wondered why, if his wife couldn't have borne a child, they hadn't adopted? He had the

78

sure touch with Martin, talking to him as an equal, asking questions, then listening to the answer, as if the opinion of an eleven-year-old boy was of great importance. When they came at last to the river, they sat down on a fallen log and watched Martin skimming stones across the dark green water. The dog scampered to the very edge, hesitated, then barked loudly as if to make up for his lack of courage.

'He's a coward, I'm afraid.' Polly smiled. 'He can't discriminate. If a burglar broke into the cottage, Jim would leap up and lick his hand. As a guard dog he's about as much use as a day-old kitten.'

Robert took off his hat and laid it down on the log in between them. 'The boy's like you,' he said. 'But Gatty? I take it she's like your husband?'

Polly nodded. 'In looks, but not at the moment in ways, I'm afraid. She's so *contrary*, if you know what I mean. Giggling at the table like that, almost hysterical. Just lately I'd have sworn her face would crack if she smiled, but put her with Winnie and, well, you saw. What did you make of Winnie?'

'Sharp,' he said at once. He was looking at her directly, eyes steady. 'But they're young. I wouldn't worry.'

'Who said I'm worrying?'

'Well, *something's* worrying you, love.'

Polly looked away quickly, embarrassed at the unexpected endearment, and saw Jack Thomson loping along on the far bank of the river, flat cap pulled down low on his forehead, hands thrust deep into the pockets of his jacket. Martin and the dog had moved back into the fringe of the wood behind them, so that it would look, Polly realized, as if she and the tall man were quite alone.

To add to her discomfiture Jack stopped, faced them,

head lowered, green eyes at that distance expressionless. For what seemed to Polly like an eternity he stayed there, deliberately assessing, frankly staring. Then he laughed, a deep-throated chuckle carried to them across the river, shoulders shaking as if in some private amusement, before turning and walking on.

Immediately for Polly, the easy familiarity she had felt sitting there in the soft October sunlight was gone. She shivered, turning up the collar of her coat. 'I think we'd better get back,' she said in a flat voice.

'Must we?' Robert turned and smiled at her. 'You know something? I haven't felt like this for a long time. At peace, I suppose.' He touched the sleeve of Polly's red coat. 'You're not cold? The sun's quite warm down here. I was fancying I might get a bit of a tan.'

'Well, all right, then.' Polly lifted her face to the sun. 'If I get one it'll make a change. We once had a week's holiday at Blackpool, and though I lay on the beach on a striped towel every day, really trying to go brown, all I got was a few freckles and the skin off my nose.'

Even the light was soft that afternoon. The river flowed sluggishly with here and there a flurry of white froth as the water gurgled over small boulders in its shallower reaches. The fields merged into the far distance, their summer green faded to a dull brownish yellow. Out of sight, round the bend, came the sound of oars splashing rhythmically, and the creak as they moved in their rowlocks. Jack Thomson was coming across, saving himself the walk down to the bridge, using the boat when he'd no right to, because it didn't belong to him, and not giving a damn.

Suddenly Martin appeared from nowhere, his face with its tell-tale expression obnoxiously smug. 'Jack Thomson's taken the boat again! Old Mr Bleasdale'll

give him what for if he catches him. He told me he'd
have the police on him if he did it again.' An expression
of hope gladdened his eyes. 'Do you think I ought to
run round the bridge and tell on him? Or get in the
boat and row it back, Mam? There might be somebody
wanting to get across, ringing the bell for Mr Bleasdale
an' everything. Oh, go on, Mam! I can do it. You could
watch me. Scout's honour I could do it!'

'We're not interfering.' Polly's voice was firm. 'For all
we know they may have come to some arrangement
between them. Hardly anyone uses the ferry these days,
especially not at this time of the year.'

'Mam. . . ?'

'No!'

Martin kicked out at a stone. 'You're rotten,' he
mumbled. 'You won't let me do nothing! Me dad
would've. He wouldn't have stopped me rowing that
flamin' little boat across. I wish he'd come home. He's
not rotten like you!'

'He's quite a nice boy, really.' Polly's expression was
so calm, her face so serene that Robert laughed out loud.

'Do you ever lose your temper, Polly?'

She seemed to be considering. 'With Gatty often. With
Martin hardly ever.' She brushed a fallen leaf from her
coat. 'Martin said what he did because he's missing his
dad. When Gatty cheeks me she's not thinking about
anyone but herself. I read somewhere that adolescents
have to go through a period of rejecting their parents in
order to come out on the other side whole and independ-
ent. I just pray that's true.'

Robert was holding out his good arm to help her up
when she saw Martin running from the wood, the dog
leaping excitedly round his heels as if it were a game.

'It's Jack Thomson!' Martin's blue eyes were standing

81

out with fear. 'I was spying on him and our Gatty through the trees, an' he was talking to her, then he pushed her over an' she fell down. . . .'

'Show me! Show me where!' Polly had never known she could run so fast. With heart pounding, she kept up with Martin's flying figure, her mind only half acknowledging the fact that Robert Dennis was right behind her. Her feet slithered on mounds of damp moss; a branch caught in her hair, tugging it viciously away from her scalp, but she ran on heedless of anything but the urgency of getting to Gatty.

When they came to a clearing and she saw them, it was something of an anticlimax. Jack was holding an upright Gatty by her arm, keeping her by his side, his handsome face serious and intense, while Gatty, startled by their sudden appearance, turned to gaze at them mutely, dismay clouding her face.

Or guilt. In that single moment it was the guilt that registered with Polly. 'What's going on?' She heard her voice high and shrill. 'For heaven's sake, what *is* going on?' She took a step forward. 'Let go of her, Jack. Can't you see you're hurting her?'

The sneer spreading over Jack's face chilled her blood. Before she could intervene a small bundle of black fury hurtled past her.

'Flamin' 'enery!' Martin was beside himself with excitement as Jim's sharp teeth buried deep into Jack Thomson's trousered leg. 'Give him what for! Go on, lad. Let him have it!'

Pushing Gatty violently aside, the big man grabbed Jim's collar. Before anyone could even think of moving, he swung the little dog round, bashing him hard against the horny trunk of a tree.

'Bloody mongrel!' Jack's face was contorted with rage

and pain. His throat, rising from the open neck of his striped flannel shirt, seemed to swell. Viciously kicking the dog aside as he lay yelping with fear at the foot of the tree, he glared at Polly, green eyes smouldering beneath heavy dark brows. 'I'll do for that blasted mongrel one of these days, see if I don't, an' for that daughter of yours, pestering a man on his way home from work.'

Clutching his thigh, he turned on his heel, limping away into the wood, muttering to himself, mouthing curses, the great width of his shoulders bowed almost double.

It was unbelievable; it was a nightmare happening there in broad daylight. Gatty ran from them, pleated skirt swinging round thin legs, but Polly stood as if rooted to the ground, shame flooding over her in a warm tide.

Martin cradled the little dog in his arms, turning a horrified face in their direction. 'He's broken Jim's leg!' he wailed, his young voice cracking with pain. 'Look at it! He's gone and broken Jim's leg!'

'The bastard!'

Polly stared in amazement as Robert caught up easily with the man stumbling away into the trees. Polly saw him grip the back of Jack's jacket, swinging him round, and even as she cried out in alarm she marvelled at his courage. Robert held Jack off with his good arm, his face dark with anger.

'Little girls, and little dogs,' he said from between clenched teeth. 'What kind of a man are you, for God's sake? If that dog's hurt badly then you're in real trouble, I can promise you that!'

Polly felt rather than saw the derisive glance Jack gave to Robert's overcoat sleeve hanging loose. In that moment she knew that if Jack Thomson had thought he was matching up to a man his equal in strength, he would have given in. Now the bully inherent in his disposition took over.

'Trouble?' he sneered. 'From you and who else?' Twisting his head he spat on the ground. 'You want to get yourself another arm before you start threatening me!'

Even as he spoke his knee came up, catching Robert in the groin, causing him to lose his grip, sending him rolling over, to fall with a thud against a black gnarled tree root, as hard and unyielding as rock.

For the second time in a space of a minute Jack Thomson lurched away, but this time, instead of cursing, he was laughing, a low almost inhuman chuckle that ran a cold trickle of dread down Polly's spine.

So much for my happy family Sunday, Polly thought, as they went slowly back up the hill, Martin carrying the dog, and Robert walking by her side, grey-faced, but swearing his shoulder hurt hardly at all.

He will think we are savages, she told herself; he will wonder whatever possessed him to leave his nice house in town and meet my family, not one of whom has behaved normally since he set foot over the doorstep. And that includes my mother with her fractured vowel sounds. He will be thinking we are like characters out of a Russian play, each one hiding dark secrets, as divorced from reality as if we'd been conjured up out of some writer's tortured mind. The sun had gone in, while a cloud like a shroud now enveloped Pendle Hill, drifting down towards them in curling tendrils of damp, cold air. He will never be my friend now, she told herself. I will never see him again after today.

Robert's emotions would have startled and surprised her. The pain in his left shoulder was a grinding ache. Only by cupping the stump in his right hand could he bear it without giving himself away. He suspected it could be dislocated, and guessed also that once back in the cottage Polly would want to tend it, would want to help him remove his jacket and even his shirt to persuade herself that no real damage had been done. And he couldn't. Not at this stage. Biting his lips he trudged on. Up to meeting her he had been in cool command of his own life, even riding out his grief at his wife's death with a calm equanimity of the spirit. Their childless marriage had been almost without storms, and he had been content to stay in that same safe harbour for possibly the rest of his life. Glancing sideways at Polly, he immediately sensed her shame.

But was there any shame more abasing than the shame of a man who had failed to defend when put to the test? It was that tearing at him, not the pain running like molten fire down his left arm, into the hand that didn't exist.

'I'll see to your shoulder when we get in,' Polly said quietly, and he answered her abruptly with a firm shaking of his head.

'There won't be the need for that. I'll be off home when I've looked at the dog. If he's really broken a leg, then I'll telephone the vet and have him come out to you. That's unless you know one roundabouts?'

'Harry always knew what to do.' Polly spoke without looking at him. 'He was good with animals and birds. He *is* good with them,' she contradicted herself. 'Everything seems to have gone wrong since he went away. He even had a lot of time for Jack, thought he was kind in spite of what people said about him.' She shuddered. 'Harry sees good in everyone, you see.'

'And you don't?'

'Not in Jack Thomson, I don't. He works all day with mental defectives, and it seems sometimes that some of their behaviour has rubbed off on him.' Her step faltered suddenly. 'Harry actually thought Jack would fill the good neighbour bit when he'd gone. Sawing logs, that sort of thing. I wouldn't be surprised if he saw Jack as a sort of father figure to Gatty in his absence, but things have gone wrong there. As you must have noticed.'

'Was Jack Thomson in the war? In France?' Robert asked the question quietly.

'Yes. He was in the thick of it, I believe. Regular army.'

'In the trenches?'

'Yes. I believe he got some kind of medal for bravery. Why do you ask? The war's been over for years. Fifteen years, now.'

'I know, love. And yet it's as fresh in my mind as if it only ended yesterday. The mind's a funny thing. It can carry memories hidden deep inside a man for years. He can persuade himself that when the guns stopped, his pain stopped too. There are men who will never be the same, Polly. You had to be there to understand. Adrenalin would be pumping through Jack Thomson's veins like a drug. For four hellish years. Some can switch it off and get on with what's called normal living, but others crack. It might take five, ten, even fifteen years, depending on their temperament. Physical wounds heal, but the other kind can burst open at any time. My guess is that your neighbour is more to be pitied than condemned.'

'You mean he can't stop fighting?'

86

'Something like that.'

'So hitting his wife isn't his fault? Because in his mind she's taking the place of the Germans?'

They were walking up the cinder path to the cottage now. Edna met them at the door wearing her hat and coat, a bulging handbag over her arm.

'I'm going now.' She nodded towards the distant hill. 'I don't want to be caught in the rain, and if I get a move on I'll catch the four o'clock bus.' She glanced at Martin cradling the dog tenderly in his arms. 'What's up with everybody? Your Gatty came in a while back and went straight upstairs. Took her all her time to answer me civil when I asked her if she wanted a cup of tea.' She smiled politely at Robert, changing her accent completely. 'It's been a right pleasure to meet you, Mr Dennis. I hope you enjoyed your little walk.'

'You'll be all right, Mam?' Polly looked up at the lowering sky. 'I'd come down the hill with you, but. . . .' She gestured helplessly towards the open door. 'Be careful then.'

'There's summat up,' Edna told herself, as she started down the hill. 'An' it's to do with Gatty, that's for sure.' A pain shot through the sole of her best Sunday shoes as she forgot to step round a sharp stone. 'Live like gypsies and kids'll grow up like gypsies, running wild in this God-forsaken place.' On she went, small mouth working, muttering, chuntering, worriting at her brain till she felt one of her heads coming on. There *was* summat wrong, summat she couldn't put a finger on. When she'd gone upstairs to have a nose round like she often did when she got the chance, she had *felt* proper queer. Edna snorted out loud. An' that was daft for a start. She didn't hold with cyclic feelings, never had, but all the same she'd been glad to get back down to the fire and the kettle singing on the hob. Yes, she'd be happy to get back to her own little house with a good neighbour either side of her, and not a single blade of grass nor a view in sight.

As she passed the Thomson's tumbledown cottage she heard shouting voices raised in anger, one deep-throated, and the other like the squawking of a tiny bird, interspersed with the wail of a baby's hungry cry.

The bus was waiting there by the little general store-cum-post office, red and reassuring, the driver winking at her beneath the neb of his peaked cap.

And as it drove away down the winding road, leaving the village behind with its muddy winter fields and the hump of Pendle rising from its east side like a dark and brooding backdrop, Edna settled herself in her seat, staring straight ahead, already in her mind back home, putting the kettle on.

Biting his lips hard in an attempt to stem the pain now crawling round his shoulder blade and down his spine, Robert knelt on the floor by the dog's basket. Carefully he held the bent leg in his hand, running his fingers up the bone. Whispering words of reassurance, he slowly straightened the leg, studied it for a moment then, holding his breath, bent it back again.

'Put his dish over there. Right by the door.' He nodded at Martin. 'That's right. A bit farther away.' He straightened up. 'Now rattle it on the floor and call his name.'

'But he can't walk!' Martin's indignation showed in his voice. 'You *know* he can't walk.'

'Call him over. That's a good lad.'

'Do as Mr Dennis tells you.' Polly exchanged a glance with Robert, and thought she saw him wink.

Snug in his basket, the dog seemed to be weighing the odds of the situation. Rolling his liquid brown eyes back, he then slewed them in Polly's direction in an attitude of abject pleading.

'How can you be so cruel?' he seemed to be saying.

'Call him again.' Robert was smiling now.

'Come on, Jim! Gran's scraped the hotpot dish on top of your biscuits. See!' Holding the dish out, Martin tried again.

For a moment the shiny black nose quivered. Rising slowly the little dog gingerly took his weight on the injured paw, tested it further by stepping out from the basket before running four-legged over to the round, brown dish by the door.

'The little fraud!' Martin's face was a study in amazement. 'How did you know he wasn't hurt bad, Mr Dennis?'

'I didn't.' Robert got to his feet too quickly, the sudden movement sending pain springing in his armpit. He reached for his trilby, picking it up from the table where he'd skimmed it on coming into the cottage. 'And now I'll be going.' He jerked his chin upwards. 'You'll be wanting to talk to Gatty. She won't want me around when you do that.'

Polly went with him to the door. 'I wish you'd let me look at your shoulder first. The dog might have been putting it on, but you're not, are you? You went with an almighty crash down there in the wood.' Her blue eyes were troubled. 'I'm sorry things turned out the way they did, and I appreciate the way you went for Jack Thomson. But I'm not as tolerant as you. I can't make excuses for him the way you did. He's an evil man,

Robert. Bad, through and through. Harry would know what to do, but he's not here, and I'm certainly not going to write and worry him. I've a feeling things aren't going right down south. Harry might come home if I told him the truth, and that's the last thing I want. He's got to try to make a go of things first. Coming back now would mean we're back to square one. You can see that, can't you?'

They stood silently for some seconds. She was so vulnerable, he had a sudden urge to draw her to him, promising his protection. His feelings for this lovely, troubled, young woman needed clarification in his analytical mind. Leaving her in these isolated backwoods was tearing at him with a pain as acute as the agony of his injured shoulder. Their eyes held hard for a moment as a flicker of awareness passed between them. He forced a smile.

'Thank you for that wonderful hotpot, Polly.' Taking her hand he squeezed it briefly. 'Take care, love. And don't worry. It'll all come out in the wash.'

Slowly Polly closed the door. There was so much she had wanted to tell him, so many worries to unload. He had come into her life at a time when her need to confide was overwhelming. He was virtually a stranger, and yet she had known the way he would have listened without uttering a single word of advice.

'People have to work out their own salvations,' he had said, as they sat together in the sunshine. She guessed he was a man of great tolerance. And it was odd and somehow disturbing the way his friendship meant so much, even in the short time she'd known him. He had a way of seeing things straight on, tempering them with wisdom and compassion.

Now she would never see him again. Polly imagined

him returning to his house, looking back on his Sunday in the country with utter disbelief. For a fleeting second she had an urge to open the door again, run after him, and beg him not to go.

'We're not like this,' she wanted to say. 'Before Harry lost his work and with it his quiet happiness, we were an ordinary family. I wanted you to see us as we really are, and more than that. I believed there was in you a need for laughter and friendship, and I wanted to answer that need.'

Sighing deeply, she started up the stairs and the necessary confrontation with Gatty.

'Jack Thomson said you were *pestering* him!' Polly came straight to the point, closing the bedroom door and going over to the bed where Gatty lay, one arm over her face, thin legs in pale lisle stockings stretched out on the patchwork quilt. 'What did he mean by that?'

'Search me.' Gatty's voice came back, muffled but defiant. 'He had to say something, didn't he, when you and that man came bursting through the trees like Robin Hood and flamin' Little John.'

'Gatty . . .' Polly prayed for control, fighting down a desire to yank her daughter to her feet and shake the truth out of her. 'If Jack was trying anything on with you, and you've more or less admitted it wouldn't be the first time, I'm going to tell the police.' She found she was actually wringing her hands. 'It's the last thing I want to do, but you're my responsibility. Even more so while your dad's away. Jack has got to be warned off. Surely you can see that?'

The arm over Gatty's face twitched a little, but she gave no sign of having heard a word her mother said.

Polly tried again. 'Where was Winnie?'

'Gone home.'

'Why so early?'

'Because there's nothing to do out here of a Sunday night, that's why.'

'And there *is* down the town?'

'She goes with some mates on the road, that's all. Just larking about, linking arms and talking to lads sometimes. Everybody goes.'

Polly knew all about the 'road'. A few of the girls at school had done it, Sunday after Sunday. They walked in twos and threes up and down the main road, as far as the park gates and back. They even went into the park at times, if they were picked up by a boy, to sit on the benches bordering the Broad Walk and lie in the grass fronting the Conservatory, if they were bold enough.

'I never wanted to do that.'

'Well, you were *courting* at my age, weren't you? More fool you.'

'So you met Jack accidentally, walking back from seeing Winnie off on the bus?'

'That's it.'

'Why were you in the wood then? The way from the village is up the hill.'

'Because I was looking for you. I knew you'd gone for a walk and so I was looking for you.'

'And that's the truth?'

'God's honour.'

'Martin said Jack pushed you over.'

'Only because I gave him a bit of cheek.' Gatty's tone was infinitely weary. 'He said something rude to me so I gave him a mouthful. He thinks he's that flamin' handsome, it was time somebody told him he's just a nowt.' Her voice wobbled. 'I *hate* him, if you must know. One minute he was laughing at me an' the next he looked as if he could kill me. You know what he's like, our Mam.'

It was all so plausible, so reasonable an explanation, Polly felt the tension ebb away from her. Sitting down on the narrow bed, she lifted Gatty's arm from her face. She spoke softly. 'Don't give him any more cheek, love. He's always had a bad temper, and Bella says it's got worse lately.' She coughed nervously. 'Mr Dennis said it could be because of what happened in France during the war. Jack was in the thick of it for almost the whole time. You didn't know that, did you? So we have to make allowances.' Polly held Gatty's hand to her face for a moment. 'Just keep away from him, love, as much as you can, and don't provoke him. Promise?' She tried not to notice when Gatty immediately snatched her hand away. 'I know it's not much fun for you living out here now you're older. It was all right when you were a little girl going to the village school and following your dad around like a little lapdog. Sometimes I tend to forget you're all grown up.'

Oh, God, would she never stop talking? Gatty knew she couldn't bear another minute of it. What did her mother know about it? What did she know about *anything*, come to that? And why did she always have to be so flamin' patronizing? Oh, God, why did she just have to BE when all Gatty wanted was to be alone, cut off from living till things came all right again?

Before her mother had closed the door, Gatty could feel the terror taking over. Sitting up she laid her forehead down on her bent knees. The fear inside her swelled and swelled until she was faint with the feel and smell of it. If Polly hadn't got up and left the room, Gatty knew she would have blurted out the truth. But the truth was too horrible even to contemplate.

She bit hard on her finger to stop herself from crying aloud. Over and over in her imagination she went through every single detail of what had happened to her. . . .

It was the Sunday before, and she'd been down in the little wood like today. But not looking for Jack Thomson, just gathering sticks for the fire with Martin, quarrelling with him, as usual. Gatty swallowed hard, feeling the swelling come up into her throat again. Crying wouldn't do any good. Puffy eyes would only get her mother going again, asking her everlasting questions, ferreting out the terrible something that might never need to be told.

Gatty stretched her eyes wide. The thing to do was to keep calm, and not worry. It was three whole weeks before her next period was due, even if it came on time which it hardly ever did. Sometimes she went five or six weeks. Doctor Mansfield said it was because she was anaemic, and that lots of girls were the same at the beginning.

Gatty started to tremble, forcing herself to go over what had happened, picturing it in detail, striving with all her being to rid herself of this tearing anxiety.

Gran had been for her dinner, sitting round the table with her hat on, chewing with her mouth open the way old people did sometimes. Gatty remembered watching her in disgust, deciding never to grow old like that. Fifty would be a decent age to die, she'd decided. Before her neck went scraggy and she needed to wear glasses, anyroad.

It had been a misty day, with the whale-shape of

Pendle hidden by cloud. By four o'clock it was going dark, and that was when Martin said he was going home.

Or was it when the cat, sleek and black as night, had streaked across their path? 'A witch's cat' Gatty had said, trying to scare her brother. 'It's not true that the witches lived on the hill all those years ago. It was down here where they lived. I bet that cat wasn't real, our Martin. I bet if we'd touched it, our hands would have gone right through it.'

'I'm going home,' Martin had told her, going all funny the way he did when he was trying not to show he was frightened. Taking a piece of string from his pocket, he'd tied the sack of sticks at the top before slinging it over his shoulder. 'That old cat *was* real, our Gatty! I've seen it many a time, sitting on the counter at the shop. Mrs Bebson says it comes in with fleas, and ghost cats don't have fleas. If that old cat was a ghost, then I can knit fog, so yah to you!'

The peevish, brotherly face he pulled made Gatty want to hit him, to run after him, grab his hair and roll over and over on the ground with him as they'd often done when they were younger. In that moment she hated Martin so much, she could feel the hatred swelling up inside her, thick and hot. But she was wearing her only pair of unmended stockings and her new pleated skirt, and besides, she was too old to fight. She stood watching him go, the sack over his shoulder, tall where she was small, fair where she was dark, clear-skinned where she was sometimes spotty, clever where she was not.

'Oh, God!' Deliberately she shouted the blasphemy aloud. Oh, how she *hated* Sundays! Hunching her shoulders and digging her hands deep in the pockets of her swing-back jacket, she trudged away in the opposite direction, scuffing the wet fallen leaves with her shoes, seeing the toe-caps turning black and caring not at all. Shoes . . . she *hated* shoes. She hated the rows and rows of boxes on high shelves, the climbing up to get them down and then the kneeling on haircord carpet and pushing them on to feet. Big feet, small feet, sweaty feet. . . . Gatty grimaced as if burdened by a sudden pain. If it wasn't for Winnie, she wouldn't stop at the shop another day.

'There'd be a hundred girls queueing up for your jobs,' Mr Arnold had told them the day he'd found them smoking in the store-room at the back. 'Do you fancy yourselves in the ranks of the unemployed, queueing up for the dole and lying in bed every morning for want of an occupation?'

Every single day like Sunday, Gatty reminded herself, and stopped, the endless prospect of a whole week of Sundays almost too terrible to contemplate. She tried to imagine waking up in the cottage with nowhere to go, nothing to do. She sighed. It was a bit thick when the alternative to doing what you didn't want to do was doing nothing at all. Life itself was a bit thick, come to that.

Always a slow thinker, Gatty sat down on a fallen log and tried to rationalize her depression. It was just that nothing was fair. Nothing in the whole rotten world was fair. Her father, before he went away, was always reminding her that she lived near the loveliest village in Lancashire. In the country, come to that. It had a gurgling brook, a village green with stocks, and a church built in fourteen something. And nothing happened. Nothing! Nothing! Nothing! The stupid sheep on the hillside, with their silly black faces and potty vacant staring eyes, had more interesting lives than she had.

Suddenly Gatty started to cry. It was a meaningless,

vapid, silent habit of weeping, and one she'd indulged in a lot lately. In a strange way she enjoyed it, this feeling of tears slipping down her cheeks and her tasting the sad saltiness of them as they ran past her open mouth. Sometimes, when she cried in bed, she pretended she was crying for her father, missing him, but she knew that wasn't strictly true. For a long time now, for the last year at least, she hadn't been all that interested in anyone except herself. Taking a tiny mirror from her pocket, Gatty gazed at her tear-stained face with lingering concentration. Seen that way, with tears glistening like glycerine on her cheeks and on the ends of her long black eyelashes, she looked quite pretty. Winnie wet her hair with sugar and water and put Dinkie curlers in every night, and she was always telling Gatty how much nicer she'd look if she at least waved her fringe with kirby grips crossed over her hair made into little round snails. The tears forgotten, Gatty pushed her fringe away from her forehead and pouted, not too sure of the effect.

That was the face Jack Thomson saw turned towards him as he came up behind her, walking soft-footed on the mossy undergrowth of the little wood. A young face, wet with recent tears, wide mouth quivering, dark eyes limpid with a longing she didn't even begin to guess was a longing. Even before he sat down beside her the familiar excitement grew inside him, tightening like a low-down pain. He smiled at her, reaching out a hand to smooth her ruffled hair.

'Crying, Gatty? All by yourself on a Sunday afternoon? What's wrong? Your boy-friend chucked you? A pretty girl like you? He needs his head seeing to.'

There was the added warmth of the best part of half a bottle of whisky inside him. Bella had been downstairs seeing to the baby, leaving him lying upstairs in bed, partaking of what he'd called his liquid breakfast. He'd tried to pull her down beside him as she'd walked past the bed, but she'd jerked away, nagging on about the whisky, warning him he'd get caught one of these fine days pinching it from the patients' lockers.

'Who's to know?' he'd said. 'They're not supposed to have it, anyroad. If their relatives are daft enough to smuggle it in, then I'm doing them a good turn taking it away. It's wasted on them, anyroad up.'

'I haven't got a boy-friend.' Gatty fluttered her eye-lashes at him, flirting without realizing she was being provocative, enjoying the nearness of the big, good-looking man with his strange green eyes and his teasing ways. It was a way Jack had of looking at her, the way he was looking at her now. Jack Thomson always managed to satisfy her craving for masculine attention and flattery; a craving Gatty didn't know she had. She shivered.

'A goose walk over your grave?'

She nodded. She could smell the drink on his breath, and a little warning bell rang in her head, but it was too late. When he slid a hand underneath her hair at the back of her neck, she felt a queer melting sensation inside her. She knew he wanted to kiss her, and her wanting to be kissed was just an extension of her tears, an added feeling of the unbearable sadness deep inside her. It didn't have to be Jack; it could have been any man with arms to hold and a whispering voice telling her she was lovely.

What she hadn't expected was the change in him after the long, searching kiss ended. Jack's face was burning so hot she could feel the heat on her own cheeks. His green eyes were glittering, and he seemed to be finding it hard to breathe. Gatty was filled with wonder. He was

98

trembling now, and as his hands slid down her body she felt a strange power. That she, Gatty Pilgrim, could make a grown man feel like this!

'That's enough,' she whispered in her light young voice. 'Stop it, Jack!'

But this was no young boy cuddling her on a settee at a party. This wasn't a boy canoodling on the back seat at the pictures and grinning in the darkness as she slapped his hand away.

Before Gatty knew what was happening, she was lying flat on her back with the weight of the big man on top of her. He was tearing at her underclothes, struggling with his own, and as she felt the hardness of him against the inside of her thighs she opened her mouth to scream, only to have his hand across her mouth suffocating the very life out of her. . . .

Now, sitting up on the bed, staring wide-eyed at the wall, this was the part she had to remember clearly. In her terror she'd twisted, fought, felt a sharp pain; she had thrashed about, jerking her legs, biting the hand across her mouth. She remembered sweating and crying, and then, almost unconscious, feeling him grow suddenly limp. Rolling away from him to pull at her disordered clothes, she'd felt sticky and horrible as if she would never be clean again.

Whimpering now, Gatty choked back the tears in her throat. Reliving it hadn't helped. She still didn't know *exactly* what had happened. It had been too quick. *Surely* it had been too quick? Making a baby couldn't be like that. There had to be love, hadn't there? Soft words spoken, not just a terrifying, over-in-a-minute struggle, lying on her back in a wood on a late Sunday afternoon? Gatty gulped back a sob.

It had taken all her courage to seek Jack out that

afternoon to ask him if she would be all right. She had never wanted to speak to him again, but she needed his reassurance so badly she had felt she couldn't get through another day without it.

Closing her eyes, she went over what had happened, trying to persuade herself that Jack's anger had been because she was stupid enough to worry, not because he was worried himself.

'You only got what you asked for,' he'd told her. 'An' if you're not all right then it's none of my doing.' He'd called her a bad name and pushed her away.

'Gatty?'

Polly's voice spiralled upstairs, and wearily Gatty swung her legs on to the sloping floor and stood up.

Jack Thomson was right. She *was* a silly what he'd called her. She knew nothing, nothing at all, not even if there was a need for this worry eating away at her. Taking her brush from the wash-stand, Gatty stroked her hair listlessly. The thing to do was to hold on, keep the dreadful secret tight inside her. Talk and eat, just as if nothing had happened. Go through the motions of living, even though the worry was so overwhelming she feared she might die of it.

'Gatty? I've made a pot of tea, love. Aren't you coming down?'

'Oh, Mam.' For a moment Gatty stared wide-eyed into the mirror on the wall. The urge to run downstairs, hurl herself into Polly's arms and blurt it all out was so powerful she could almost feel it happening.

'Just coming!' she called out, then because the fear was like dark treacle cloying in her throat, her voice tightened with irritation. 'I heard you the first time.'

She sat down at the table, the all-pervading numbness taking over again. It was better this way with the worry temporarily paralysed. This way she could even eat and drink as if everything was normal. Gatty took a piece of bread and butter from the plate in the middle of the table, asked Martin to pass the jam and spread it carefully right to the crust, as if she was hungry and looking forward to enjoying her tea.

— Five —

From Polly's long table in the middle of the factory floor, she could see rows of heads bent over the uniformly spaced sewing machines. There were heads trimmed with rows of Dinkie curlers and tousled heads, all drooping over the drab material as they guided the foot of their machine swiftly round pockets, belts and the cut-out pieces of Mr Goldberg's utilitarian raincoats.

That morning, on her way to work, Polly had sensed a definite lethargy in the air itself as she'd walked from the Boulevard, taking a short cut through streets silvered with a gently falling drizzle. It had beaded her red coat in tiny globules, more wetting than a proper downpour, muckier, she'd decided, than the soft rain sweeping down from Pendle Hill as she'd left the cottage.

With more mills closing down, or putting their workers on short time, it had seemed to her as if the whole town was dying. Blinds still drawn on a great number of the terraced houses spoke to her of whole families lying abed. Father, sons and daughters having a Monday morning lie-in because there was nothing to do and nowhere to go.

She walked on through silent cobbled streets which

not so long ago had rung to the hard clatter of clog irons. The flagstones were shiny-black wet, but some of the window bottoms showed rims of yellow stone where the rain had not quite washed it away.

Smoke billowed from chimneys, and she imagined fires being lit in back living-rooms, with the aid of a newspaper held against a shovel. Fires for a mug of shaving water or that first comforting pot of tea.

A man in shirt sleeves, with his braces dangling over his trousers, gazed hopelessly at the lowering sky. 'Nasty morning, love,' he called out, and Polly smiled an agreement from beneath her dripping umbrella.

It wasn't much more cheerful out of the wet that morning. Polly stared up at the high ceiling, imagining how it must have looked with the whirling leather belts of the machinery driving the looms of the weavers. She remembered the day her mother had taken her as a child to stand in the wide doorway of the mill round the corner. She'd never forgotten the noise. Or the cotton dust floating like dandelion clocks in a summer breeze round the heads of the weavers standing on damp stone floors, with their fent aprons worn cross-over style. Or the weavers and overlookers, tacklers, engineers, oilers and greasers, lip-reading each other above the noise of the looms.

'If you get your scholarship there'll be better for you,' Edna had said, and yet here her daughter was, standing in such a shed doing a job with far less dignity to it than that of any weaver at her loom.

Polly shrugged her shoulders. There was never any point in *dwelling*. Situations *dwelt* upon never improved. Anyway, she didn't have the right face for it, not with her pink cheeks and what she was sure was an incipient double chin. She gave the totally imaginary fullness a hearty slap. If her looks really pitied her that Monday morning, she would be grey and haggard, with a nerve twitching away at her jaw-line.

No, the trouble with folding coats was that it left the mind free to wander down dark paths. That was if you were daft enough to let it. She patted the folds of a finished coat into place and added it to the growing pile on a side table, ready for packing and distribution.

Harry had been away for not much more than two months, yet she was finding it hard to bring his face to mind. That scared her a little. His letters had dwindled to a few hastily scrawled lines every other week, telling her nothing, not even passing comment on the news she'd given him in her longer replies. There was nothing *intimate* in them, no lovey-dovey bits for her to sigh over. She sighed now, and reached for another coat. Harry had always been an inarticulate man, hating putting pen to paper as he called it, but it hadn't used to matter. Harry's was an untutored intelligence, for heaven's sake, Polly reminded herself angrily. Then wondered at her anger.

He had got his school-leaving certificate at twelve, worked half-time in the mill, then at thirteen he'd been out on his own, determined to turn his back on the ear-splitting noise of the weaving shed, gladly exchanging it for bird song and the sound of the wind in the trees. He'd slept in barns, worked for nothing more than his keep, until now, as Martin had said, he could grow a plant from a lump of granite.

Bending down to pick the matching belt from a hamper on the floor by her side, Polly slotted it through the loops of the coat on the big table. She fastened the buttons, checked for loose threads, then turned the coat

104

over ready for folding into the required neat oblong shape.

Another coat, another belt. Polly's mind wandered free. . . .

Would Harry have known how to deal with Gatty and her moods which seemed to have grown blacker since her father went away? Would Harry have known what to do about Jack Thomson? She suspected that even Harry with his live-and-let-live attitude to life would have been shaken out of his quiet complacency by the sullen withdrawn girl, who had stared unseeing at her oatmeal porridge that morning with the eyes of a woman twice her age. Would Harry have squared up to Jack Thomson and demanded to know what the hell was going on?

'Good morning, Polly!'

Manny Goldberg walked past the long table, darting a glance at her from beneath his dark wandering eyebrows. He stopped and smiled. Just the sight of Polly Pilgrim was enough to lift his spirits on a morning when the sky outside seemed to be resting on the tops of the tall mill chimneys.

There, he told himself, was a young woman totally at peace with herself and the world. In her yellow knitted jumper and blue tweed skirt she was a welcome splash of colour in the drab surroundings of the factory. She didn't even seem to feel the cold, not like the majority of the machinists working in their jackets, faces pinched with a cold the newly installed oil heating wasn't apparently doing much to alleviate. Polly's warmth came from inside her, Manny decided sentimentally. He turned back the lapel of a coat to check the stitching.

'Everything all right, Polly?'

'Fine, Mr Goldberg. Just fine.'

Her wide smile gladdened his heart. 'Any further progress with the shorthand and typing?'

'I'm afraid not, Mr Goldberg. It was a daft idea me thinking I could go on to night school after finishing work. I lost my chance to do that when I was seventeen.' Her blue eyes twinkled at him. 'We live too far out for one thing, and for another, my two kids seem to need watching even more than when they were babies.' She pulled a raincoat towards her. 'I'll just have to wait till my husband comes back before I start fancying myself as a secretary.'

Manny fingered his top lip. She was *wasted* doing the job she was doing. He felt a hurt seeing her standing there, hour after hour, doing a job that an intelligent nine-year-old could have done, given a box to stand on. Manny compressed his lips, chiding himself for taking too much of an interest in one of his workforce. Impartiality and fairness – that was the only way. Still he lingered.

'Your husband hasn't got himself fixed up with a job down south yet?'

'Not one good enough for him to feel he can settle, or even think of sending for us. What he had in mind was a job with a cottage to go with it. In the grounds of some big house maybe. One where you don't need the paper qualifications they seem to insist on at Kew.'

'Ah, certificates,' said Manny, with the proper disdain of a man without a single paper qualification to his credit. 'Ah, well. . . .' He turned away. 'Keep hoping, Polly. That's all any of us can do these days. Just keep on hoping. What else can you do?'

What else indeed? With nimble fingers Polly turned the coat inside out to examine the lining. But hope didn't exactly buy the baby a new bonnet, did it?

At dinnertime she ate her sandwiches quickly, then

went outside into the short street fronting the loading area of the mill to where a telephone booth stood on the corner. Manny Goldberg would have been surprised to know that she had used a telephone only twice in her life before, and then only in dire emergency; telephones were akin to cars, and therefore well out of the range of the average pocket.

Ensconced in the booth, Polly flipped over the pages of a local directory which was tethered to the wall by a long chain. As she dialled the number, she remembered the only time she had seen her mother use a telephone. Gripping the receiver as if it were greased and might slip from her grasp, Edna had bellowed her message as though the party she was calling lived in Outer Mongolia.

Carefully monitoring her own voice, Polly made her request. 'Accounts Department, please.'

'Hold the line a minute. I'm putting you through.'

Polly nodded. 'Thank you. Very much.'

Even Joan Crawford in that film where she wore a little white dress and a frilly white organdie collar couldn't have done better than that, she told herself, well satisfied.

'Accounts Department here.'

Polly chided herself silently for the unexpected blush staining her cheeks. 'Could I speak to Mr Dennis, please?'

'Who is calling?'

'Just a friend.' The blush deepened.

'I'm sorry, but Mr Dennis hasn't come into the office this morning. Can I help in any way?'

For a moment Polly hesitated. The voice at the other end was so cool, so impartial. Not homely, not one you could question further. A deep masculine voice with the suspicion of a chuckle in it. Polly shook her head, then remembered whoever it was couldn't see her. 'No, thank you. I'll ring up again. Another day. Goodbye,' she added quickly, and replaced the receiver.

Before pushing open the heavy door she stood still for a moment, one half of her mind registering the rude word written on the wall in front of her, and the other registering the embarrassment flooding over her in a deep wave of prickly heat.

What in God's name was she, Polly Pilgrim, a married woman, doing rushing out in her dinner hour to telephone another man? In that moment she was all her mother, narrow-minded to the point of idiocy, a product of her upbringing, her round face stern with puritanical disbelief. In that moment Edna would have been proud of her.

But as Polly hurried back down the short street, her commonsense took over. It was only natural that she wanted to know how Robert was after the fiasco of the day before. She frowned. His shoulder must have been badly hurt for him to take time off from his office. Even on their short acquaintance she guessed he was no malingerer. Had he gone to the doctor? Was he now sitting up at the Infirmary, waiting to be seen by a specialist? In pain, his face lean with suffering? Pale grey eyes cold with contempt as he dwelled on the reasons for him being there.

She glanced up at the leaden sky. They were in for a real downpour by the look of it, and if so, she wished it would get a move on and get it over with.

Putting Robert Dennis's face from her with an effort, she imagined Martin walking up the hill from the bus, school satchel bouncing in his back, prized long trousers soaked by the rain sweeping down from the fells. Hurrying home to an empty cottage, cold as the grave, with a fire-lighter and a pile of sticks in the grate instead of leaping flames to greet him.

Lifting her head, she felt the rain on her face and began to run.

When she took her stand at the folding table she was smiling again, joining the girls in a spirited rendering of a Methodist hymn.

'Tell me the stories of Jesus,' she sang, her expression as serene as if not a single anxiety clouded her mind.

The storm broke late that afternoon. On the road running parallel to the river the bus had to plough its way through a foot of water. Lightning ripped through the sky, and just short of the village the driver had to make a slight detour because of a fallen tree.

The Thomson cottage was in darkness, its tiny windows blinkered like bandaged eyes. Polly hesitated, then with her head bent against the driving rain, trudged on. At any other time she would have made her way up the weed-trimmed path, lifted the heavy iron knocker on the door, even pushed it open and called out. But all she could think about was getting home to Martin, alone in the cottage and terrified of the storm, cowering in the corner furthest away from the window, hands over ears, his entire body given over to fear.

Gasping for breath, heart pounding, a stitch in her side as sharp as the thrust of a knife, Polly muttered to herself about the stupidity of Bella having the baby out in weather like this. The pram she used on short excursions to the small grocery shop in the village had a hood that wouldn't stay up, and wheels that looked as if they'd belonged to something else, a long time ago. The baby dribbled so much he put people off bending down to coo at him, and his little knitted bonnet had shrunk and felted so much in the wash that it lay on his head like an extra layer of matted hair.

Poor little Bella, counting her blessings when in truth she had none really worth the counting. Polly opened the door of the cottage and felt her mouth drop open in a wide 'O' of surprise.

'Bella!' she gasped. 'What on earth. . . ? What's happened? Oh, my God!'

The blasphemy was instinctive as Polly went down on her knees by the rocking-chair drawn up to the fire. If she lived to be a hundred, she told herself, she would never forget that first sight of Bella's face.

Puffed up like a water melon, Bella's sandy-lashed eyes were mere slits in the cushions of her swollen flesh. Her lips were twice their normal size and a thread of dried blood ran from one corner, giving her expression a grotesque twist. Bella sat on the very edge of the chair, staring straight ahead. Her hands were clasped over torn and muddied stockings, and when Polly touched her she shied away to clutch the familiar grey shawl closer round her throat.

Martin, still in his school uniform, sat back on his heels from his position on the rug and his task of adding small cobs of coal to the already glowing fire. His blue eyes blazed with the excitement of finding himself the centre of a drama better than any he'd read about in his comics.

'He nearly killed her, Mam! Jack went for her with a big stick, an' she was unconscious on the floor for ages. That's right, isn't it, Bella?' The words tripped over themselves in his effort to get them out quickly. 'The postman called an' when he saw he sent for the police, an' they took Jack away to the hospital. The Institution

110

where he works. You *know*, Mam.' Putting a finger to his temple he screwed it around, trying to convey a meaning he obviously felt was too indelicate to put into words.

'What is it, Bella?'

Polly put up a hand and gently lifted a lock of the sandy hair falling forward over the terrible purple mask that had once been Bella's face. 'You're all right now, love. You're quite safe here.'

'A straight-jacket, Polly. They put my Jack in a straight-jacket.' A single tear slipped from beneath a reddened eyelid and ran down Bella's cheek. 'He's gone mad, Polly. It's being with those loonies all day. He's catched it from them. Oh, my poor Jack.'

Martin broke in eagerly. 'He's broken all the furniture, Mam, and all the pots! But he never touched the baby, did he, Bella?'

As Polly looked round, he pointed importantly to the stairway. 'I put him on my bed asleep. He cried a lot, but I carried him up the hill and he dropped off again. He's got a dirty nappy on, Mam.'

'You're a good boy, Martin.' Still hardly able to believe the evidence of her own eyes, Polly tried to pull the shawl away from Bella's throat, only to have it firmly pushed down again as Bella moaned with pain.

'It's my back,' she whimpered. 'I tried to get the stick away from him, but he was too strong for me. Have a look what he's done to my back.'

Polly looked, then closed her eyes in horror. Bella's blouse, ripped to ribbons, hung tattered from her thin shoulders. The grey shrunken vest had stuck to deep flesh wounds, the blood blackened into hard ridges in the pattern of the ribbing.

Swallowing the nausea rising in her throat, she spoke

111

quietly: 'I'll have to bathe your vest off, love.' Nodding to Martin, she motioned to him, telling him to push the kettle on its trivet over the leaping fire. 'It will hurt, but we've got to get it clean. I think there's a tin of Germolene in the cupboard. Harry always swore by Germolene. It's antiseptic,' she explained, getting up and going over to the dresser. 'But first you must drink a cup of tea.'

'With a lot of sugar in it,' said Martin, still feeling the weight of responsibility. 'I learnt that when I was in the Cubs.'

With the dropping of the shawl, Bella's childish breasts were exposed, no bigger than walnuts, mere swellings in the flatness of her narrow chest. Polly glanced quickly at Martin.

'Go up to my room, there's a good boy. Light the stove and start your homework. See, I'll light this lamp, then you can take the one from the window.' She was making signs at him from behind Bella's back. 'The storm's passed over now, so there's nothing to be afraid of.' When he set his face determinedly, she raised her voice. 'Martin. D'you hear me? Bella won't want you here when I bathe her back. You've been marvellous, and when I write and tell your dad he'll agree with me, but just for now do as I say. You don't want to upset Bella, do you?'

'I won't look, Mam,' Martin whined. 'See. I can sit here at this end of the table and I can't see nothing. Don't make me go upstairs, Mam. Please?'

Polly shook her head from side to side as if wondering what to do with him. This precious son of hers, brave to the point of heroism about things he felt could be explained, such as a man beating his wife almost to death, but as nervous as a puppy about thunder and things that went bump in the night. She gave in weakly,

112

then set about taking a bowl down from a high shelf and tearing a clean tea-towel down the middle in readiness for the task she was dreading with all her heart.

The effort of drinking the hot tea was too much for Bella. As soon as she put her lips to the rim of the cup she cried out in pain.

'I'll put more milk in it.' Polly handed it back to her. 'Try again, please, love. It'll make you feel better. Just a sip or two. . . .'

'Jack's ill.' Bella's hand trembled so much she could hardly hold the cup. 'He didn't know what he was doing.' The dignity, the proud withdrawal was there again. Polly recognized it immediately and marvelled at it. 'It's been coming on him a long time.' The pale eyelashes quivered like butterflies' wings. 'They'll make him better at the hospital 'cos they're used to dealing with what's wrong with Jack. He'll be put to bed and they'll give him food, proper food, not bread and scrape like what I've been giving him. He's not been giving me hardly any money of a Friday, 'cos of spending it all on the drink.' Just for a moment the treble of the tiny voice hardened. 'How could I get fat like he wanted me to be when he was drinking all the money away?' She glanced down at her skinny chest. 'They'll calm him down with special medicine, Polly. You'll see.'

Polly turned round from pouring hot water into the bowl. 'It may take a long time, love. Minds don't heal as fast as bodies.'

The purple rubbery lips chewed on nothing. 'Aye, that's right. The doctor told me you can be sick in your mind as well as in your body. He wasn't in a hurry or nothing. He just sat down and talked to me when they'd taken Jack away.'

113

'In a black van,' said Martin at once, only to bend his head over his books again at a look from his mother.

'And you showed him your back?' Polly knew the answer before it came.

'No. I never let on. I kept me shawl on.' Bella put the cup down and pressed joined hands over her heart. 'I wasn't going to let them take me away as well. Not from the cottage.' She coughed. 'I've got to get back home when you've done me back, Polly. I've got to set things to rights.' She glanced at the dresser with its row of blue willow-patterned plates, and in spite of her pain her small face hardened with envy. 'I'll save up some money somehow. I will! Then when the pot fair comes to the market at Easter I'll get some cups and some saucers. With flowers on and gold rims. You just see if I don't.'

Polly squeezed out the cloth and, holding her breath, tenderly applied it, steeling herself against the sudden stiffening of Bella's whole body. 'I'll find you some bits and pieces, then when you've had something to eat I'll go down with you and help clear things up. That's if you wouldn't rather stop on here. You can sleep with me and we'll put the baby in a drawer lined with a blanket. I'll go down and get his things.'

'No!' All Bella's wavering strength went into her refusal. 'I've got to go home. Jack might get worse in the night, and if they send for me then I've got to be where they'll come looking.' She shuddered. 'They won't be hard on him, will they, Polly? That policeman wanted me to speak against him, but I wouldn't. Jack's wife kept on hounding him through the courts, an' I won't do the same. I couldn't be that cruel.'

At the mention of Jack's wife, Martin's head came up. 'Has Jack got two wives then, Mam?' His eyes bulged.

114

'He'll cop it if he gets found out, won't he?' The stretched eyes narrowed to slits. 'Mr Dennis said Jack was going the right way for real trouble, didn't he? You *know*, Mam. Yesterday when Jack nearly broke our Jim's leg.'

Hearing his name, the little dog perked up his ears and cocked his head to one side in a listening position. 'I told Bella about Jack frightening our Gatty,' Martin went on in a conversational tone. 'I told you, didn't I, Bella?'

'Gatty asked for anything she got.'

Polly, intent on shutting Martin up before he came out with any more revelations, said in a tired way: 'What did you say, Bella?'

'Nothing.'

Bella clenched her teeth together to stop the hurt making her sick all over Polly's multi-coloured rug at her feet. She chewed her lips trying not to speak out of turn, but she'd had enough of Gatty Pilgrim hanging round the cottage pretending she'd come to see the baby when all the time it was Jack she was sweet on.

'All the girls fancy their chances with Jack.' It was all too much. The stinging agony as Polly applied the ointment, the finding out that Jack had been in the woods with that Gatty when all the time his dinner was drying up. She put a hand over her swollen mouth and began to sob. 'It's with him being so good-looking.' She cried aloud with the agony of it all. 'He laughs at them if only they knew it. Silly young buggers, he says. An' then he laughs. Ha, Ha, Ha.'

The sound of laughter was terrible. Polly set down the bowl.

'I'm going to find you one of my blouses, Bella,' she explained. 'Then I'll take you home.'

Upstairs in her bedroom she set the candlestick high on the dresser. Gatty's blouses would fit Bella better, but somehow she couldn't. It wouldn't seem. . . . She put a hand over her mouth in a small gesture of comfort, swaying to and fro.

Gatty wasn't like that. Her own daughter wasn't like Bella had implied. She wasn't. Oh, dear God, it just wasn't true! Polly held up a striped blouse, her face reflecting her thoughts. Her mouth quivered. Jack had behaved badly, abominably, but Gatty had egged him on. She was sure of it. Polly knew that her imagination was running riot, the way it always did when she was worried, but at that moment she had no control over it. She forced herself to face the unpalatable truth.

There was something inherent in her daughter, a trait glaringly obvious even when Gatty had been no more than twelve years old. Gatty liked men. Anything in trousers, as Edna would have said. Before she'd decided her parents were beyond the pale, she had flirted with Harry, making him laugh by the way she sat on his knee, leaning back against him, fluttering dark eyelashes when she wanted her own way. Innocently, of course, but the inference had been there. Sexy. Polly's mind shied away from the very sound of the word in her head. Connecting it with her own daughter was tantamount to blasphemy, but such things did happen. She closed the drawer and took up the candle. There'd been a girl at school when Polly was in the fifth form, a girl who dyed the front of her hair, bleaching it to a candy-floss over her forehead. Once she'd had to go in front of the headmistress for putting pancake make-up on her face. She boasted about her conquests with the boys at the Grammar School to her own circle of friends, and laughed at Polly when she saw Polly's interest owed more to curiosity and nothing to envy. She was expelled in disgrace when the box pleats of her gym-slip divided because of her bulging stomach, the rumours being that the baby she was expecting could have had any one of four schoolboy fathers.

But Gatty? Oh, dear God, not Gatty.

Polly walked to the door, giving herself a mental kick, telling herself to stop *exaggerating*. Talk about Samuel Grundy, born on a Monday. *His* day had been one big laugh compared to this. Bella, sitting there in Harry's chair, had said things not even remotely true, trying pathetically to take the edge from her own despair.

Holding the candle high, Polly resisted the overwhelming urge to glance up at the ceiling, knowing that if the light was there she wouldn't be capable of finding a rational explanation for it. Not today.

When Gatty came home she would talk to her, spell it out, woman to woman: no glossing over words, using euphemisms, just straight questions, demanding straight answers.

But when she got back later that evening from Bella's cottage, tired half-way to death, Gatty had piled her tea things in the sink, leaving them unwashed and gone up to bed. She lay there apparently so fast asleep that Polly hadn't the heart to wake her.

The next morning, with the rush of getting them all out of the cottage in time, with Martin doing his Maths homework at the breakfast table and Gatty mooning into her porridge, the events of the day before took on the semblance of a nightmare, better ignored, easier forgotten.

Jack Thomson had been put away. Not for a long time, perhaps not ever again, would he walk the woods soft-footed, cap pulled low over mocking green eyes.

With Jack gone, life could surely return to normal, the way it had been before Harry went away.

The red-haired woman answering the door early that morning heard Harry out, then shook her head.

No, she was sorry but she did the garden herself, apart from a little man who came to do the lawns every other week in the summer. She closed the door firmly in his disappointed face, and went back to the telephone to carry on with her conversation with a friend in Guildford who had been telling her about a day dress she'd got from Dickens and Jones in Regent Street. Lilac angora wool with a small shoulder cape, and a flat bow looped through a slot high on the bodice. Then taking a taxi to Harrods' Food Hall, she'd ordered a whole ham in time for Christmas, which at fourpence a quarter she felt was good value. Didn't her friend think so?

By the time the red-haired woman had put the receiver down, Harry had knocked at four more doors down the long winding avenue, getting the same answer each time.

'Nothing. No, thank you.'

Raised eyebrows at Harry's broad Lancashire vowels, sometimes even a hint of amusement in a curled lip before yet another door slammed shut.

At the end of the avenue Harry stopped by a high privet hedge, bowed his head, and gave in for a moment to the sense of hopelessness flooding over him, leaving him trembling with weakness and anger.

He wasn't begging! For God's sake, he wasn't asking owt for nowt! All right, so late November wasn't exactly a good time for gardeners to find work, but there were fruit trees needing root pruning and useless bushes burning; strawberries to be put under forcing frames, crops lifted for storing, and stable manure to be stocked. Not forgetting bulb planting, even if it were a bit late for that. Dahlias to be dried and put away for the winter, gladioli and montbretia to be stored, lawns to be swept clear of leaves, and compost heaps to be nourished. Perennials to be bent down, never cut if you wanted to preserve their crowns, and chrysanthemums put in frames to give cuttings later.

The list was endless.

Harry held his hands out in front of him, turning them over and over. Idle hands, blue with cold, the same hands that could work outdoors all day in the worst weather the elements could throw up, without ever feeling or looking the way they were today.

Coughing, shivering, his mind overwhelmed with despair, Harry forced himself to turn and walk up yet another driveway. Turning up the collar of his jacket – what did it matter if it didn't look as smart as when laid flat – he asked himself why he had never felt the need of an overcoat in his whole life before coming down here? Even with a cutting wind sweeping down from Pendle, he'd managed to work on with maybe a piece of sacking across his shoulders to keep out the worst of the wet. Raising a hand, he lifted the knocker on a mock-Tudor door, and saw a lace curtain twitch slightly.

The cold was inside him. It was a chilling half-death creeping through his bones, a part of the anger and bitterness he couldn't control. Harry told himself that if he'd been a man of violence he would have kicked at the black and white door, scarring it with his boots, yelling at the woman to come out from behind her blasted lace curtain to tell him to his face that she thought he was the scum of the earth.

'I fought for you!' he wanted to shout. 'You and your

kind hung over my stretcher when I was lifted down on to the platform at Victoria Station in 1918. You wiped my forehead with your little white hankies, you gave me chocolate and a packet of fags. I nigh on *choked* for you, and now you hide, too toffy-nosed even to open the door. . . .'

As he walked back down the path, Harry looked like a drunken man weaving his way to the next pub, the next pint, craving his whisky. But in his case it was the craving for work setting him literally off balance, guiding him as if walking through water to the next disappointment. The thin whippet lines of Harry's face deepened into creases, etched by the hunger of his despair.

'I'll do owt,' he told the woman at the next house. 'Odd jobs. Feckling that broken catch on yon gate.' He nodded through the wrought-iron side gate at a spade left unforgivably outside, standing bolt upright in a mound of compost. 'Siding your tools away in the shed an' polishing them up fost.' Lapsing into broad dialect in his distress, forgetting that the woman staring at him with her hat and coat on all ready to go out wouldn't understand a word he was saying; taking off his cap for some reason, and standing there with the wind blowing his black hair and bringing tears to his eyes as he tried not to cough.

He'd got into the habit of staying out, only going back to his lodgings when it grew dark. Since being laid off from Kew Gardens three weeks before, he had kept his dismissal a secret from his hard-eyed landlady, determined to find another job before he wrote and told Polly. Knowing that if he told Polly, she would be likely to write straight back telling him to come home.

Thrusting his hands deep in his pockets, he walked aimlessly on. He wouldn't put it past Polly coming down

120

on the train and *fetching* him back if she once got wind of the way things were. Harry experienced a fierce and grinding ache for his wife low down in his stomach. Definitely not a weak man, Harry's strength lay in his gentleness, and if anyone had dared to suggest that his wife was the boss he would have agreed, feeling even more of a man for his admission.

Oh Polly, Polly. . . . They didn't grow women like her down here. Or at least if they did he'd still to come across one. The little boy in him ached to let the tears inside him spill over, but he deliberately focussed his mind on the effort of placing one foot in front of the other, postponing the time till, alone in his attic room, he could allow himself the luxury of a good old wallow in homesickness.

Practical Polly. She must be missing him, too, but Harry knew she would never let on. And Gatty and Martin. Especially Martin, in his new school uniform, with marbles in his pocket, an embryo schoolteacher if ever there was one.

Away from the big houses now, Harry found himself on the bridge at Kew, with the wind biting through his jacket, freezing his breath till it rattled in his throat with the onset of another bout of coughing. Stopping by the parapet he stared down into the muddy brown water, riffled into creases like the skin on a pot of cocoa. Certificates would be what Martin had to show for any knowledge he acquired. Bits of bloody parchment, framed for good measure, proving that what he'd learned had been put on paper and not stored in his noddle where apparently it made no odds.

He'd best get on his way. The rain falling now was laced with sleet, and soon, if he wasn't careful, Harry knew he would meet the men going home from work, home to their wives, to sit round a fire listening to the wireless, or even braving the weather to queue for the second house pictures. He looked up as he walked past a cinema announcing a new film star in a picture called 'Morning Glory'. Katharine Hepburn stared out from her framed photograph with bold eyes and white teeth gleaming. Harry decided he didn't reckon much of her. Not a patch on his Polly when it came to looks.

Lights were showing in the front windows of houses now. It seemed that folks used their parlours more down here. Street lamps emphasized the driving sleet, and on the corner of Harry's road, outside the little newsagent's shop, a poster meshed into its frame shouted headlines proclaiming that the man called Hitler over in Germany had pledged that his fight would be for the peace of the whole world.

The front door of Harry's lodgings opened on to a square of chipped and weathered crazy paving, fronted by an iron railing. In desperation one Sunday morning he had offered to dig up the edging and plant a row of perennials, anything to keep his hand in.

But Mrs Cook would have none of it. 'Who's going to keep it weeded when you've gone?' she'd asked. 'Not me, that's for sure. I've got enough to do without making more work. It suits me as it is. I can go in the park if I want to stare at flowers.' Her small eyes had regarded him suspiciously. 'I'd have thought you had enough of digging through the week, Mr Pilgrim.'

Sighing, Harry turned in at the gate, hanging by its hinges, left perpetually open, barely glancing at the black saloon car drawn up to the kerb. When he heard his name called out he whipped round smartly, thinking at first that he must have imagined it.

'Mr Pilgrim? Mr Harry Pilgrim?' The voice was low,

a cultured London voice, coming from the wound-down window of the car. 'I'd like a word with you, if I may.' Then, as Harry hesitated: 'Oh, do come round and get in. I've been sitting here for at least half an hour watching it rain, and I'm damned if I'll get out and stand on the pavement talking to you.'

Slowly, cautiously, Harry did as he was bid, taking off his cap and holding it self-consciously on his knees. He was very wet, very cold, and his profile, averted from the curious gaze of the young woman in the passenger seat, spoke to her of his shyness and bewilderment.

'I'm Harry Pilgrim, aye,' he said. He turned to face her. 'But I can't place you.' He turned back to stare through the windscreen, remembering his manners. 'I haven't had that pleasure, Miss. . . ?'

'So you think it would be a pleasure, then?'

The voice was teasing, light and controlled. 'Can't you guess who I am, Mr Pilgrim? People do say the likeness is a family one. Oh, do look at me properly. I promise I won't bite.'

Forced now to study the young woman as she'd asked, Harry turned to stare at a heart-shaped face, eyes slanted a little at the corners, a pert nose, and wings of dark hair curving forward, almost touching a mouth clearly outlined in purple lipstick. Or was it the light from the street lamp turning it into that garish shade?

'Aye,' he said slowly, 'there's something somewhere.' He shook his head. 'I know nobody down here, Miss.' Especially somebody like you, he wanted to add. As beautiful as you, smelling of scent and making fun of me just because you choose to do so.

She was enjoying herself. Harry's fingers were fidgeting with his cap, his embarrassment obvious. She knew she was being impossible, and half despised herself for it, but the house and the woman who'd said she could sit and wait in the kitchen had appalled her. And now here was a man totally unaware of his own shattering good looks, and that in itself was a novelty. A man so dark there could have been a touch of the Spanish in his ancestry, with soft black hair curling over his forehead and down into the nape of his neck. With an accent of wide-vowelled intonation that spoke to her of moors and wild winds, tempered with a calmness of the spirit. A reserve, too, telling of pride deeply inherent in his make-up. She decided to put him out of his misery.

'I'm Yvonne Frobisher,' she told Harry, holding out a hand. 'Yvonne Craven that was. The black sheep's sister. I've come to thank you for all you did for my brother, and for writing to tell my parents of his death.' She made no move to take her hand from Harry's grasp. 'He broke my parents' hearts, you know, and they would have come to the funeral if they hadn't been abroad when your letter came. It lay unopened all these weeks.'

Harry nodded without speaking, then he whispered: 'Roger was a fine man. I was proud to be considered his friend.'

'He should have come home.' Her voice had lost its light bantering tone. 'The Prodigal Son's welcome would have been like a mild hello to the one Roger would have got. They never stopped hoping he'd return, you see.' She gave a little squeeze to Harry's wet sleeve. 'So now they want to meet you. Will next Sunday be okay? They're only half an hour's train journey away from Baker Street.'

She moved her hand to adjust a stray strand of hair, and Harry saw the wedding ring on her finger. 'I've written the address down and how to get there from the station. It's on a straight road. You can't go wrong.'

He took the slip of paper from her, frowning at it in the half light. 'Will you be there?' The question seemed to ask itself as he hesitated, shy as a young boy. 'It's just that . . . well, I don't know quite what to tell them. Your brother would have hated them to know exactly the way things were.'

'That he died in squalor?' The close-fitting hat jerked towards the house with gas light filtering from a window through a torn blind. 'They'd given him up for dead, Harry.' She smiled. 'I may call you Harry? Mr Pilgrim sounds too much like that worthy chappie conjured up by John Bunyan growing more sanctimonious with every step he took.'

'But his progress was more rewarding than mine's been lately.' Harry smiled, pleased at his own unexpected wit, then sat silently again, wondering what to say next.

'You're a nice man, Harry Pilgrim.' Roger's sister smiled too. 'And yes, I'll be there. Why not? A day in the country could be just what the doctor would order.'

His hand was on the door handle when she spoke quickly. 'No point in you going out to Amersham by train. I'll pick you up at eleven. Okay?'

By the time he was out on the pavement, lifting a hand to wave goodbye, the small black saloon car had drawn away from the kerb, its tail lights like red glowing eyes in the darkness of the late winter afternoon.

Feeling rather foolish, Harry lowered his hand and turned towards the house, going straight into the kitchen to the unlovely sight of Mrs Cook standing at the cooker with the soup ladle at the ready.

— Six —

Manny Goldberg believed in putting the facts to his employees. It wasn't going to be easy breaking such depressing news, but it had to be done.

With his workforce gathered round him in a large semi-circle, he began: 'You don't need me to tell you how bad business is these days.' The jowls of his big face drooped like a bloodhound's as he tried to find the right words. 'Being in business is a chancy thing at the best of times. You think everything's going all right, then before you can turn round you're stockpiled with goods that won't shift. And because they won't shift, then where's the capital to buy new material?' He closed his eyes to shut out the ring of faces, each one stamped with apprehension, clouded with a creeping fear of what they guessed was coming next. Manny raised his voice slightly. 'The only protected areas, as far as I can see it, are the Civil Service and local government. They have sustained fewer casualties than most in this never-ending slump.'

'Tell us the worst, Mr Goldberg. We don't need no telling about Civil Servants. Sat out the war on their backsides, that jammy lot did.'

Manny nodded at the speaker, his chief cutter, a tiny man with the stooped shoulders of his profession. 'All right then, Arnold. I won't beat about the bush. For the time being, for quite a time to come, I'm going to have to put you all on half-time.'

'An' half bloody pay,' a woman in curlers said.

Manny agreed sadly. 'So if any of you would like your cards, come with me into the office. You can try signing on at the Labour Exchange if you think you'll be better off.'

The cutter gave a loud snort. 'What? And get no more than would keep us in shoe leather while we tramp the streets looking for another job? Nay. I for one'll stop with you, Mr Goldberg, and hope for better things to come. Plaiting sawdust would be easier than finding a job in my line these days. Nay, tha's been fair to us, so I reckon most of us will want to play fair with thee.' He looked round at the nodding heads. 'We're all of like mind, Mr Goldberg.'

Manny relaxed a little, releasing his breath on a deep sigh of relief. There were sentimental tears behind his eyes, but he blinked them away angrily. Was there, anywhere in the world over, a prouder lot than these northerners?

He'd thought his own race had the prerogative in that line, but now he wasn't too sure. Watching them going quietly back to their sewing machines with no more than a bleakness of expression to betray their feelings, he marvelled. Was it because their upper lips were stiffer than usual, or had they been knocked down so often in their past history they'd come to expect less than their share of the world's benefits? What could you do with people like this? In the name of God, what could you ever hope to *do*?

He turned to look at Polly, determined to shake off his deep lethargy of the spirit. There was no room for muddled thinking, not with his accountant sitting waiting for him back in the office, briefcase stuffed with sheets of figures refusing to balance.

'Will working mornings suit *you* all right, Polly?'

Already her bright head was bent to her task, but she looked straight at him in her usual direct way.

'As a matter of fact, Mr Goldberg, mornings will suit me fine.' She slotted a belt through its accommodating loops. 'It means I'll be home in time for that young lad of mine finishing school. He's as soft as me pocket, even though he's eleven. I thought he'd toughen up when his dad went away. You know, be the man of the family and all that, but it hasn't worked that way. Not entirely.'

'And the money?' Manny wanted to ask, but knew he dare not. This lass would starve before she'd let on, he'd bet his last penny on that. He glanced at her shrewdly for a moment. This lass, this *bonny* lass, as he called her privately, had changed imperceptibly from the golden girl who had bounced into his office to apply for the job as his secretary. The smile was still there, but her eyes had a bruised look about them as if she had slept badly. He hesitated, then walked on, a stocky, thickset man, bowed down with too much responsibility, too many nights lying awake wondering how he could borrow yet more money, seeing as he tossed and turned his stock piling up, and his buyers dwindling to a mere trickle.

Even his southern outlet was closing in on him. Londoners didn't go for the heavy-weight type of rain-coat he produced, preferring something lighter. And up here, the only people with the money to invest in rainwear were making do till things took a turn for the better. Christmas was on the horizon, and after that the

128

hope of spring and summer. Decent shops were closing, one after the other, to be taken over by second-hand clothes dealers, offering to buy old iron, rags and even furniture as a sideline. And lined raincoats were becoming a luxury and not the necessity he had thought they would be when he offered for the mill. All pitfalls even his astute business mind had failed to foresee.

The newspapers said that the worst of the Depression would exhaust itself by 1935 or 1936, giving as a reason for their cautious optimism the signs of improvement in the building trade. Londoners were moving out from the centre of the city, buying houses for twenty-five pounds down and twenty-five shillings a week for the next twelve years. Flimsy houses, built with cheap materials. Manny sighed. Was it possible that he'd gone into the wrong kind of business after all? He shook his big head mournfully from side to side. No, the clothing trade was all he knew about, not bricks and mortar.

Back in his office he dismissed his accountant, took his black overcoat down from its peg, slammed a Homburg hat on his head and told his secretary he was going to keep his ten o'clock appointment at the bank.

'I'll walk,' he said. 'The fresh air will do me good.'

'It's fresh all right, Mr Goldberg,' she told him, whipping out a letter from her typewriter with a grating sound that set his teeth on edge. 'It said on the wireless this morning that the sea came right over the front at Blackpool last night. Fog and frost are forecast. It's turning out to be a bad winter right enough.'

'So it's going to be a bad winter? So we have fog and frost to contend with as well as cold hearths and empty bellies? So. . . ?' Turning into the Boulevard which fronted the railway station, Manny grimly touched the brim of his hat to Queen Victoria staring regally from her elevated position at townsfolk hurrying to catch trains or standing in queues for buses and trams. 'I wonder what you'd have made of it all, Ma'am?' he muttered, striding on down past the ornately embellished architecture of the town's evening paper, the *Northern Daily Telegraph*.

In the bank at the top of Church Street he sat on a little hard chair, stoutly dignified, holding his black hat on his knees, waiting patiently to be called into the manager's inner sanctum.

'So he tells me I've come to the end of the road?' Manny's chin shook. 'So I go back and tell those brave lasses that even working half-time is only a way of putting off the inevitable?'

And there, as if appearing in a whiff of ectoplasm, was the rosy face of Polly Pilgrim, smiling on him as if he'd done her a favour in giving her afternoons free. A long sigh escaped him. 'Bridges I haven't come to I don't intend to cross,' he muttered, a kindly man who had only wanted to do his best, then found that even his best wasn't good enough.

'Good morning, Mr Goldberg.'

Mr Ormerod, the bank manager, a spare man with tow-coloured hair arranged carefully across his shiny, bald head, came out of his room holding out his hand. With the acute sensitivity of the over-anxious, Manny searched the bland smile for its reasons. Was it a genuine 'I'm here to help you, Mr Goldberg'? Or was it a smile pinned on merely for politeness, a sort of softener before the blow fell?

There was certainly no warmth in the manager's grip as they shook hands. Like shaking a piece of salt-fish, Manny decided. He followed through the counter flap into the tiny inner office and sat down in the chair indicated, with the light from a high window full on his troubled face.

The bank manager drew a folder towards him, pushing horn-rimmed spectacles into position on his apology for a nose.

Manny twisted the rim of his hat round and round in his hands. The feet sticking out through the manager's desk were encased in shiny brown leather, topped by spats in an elegant shade of beige. Manny considered them balefully. Since the end of the war the wearing of spats had virtually disappeared, mainly on account of the cost of the necessary and expensive workmanship, but these spats looked new. With a practised and jaundiced eye, Manny did a quick calculation of the approximate price, subtracted the retailer's profit, plus the wholesaler's rake-off, and decided that even raincoats were a much more viable proposition.

The manager extracted a sheet of figures, coughed slightly. 'These are hard times for us all, Mr Goldberg,' he began.

'So what can you do?' Manny whispered, tensing himself for the blow that would surely fall in the next few minutes. 'I've put the whole workforce on half-time, starting today, and if in the next few weeks we manage to break the back of most of the bills coming in from the suppliers, I've worked out that—'

He stopped as the manager raised an imperious hand. 'Not so fast, Mr Goldberg. Hear my side of the position first, if you please.'

The eyes behind the whirlpool lenses of the thick spectacles were cold and totally lacking in reassurance. Manny apologized, and settled his face into a subservient listening expression.

'Sorry, Mr Ormerod,' he said aloud.

131

'You and your bloody spats,' he said underneath his breath.

'Mr Goldberg put us all on half-time,' Polly said quickly, when Robert Dennis opened his door to her knock. 'Starting today as ever was. So I thought I'd come and see how you were. With having this unexpected time off, you see.' She stared down at her feet as if wondering how they'd had the nerve to walk her down this long street of quiet houses, each one fronted by a small garden. Terraced, but full of character, as an estate agent would undoubtedly have said. 'I rang your office and they gave me your address. Not at first, I admit.' Her pulse was racing and her cheeks burned. 'I've been worried about you.'

He stared at her, feeling his own heart race with the shock of seeing her standing there, the collar of her red coat upturned against the cold wind, a small brown hat in the shape of a pork pie perched on the glory of her bright hair. She had been almost constantly in his thoughts, and yet she was the last person on earth he had expected to see. There was a hospital sling in some coarse cotton material supporting his shoulder, pinned across with a huge safety pin. He pointed to it with a smile.

'This is only for show. I'm going back to work next week.' He stood back to let her pass. 'I wrote to you yesterday, so it should be waiting for you when you get back home. Come in. Come on in then.'

They went through the black and white tiled vestibule into the lobby, a passageway too narrow to be called a hall. A door on the left led into what Polly guessed was

132

the front parlour, and when she hesitated he gave her a gentle push.

'Through there, Polly. The parlour's only for visitors, not friends.' He pushed open a door at the foot of a steep flight of stairs. 'This is the living-room, and on through that the kitchen.'

Politely trying not to look, Polly saw a draining-board set beneath a window festooned with red and white gingham curtains. There was a single cup and saucer set to drain, and a white tea-towel with a red stripe down the middle folded neatly at the side.

'Give me your coat.' Robert held out his hand. 'And your hat – or will you have a job to get it back on just right again? I remember my wife used to spend ten minutes doing her face and her hair, then twenty minutes settling her hat.' Laying the hat and coat down on a stand chair at the side of a polished mahogany sideboard, he pointed to a photograph of a pretty woman in a silver frame. 'That was Jean.'

Polly looked. She saw a serious studio profile of a sweet-faced, middle-aged woman wearing a dark dress with a little white lace collar, looking down as if reading a book.

'The photographer in Preston Road preferred that type of pose to what he called an inane grin,' Robert said. 'It's the last photograph Jean had taken, so I wish he'd taken her smiling.' Picking the portrait up, he studied it for a moment then put it down again. 'In a way though I suppose he was right. Jean didn't have much to smile about those past few years of her life.'

'She died of pneumonia, you told me?' Polly whispered, embarrassed, fussing with her hair where the elastic from her hat had pulled it out of shape.

'Oh yes. It *was* pneumonia at the end, and everyone

133

said it was a blessing, but for ten years before that she'd suffered from a kind of muscular complaint which meant she was housebound for two years. At the end it was affecting her speech.' He motioned to Polly to sit down in a chair by the fire. 'So I suppose everyone was right when they said it was a blessing about the pneumonia.'

'But you don't think so?'

'I'd've thought it a blessing if it had come years before!' His voice was harsh. 'It'll come one day, Polly. Maybe not in our time, but one day someone with sense will make it legal for someone who suffered like my wife to have their pain put an end to. Of their own volition maybe, and if not, assisted by a helping hand.'

'Take their own lives?'

'Yes. *Suicide*. Let's not use euphemisms. I'm a lapsed Catholic, Polly, and according to the dogma I had instilled in me, suicide is a mortal sin, promising an eternity of hellfire. But that's not my view! My wife was having her hell right here, through there in the next room, sitting like a lump of nowt, half-blind and incontinent. I'd have done it myself if I'd had the guts. Many, many times I nearly did, but I hadn't the courage.'

He put up a hand to his hair. Now what had brought all that on? Why, in God's name, had he blurted all that out to this young woman watching him in wide-eyed amazement? All she'd done, for heaven's sake, was walk in through the door to stand in his living-room looking like a coloured photo when everything else was in old-fashioned sepia. He must have frightened her half-way to death.

'You must forgive me,' he said, going to sit opposite her in a leather, velvet-cushioned chair. 'You'll be wishing you hadn't come.'

'Oh, no.' Polly looked very wise. 'It needed saying,

134

and you'll feel better for it.' After the intensity of the past few moments she struggled to sound casual. 'I must say you keep your house tidy. For a man on his own. But then I expect you had lots of practice before. . . .' She stopped in mid-sentence. Oh, Lord. She'd meant to *change* the subject, not bring it up again. 'What I mean is you must have been running the house single-handed for years now.' She blushed. 'Oh, I didn't mean. . . . Oh, Robert. I didn't mean that. Oh, what a clumsy way of putting it. My own mother says I put my big foot in it every time I open my mouth. Shall I go outside and come in again?'

His lips twitched even as he appeared to take her seriously. 'No, don't go outside, Polly. If you do that you may decide to keep on walking down the street, and that would never do.' He touched the sling deliberately. 'I got used to far more tactless remarks than the one you just made a long time ago. A one-armed man is something of a rarity even since the last war. I think my worst moment came when they removed the dressings one day in the field hospital and I forced myself to look instead of turning my face to the wall.' His eyes regarded her steadily. 'It reminded me of a sausage in a pork butcher's shop. A pinky brown colour with the skin drawn over the stump like a kitbag pulled together at the top. Not raw and red like I'd somehow imagined it to be. From then on I began to accept, and from then on everything I managed to do with one hand was a triumph. Dressing myself came first, and apart from my collar and tie, that proved easy. Once I'd worked out the drawer bit for the tie and used my teeth to bring one end of the collar round, I was away.' He smiled. 'Now that the embarrassing bit's out of the way, may I offer you a cup of tea?'

Knowing better than to make any offer of help, Polly

135

sat looking around her as he busied himself in the kitchen. In spite of Robert's brave declaration of total independence, the room did look as if it knew a woman's touch. She smiled at the cliché, feeling an unwarranted twinge of jealousy. The curtains, shiny cream rayon with orange flames flaring up their length, had been drawn back in neat folds, not merely dragged back any old how, the way Harry drew theirs if he was downstairs first. Used to draw them, she reminded herself. She didn't like Robert's curtains, Polly decided.

She then eyed the fireplace with speculative envy. Tiled in a beige mottled design, it boasted a back boiler. She could tell that by the way the fire was drawing to the back of the grate. That meant blessed hot water, and maybe a bathroom upstairs. All mod. cons in fact. She turned her attention to the floor coverings. Brown self-patterned carpet almost to the walls, with just six inches or so of stained wood by the skirting board polished to mirror shininess, she noticed. And by her feet, up against the raised tiled hearth, a hand-pegged rug. Not made with bits of old coats and snippets from a ragbag, but a handsome rug, luxuriously thick with tufted wools, and a red dragon breathing fire in the middle.

'My wife's sister pops in every day,' Robert said, coming in with a tray balanced on his right hand. 'She lives next door.' He slid the tray on to a drop-leaf table. 'She'd half kill me if she saw me using the tray without a cloth on it.' He poured milk into the two cups. 'And she'd be gravely disappointed in me to see these cups and saucers instead of those over there in the display cabinet.' Lifting the small brown teapot he began to pour. 'She tries to take me over, I'm afraid. Goes about saying what a burden I am to her, but never misses a day.' The deep-set eyes twinkled. 'It's all right. Don't look so terrified. She's been in and done her stint for today. She's not likely to come in twice.' He passed over a cup of tea. 'Not unless she was behind her curtains as you knocked at the door. In that case she'll be in any minute on some trumped-up excuse or other, just to see what's going on.'

'Oh, no!' It was more a shocked intake of breath than an exclamation. Polly put her cup and saucer down quickly on the settee's wooden arm-rest. 'I'd better go, Robert.' She looked round frantically for her coat and hat. 'Do you mean your sister-in-law would really think . . .?'

'The worst,' he said promptly. 'Nellie is a staunch member of the Ladies' Guild. She believes in one man, one woman, regardless of circumstances. When Jean was buried, Nellie would have felt it entirely in keeping for me to have cast myself into the grave on top of the coffin. In fact, I go as far as to say she'd have been right proud of me. Now sit down again and drink your tea.'

'But if she *should* come in?' Polly stared at the wall as if expecting to see Robert's late wife's sister appear through it. 'Wouldn't she think it funny me being here?'

'Funny ha-ha or funny peculiar?' He grinned. 'She'd think you were after me, if that's what you mean.' His eyes danced wickedly. 'Look, love. Let's get one thing straight. My sister-in-law is not my keeper, however much she'd like to think so.'

A sudden rattling noise on the other side of the adjoining wall made Polly jump so that her teacup shivered in its saucer, and at once Robert left his chair to come and sit beside her on the settee.

'Nellie raking the fire out,' he explained, placing his hand briefly on Polly's knee. 'Raking out the ashes prior to banking it up with slack before she puts the fireguard

137

round.' He glanced at the Westminster-chime clock in the centre of the mantelpiece. 'Today is her Bright Hour afternoon, held in the big vestry at the chapel round the corner. Nellie goes early to set out the tea things and butter the scones she's made this morning. She's been making them for the past ten years, grumbling at being put upon, and yet last year when a new member offered to take the job on, Nellie took it as a personal insult and threatened her resignation from the committee.'

Polly stared down at the hand on her knee. The fingers were long, a surgeon's fingers, she decided, or a pianist's. A different shaped hand from Harry's altogether.

'My sister-in-law is a woman born to minister to someone,' Robert was saying. 'But fate decreed otherwise. Her husband was killed in the war, on the Somme, and her only son hardly ever comes to see her. His wife and Nellie were daggers drawn from the first meeting. So . . . for a while Jean filled that need. It was only because of Nellie's kindness that I was able to keep on my job last year and now, well, I'm her life's work, I'm afraid. The money I give her ekes out her pension, and the house looks a darned sight better than it would left to me.' He grinned. 'So surely I can tolerate a bit of nosiness, when you consider.'

He took his hand away, and Polly relaxed, but she could still feel it there, through her skirt, through her stocking, almost as if he'd touched her skin. He was very close to her and for a terrible moment she had an almost irresistible urge to take his hand and hold it against her face. He was looking at her, his eyes soft, gentle and kind. They were the palest eyes she had ever seen, grey and luminous as mother-of-pearl. She wanted to look away, but she couldn't make the effort. She wanted to say something, but her mind was blank.

Through the window directly behind them a stray shaft of sunlight gleamed on the silver streaks in his hair. When she spoke at last her voice was distant in her own ears, almost a whisper.

'I *must* go,' she said. 'Now I can see you're all right.'

'How about Gatty?' He spoke as if he hadn't heard.

'Jack Thomson has been put away. You were right about him being sick in his mind. He beat Bella up badly, but the postman came and sent for the police. An ambulance came and took him away. He won't be bothering Gatty again. Martin brought Bella and the baby to me, and I saw to her. As long as nobody tries to take her house from her she'll be okay.'

Robert Dennis stroked his chin in a reflective kind of way. Polly's flippant way of speaking didn't fool him one bit. Whatever had happened had been dreadful, but Polly wasn't going to say. There was even a slight smile playing round her lips. He frowned. There was an old saying that it was impossible to tell what went on behind a face, and Polly typified that supposition. She'd been just the same when that drunken brute had hurled the dog against a tree and given him – Robert gingerly touched his injured shoulder – a night of pain he wasn't likely to forget. She was calm to the point of apparent uncaring, shelled in a serenity that wasn't quite normal. He decided to try another tack.

'And your husband? How is Harry?'

Again the lift of the chin and the tantalizing, smooth answer.

'Oh, Harry's fine. He doesn't write much these days, but then I can't expect chatty letters from a man who was often content to sit in his chair all evening when his day's work was over and never speak a word. Most of the communing Harry did was with Mother Nature.'

She smiled her wide smile. 'He'll write a proper letter when he thinks there's something worth saying.'

'I see.' Robert decided to play Polly's game. 'It came to me last Sunday as we walked back to the cottage that Pendle looks like a crouching lion, without the mane. I used to think it was like a whale, but it's not, it's like a lion.'

'I agree.' Polly's vivacity had come back, he noticed wryly, now that the conversation had reverted to trivia. 'I used to play a game of imagining shapes. Like the two trees on the hill further away. Just two, all on their own, bending when the wind blows, into the shape of witches with streaming cloaks.'

'It must, at times, be very lonely for you up there.'

Again the bright denial. 'Oh no. There's too much to do living in the country to feel lonely.' She wrinkled her nose. 'Our milk doesn't come in bottles on the doorstep like in the town. It has to be got in a can every morning or evening from the farm, and till we had cold water piped we had to take buckets to a spout over a mile away.' A dimple came and went at the side of her mouth. 'And the water coming from that spout wasn't how you imagine. It *trickled*, slowly, till the waiting nearly drove you mad, especially in the winter. There was a nearby tree to shelter under, but many a time we got back wetter than the water we'd managed to collect.'

Their eyes were meeting again, his quizzical, infinitely kind, and Polly's wide, unblinking. And neither of them could look away. Polly said the first thing that came into her head.

'Sticks. Yes, sticks. I can spot a good stick at a glance. For the oven.' There was a high desperation in her voice. 'Some are good oven pieces, and some not. But I can tell. I don't think I ever go into the cottage without a bundle of sticks I've gathered on my way up the lane. You see, living in the country means you never waste anything.'

His face was coming closer, and there was no way she could turn her head. He was going to kiss her, and if he did she didn't know what she'd do, and if he didn't she would die. There was a warmth inside her, spreading through her body. Closing her eyes, she parted her lips a little as his arm drew her closer.

'Coo-ee! Anyone at home?'

Their lips hadn't met, but the kiss was there, trembling between them. To the big-boned woman standing in the doorway, it was as plain as the nose on her face that they'd been up to something. Her brother-in-law's face was livid with rage as he got abruptly to his feet and walked to the fireplace, seeing the shock drain the blood from Polly's face as she too stood up and reached for her coat.

Nellie tightened her lips. She glared at the ring on Polly's left hand, and at her hair. Bottle-blonde, if she was any judge. 'Well!' she said, folding her arms. 'Well! Here's a nice old to-do!'

'I was just going.' Polly's voice trembled on the verge of hysteria. Her fingers trembled too as she buttoned up her coat, and well they might, Nellie told herself. Brazen little varmint, a married woman canoodling on the settee with a man whose wife was barely cold in her grave. She waited, biding her time.

'I didn't hear you knock, Nellie,' Robert said.

As shamed as he'd every right to be, Nellie noticed grimly. She gave a disgusted sideways sniff at the settee cushions she'd plumped up only that morning, squashed out of shape where they'd been lying back on them. She drew herself up to her full impressive height.

141

'So I've to knock afore I come in now, have I?' She put a cake tin down on the table. 'Fetching you some of me scones, I was. Fetching them for your tea out of the batch I've been making for the Bright Hour.' Her eyes, as small and round as wimberries, raked Polly up and down. 'So I should have stood outside on the flags waiting to be let in, should I?' She stared hard at Polly. 'I've seen you afore.' Her mouth chewed on nothing for a moment. 'I know where it was. You came with your mother to our last sale of work. Edna Myerscough – Edna Ainsworth that was. She went to St John's School with me. Little woman who was a bit boss-eyed.'

'Nellie!' Robert's voice was ragged with embarrassment. 'That's enough! Mrs Pilgrim is going now. She kindly came to see how I was.' For Polly's sake he fought to keep his temper. 'I'll walk down with you, Polly, if you'll wait till I get my coat.'

In his anger his movements were clumsy. The jacket didn't swing round as it usually did, and he made futile stabs at it with his good arm.

Suddenly Polly could take no more. Trying to make things right, knowing it was impossible to make things right, she turned to Nellie. 'I'll remember you to my mother, Mrs. . . ?' Her voice faltered, then she said the first thing that came into her mind. 'Did you get the two hundred pounds you were aiming to get at the sale of work?'

'Nobbut thirty-four pounds.' Nellie stood aside to let her pass. Nicely spoken, you had to say that for her, even if she did wear a coat that meant you'd see her coming a mile off.

At the door Robert tried to take Polly's hand, but she was too quick for him. 'Polly . . . Polly. . . .' He stepped out with her on to the short paved path. 'You mustn't mind Nellie. Her bark's far worse than her bite.'

But it was no use. Polly was almost in tears; he could see them trembling on her long eyelashes.

'Don't humiliate me any more, Robert. Please.'

She walked away from him, head bent, and he let her go, accepting that anything he tried to say would only add to her distress. And the first thing he saw when he went back into the house was her silly little brown hat sitting on the sideboard next to his wife's photograph.

'She's gone and left 'er 'at.' Nellie gave it a contemptuous flick of a finger. 'They've got dozens just like it in the hat market. Four and eleven a time.' She walked towards the door. 'I'd best be off. I'm late already, not that we ever start on time since the new minister's wife took over. Folks say she has a lie-down after her dinner.'

'Nellie!' Robert's voice was louder than he intended. 'Before you go, you'll listen to what I have to say!' He stood where he was in the doorway, barring her path. 'The way you spoke to Polly, to Mrs Pilgrim, was unforgivable.' He clenched his right fist, fighting for control. 'You have no right to barge into my house like that to begin with, and no right at all to speak to a friend of mine in such a way.' He seemed to slump downwards. 'I know you do a lot for me, and I know you did a lot for Jean, but that doesn't give you the right to walk in without knocking.'

'Well!' Nellie closed her small wimberry eyes for a moment. 'So that's the way it is! I can let meself in with a key to come and scrub and clean for you. I can shop and wear me fingers to the bone keeping two houses going, but it's a different story when you're lying on the settee with your fancy-piece!' Her bosom swelled. 'It's coming back to me what I heard about your so-called friend. Nearly broke her mother's heart she did, going off straight from school and marrying a gypsy.'

Her voice rose in triumph. 'An' you don't need to look at me like that, Robert Dennis! Your friend's husband's grandfather was a proper one. Clay pipe an' all! Used to come round the backs with a donkey and cart. A rag and bone man! Lived out Downham way in a house no better than a lean-to shed.'

'A cottage,' Robert said automatically.

'So you've been there!' Nellie's thin mouth wrenched itself sideways in a spitting motion. 'So we've really touched rock bottom, have we? A fine thing if your cronies at the office find out.' Moving forward with a swift snatching motion, she took the tin of scones and held it in front of her like a shield. 'You can eat shop cakes from now on, and find out the difference! And I hope you know what you're doing!'

There was nothing else for it but to let her go. As Robert's anger began to leave him, he realized that the shock of what his sister-in-law had seen, or what she thought she had seen, had forced her into an exaggerated display of righteous indignation. He picked up the tray and carried it through into the kitchen.

One-handed, he rinsed the cups underneath the tap with no realization at all of what he was doing. Polly he would come to later. For the time being all his mind was concentrated on his sister-in-law. Nellie, salt of the earth Nellie. Almost twenty years older than his wife, how often had she boasted that she'd brought Jean up herself after their mother had died? Nellie, with principles so deep-rooted that even the sliding lava from a volcano wouldn't shift them. Nellie, who firmly believed that infidelity was the greatest sin of all, far greater than

144

lying, cheating and possibly even murder. Robert slid the tray into its place at the side of the gas oven.

Nellie at that very moment he guessed would be joining her friends of the Bright and Shining hour in the opening hymn, sure of her place in heaven when her time came to go; to be reunited with her husband who had been waiting for her ever since the day a German sniper's bullet had shattered his gullet and left him choking on his own blood. Nellie, so good, so staunch, so loyal, so straight . . . Robert said each word aloud, the last one at a shout.

'Damn and blast the Nellies of this world!' he shouted. 'May heaven preserve their pious souls!'

Cleverly he folded the tea-towel and laid it carefully down in its appointed place, regarding it balefully. It was white as the driven snow, due to Nellie's attentions. Boiled first, then rinsed in water tinged to the right shade with dolly-blue. Nellie was inordinately proud of her whites. Childishly he took it up again to toss it down crumpled, any old how.

'Nellie . . . oh, Nellie,' he muttered, shaking his head.

Slowly he walked back into the living-room, sat down heavily on the brown velvet cushioned settee, and allowed himself to think about Polly.

He hadn't wanted, he hadn't *needed* that kind of complication in his life. Not yet. Not, as Nellie would say, with his wife barely cold in her grave. He tugged at the restricting sling, his expression bleak with a kind of despair. It wasn't as if he were the sort of man who found it hard to exist without a woman. His enforced celibacy during Jean's long illness had proved that. Robert stroked his chin, staring into the fire. A casual encounter with an easy-come easy-go type of woman hadn't been on the agenda at all. His love and concern

145

for his wife had taught him that desire could transcend the flesh. He flinched at the platitude, but it was the truth. And the war in France and the loss of his arm had somehow produced yet another kind of maturity, so that he had imagined he was immune from temptation.

Pleased that he was thinking now instead of merely *feeling*, he leaned forward, took a decent sized cob of coal from the scuttle and placed it right in the middle of the fire. That was what was needed. Calm rational reasoning. He hooked the tongs back on the tidy.

But nothing had prepared him for the tenderness and overwhelming sense of responsibility he felt for Polly Pilgrim. From their first meeting he had sensed a vulnerability in her, a vulnerability at total variance with her flippancy and the radiance of her bright smile. She needed him, and that in itself was crazy when she had a husband who through no fault of his own was well over two hundred miles away. Polly was a happily married woman, and her husband would either return defeated and disillusioned, or filled with triumph at having found what he had gone down south to seek.

Yet, when he had drawn her close her eyes had been filled with longing. She had wanted to be kissed.

Robert sighed an audible sigh.

'I hope you know what you're doing,' Nellie had said.

But he *didn't* know, that was the devil of it. All he did know was that he had to see Polly again. Soon . . . the sooner the better.

— Seven —

The snow came early that year. It fell, not like a covering blanket, but as fine powder, coating the roof tops like icing sugar. It turned the streets of the town into picture postcard prettiness during the day, then into a sea of slush as darkness fell.

With another hour to go before closing time, Mr Arnold came out from the back of the shop with a pile of shoe-boxes wedged precariously beneath his chin. Thus encumbered, he addressed his remarks to the ceiling.

'We're not likely to get many more customers tonight. Not by the way that snow's set in.' He risked a nod at the two girls standing idly by the small cash counter and gave what could, on a dark night, have passed for a smile. 'So you can knock off, the pair of you. I reckon I can manage till closing time.'

'Thank you, Mr Arnold.' Winnie smiled an ingratiating smile. 'We've cleared up ages ago, haven't we, Gatty?'

'Yes. Ages ago.' Gatty Pilgrim, nudged into some kind of response, pushed herself away from the counter as if reluctant to deprive herself of its support. 'Thank you, Mr Arnold.'

147

'What's up with you?' Winnie took Gatty's arm as they left the shop. 'You've hardly said a blinkin' word all day.' She peered sideways into her friend's averted face. 'You've hardly said a blinkin' word all week, come to that.' Her feet slipped on the melted snow, and she let out a squeal. 'Why don't we go to the second house pictures? It's Boris Karloff in "The Ghoul" at the Rialto an' it's only a hop, skip and a spit to your bus stop from there. Aw, come on, Gatty. Give over looking as if you've lost half-a-crown and found a threepenny bit. An' put your beret on. You're beginning to look like Mother Christmas with all that snow on your hair.'

Stopping suddenly, Gatty burst out: 'I don't care! I wish I *was* flamin' Mother Christmas, if you really want to know. I wish I was anybody but me! I wish I was dead!'

There was a small silence for a moment. Winnie, her sharp features quivering as if she'd smelt something nasty, stared in acute and genuine dismay into Gatty's strained white face.

She was Gatty's best friend. They had been best friends ever since Gatty had walked into the shoe shop to start work on her fourteenth birthday. Together they had shaved the soft down from their legs, smoked their first cigarettes, giggled themselves sick at nothing, sat on the double seats in the back row at the Majestic cinema, and allowed themselves to be furtively squeezed by a succession of boys. Untouched by any of the finer feelings of love, they had stood in the darkness of shop doorways, exchanging long hard kisses with the boys of the moment, made dates they had no intention of keeping, comparing notes the morning after, in between trying on shoes in their dark green dresses.

Now, as Winnie stared in dismay at Gatty's woebegone

148

face, her sharp mind was working overtime. Apart from sudden death in the family, there was only one kind of trouble bad enough to make her friend wish she was dead. Winnie's small eyes narrowed into suspicious slits. But Gatty wouldn't do . . . wouldn't do *that* without letting on. Surely?

The youngest of three sisters, Winnie knew more than most what doing *that* could lead to. Both her older sisters had got into trouble and been forced to get married; Mollie crying right through the service in a grey two-piece, and Doreen brazen as brass, with a stomach on her like a load of hay. Winnie blinked the feathery snow from her sparse eyelashes.

'Right then! Instead of going to see Boris at the Rialto, let's go round to my house and pick some chips up on the way. We can eat them out of the bags and put our feet up on the fender. Me mam's always out of a Saturday.' She gave Gatty's arm a little shake. 'C'mon. We can't stand here, me feet's freezing.'

Gatty stirred, as if coming out of a dream, but she allowed herself to be propelled across the street, welded to Winnie by their linked arms. As they hurried down past the Arcade, heads bent against the whirling, dancing snow, they could have been taken for little girls in their cheap coats, with their thin legs in rayon stockings and shoes better fitted for walking along some seaside promenade at the height of summer. Every now and then Winnie stole a look at her friend's averted face, but she didn't speak. Time enough when they were in out of the cold, with their chairs drawn up to the fire and a pot of tea apiece to wash down the vinegary chips. In spite of her anxiety, her mouth watered at the prospect.

'Now then,' she said, when, after no more than a few minutes' wait at the chip shop, they'd been served with four pennyworth of glistening chips apiece, ladled into little paper bags then wrapped warmly in newspaper. 'We'll soon be at our house, kid, and just hope me mam's left a good fire going. Me bum's numb.'

Winnie was like that. Sprinkling her conversation with rude words like 'bum' never failed to make Gatty giggle. Winnie and her mother used them all the time, but Polly thought it was awful talking like that. She'd said so, many a time, and privately Winnie had decided Mrs Pilgrim thought she was a cut above.

'Your mam won't have to mind you being a bit late,' she said, as they hurried along carrying the fragrant parcels. 'She can't keep tabs on you all the time. You're fifteen, for heaven's sake.'

The snow by now had turned to sleet, stinging their faces like the prick of fine dressmaker needles. Winnie opened the door of the first house in a terraced row, and hurried down the lobby to turn up the gas in the back living-room.

'Now then,' she said again, poking the fire into life. 'Come and get your chair up and your feet on the fender.' Eagerly she unwrapped her own chips. 'Get stuck in, Gatty, then tell me what's up. You didn't say you wished you was dead for nothing.'

'They'd choke me.' Gatty stared down at the chips. 'I can't eat nothing. You'd best have mine.'

Every one of her senses seemed to be sharpened to the point of actual pain. The chair she sat on was one of a set of four, covered with long silver horsehair which pricked the backs of her knees. The cut steel of the fender beneath her feet hadn't known the touch of emery paper in years, she guessed, and the ashpan was so full it jutted forward into the hearth. Her Grandma Myerscough would have died of shame rather than see her fire-irons unpolished like that, and there was a half-drunk cup of tea on the mantelpiece with a lipstick mark on its rim.

It was funny she hadn't noticed these things before. Gatty bit into a chip without really noticing what she was doing. Winnie's house was dirty. She, Gatty Pilgrim, was dirty. Not outside, but deep inside her with the memory of what had happened to her in the wood that day.

'I've done something awful,' she said suddenly. 'I let a man do something bad to me, and I might be going to have a baby.'

There. It was said. The terrible secret was out and with its release the tears came. Her wail of anguish was that of a small animal bewildered by agony and fear. The bag of chips slid from her knees into the hearth, and the tears spurted from her eyes as if from the rose on a watering can.

Winnie, at no small sacrifice, wrapped up her chips and laid them down close to the fire to keep warm. Silently she fished up the sleeve of her green dress and handed Gatty a rather grubby handkerchief.

'A man?' she whispered. 'Which man?'

Gatty held the handkerchief screwed up tightly, making no attempt to wipe the tears away. 'It doesn't matter which man. He doesn't come into it,' she snapped. 'You're like my mother,' she accused unfairly. 'Always asking questions that don't matter.'

Winnie's sparse, over-plucked eyebrows raised themselves into the wide expanse of her wide white forehead, but she bit back the sharp retort trembling on her lips. Searching carefully for the right words, she decided to probe gently. 'You was raped, Gatty. Is that what you mean?'

'No! Yes!' Gatty's voice rose in the terrible wail again. 'Rape is when a man jumps on you and strangles you unconscious. *Isn't* it?' Lurid pictures of hard-eyed men throttling the life out of innocent maidens with long hair streaming down their backs flashed into her mind, culled from illustrations to the stories in the new *True Life* magazines. 'I let him *kiss* me, Winnie! I wanted him to!' Her mouth was open. She was making no attempt to cry decently. The tears were running down her chin, making little black splashes on the front of the hideous green dress.

'You don't make a baby with kissing.' Winnie thought she began to see the light. In all her escapades with boys, the other thing, the unmentionable going-the-whole-way follow up to the hard kisses and furtive fumblings, had been unthinkable. You could do anything – well, almost anything – but not that. Doing that would have landed her in the same boat as her sisters, an' two in one family was enough. Winnie felt flabbergasted as the extent of Gatty's ignorance struck her like an actual blow. She hurried on to explain. 'Kissing's all right, even French kisses, though I don't put up with them. Too much spit for my liking.' She smiled an understanding, worldly-wise smile.

'I'm not talking about kissing!' Gatty's head drooped over her swelling throat. The horror of what had happened, and the even worse horror of what the future might bring, gave her the courage to go on. She swallowed hard. 'He tried to . . . he *lay* on me, and his hand. . . .' Her voice sank to a whisper. 'I was fighting and kicking, an' I don't know whether he . . . whether we. . . .' Terror stayed her tongue, and she sat there, huddled into herself, the tears pouring down her pale cheeks.

'So he may not have . . .' Winnie coughed delicately, 'gone the whole way?'

'I don't know! Oh, God, I don't know! It's the not knowing what's killing me!'

'There has to be penetration,' Winnie said suddenly, remembering the word from an Agony Aunt's column in a magazine. 'This girl wrote in and that's what they told her in the reply.'

She was going to say the word again, but Gatty stopped her by raising her voice in a wail of protest. The quite ordinary word filled her with revulsion. *Penetration*. Oh, God, it elevated her fear out of the realms of possibility into a distinct medical supposition. It petrified her and it made her wish she had never told Winnie.

Winnie was talking, but Gatty scarcely heard her. She had retreated into a solid mist of cloying terror where Jack Thomson laughed at her with his mad green eyes, and the thing that was his child developed inside her till she grew bloated and fat.

'When are you due next?' she heard Winnie say.

'Two weeks, or perhaps even three or four. I'm not regular,' she answered automatically. Why had she told Winnie? Winnie hadn't believed her that she didn't know properly in shameful detail what had happened. There was that awful word again. You either knew whether you had been *penetrated* or you didn't. That's what her mother would want to know if she tried to confess, and that was what a doctor would ask if she found the courage to go to one.

In a torture of mind she swayed forward, laying her head on her knees. She was whispering to herself: 'Oh, God, dear sweet Jesus. I never meant to do anything so wicked. You know that's true.'

'Have you got any symptoms?'

Gatty lifted her head to stare at Winnie. Now more than ever she wished she'd had the sense to keep it all secret. There was genuine compassion in her friend's eyes, but Winnie was fascinated. Interested and fascinated. Gatty could see that.

'Have *you* never. . . ?' she asked, knowing the answer, but needing to wound.

'What d'you take me for?' Winnie's answer came pat, then immediately regretting her lack of tact she put an arm round Gatty, drew her close and they sat like that, the uneaten chips in the hearth, their legs mottled into barbed-wire patterns through sitting too close to the fire.

'You'll be all right, kid.' Winnie's hoarse voice soothed. 'Your whatsit will come, you'll see. There's no point in crossing bridges.'

'An' you won't tell nobody?'

'Cross me heart and hope to die.'

'I'm sorry I spoilt your supper.'

'Best chuck 'em on the fire before me mam comes in.' Winnie bent down and bundled the newspaper parcels on to the fire. 'I'll go and make us some cocoa. You'll feel better for a hot drink.'

But before she could make a move, Gatty was on her feet. 'I'm going.' She glanced at the black oblong of uncurtained window. 'I'd best go now in case the snow starts to stick. You know what me mother's like. She'll have a search party out for me if I don't turn up.'

She was buttoning herself into the single-breasted coat when the front door banged back and a voice called out: 'Yoo-hoo! It's only me.'

Winnie's mother was back.

Mrs Parker was a much older version of her daughter. At first glance they could have been taken for sisters, but Eileen Parker's hair had lost its fire and curled over her bulging forehead in a sandy frizz. Living a hand-to-mouth existence on the dole since the nearby cotton mill had closed down, she spent her days in cross-over pinafores and curlers and down-at-heel bedroom slippers. But now, because she'd been out with a friend to the pub, she was resplendent in dusty-black costume and velvet pillbox hat with a veil. When she saw Gatty, her face lit up in a welcoming smile.

'Hello, love! By gum but it's parky outside!' Taking off her hat, she tossed it on to the sideboard, where it ringed a clock in a glass dome. 'It's a pity you've got to go home, Gatty.' She slipped out of her coat, revealing a scarlet jumper knitted in raspberry stitch, each bobble furred and felted by careless washing. 'You're welcome to stay with us while the bad weather's on. There doesn't seem much sense in you traipsing up yon mountainside just to slither down it again in the mornings.' She went to put the kettle on, talking over her shoulder. 'See what your mam says, love.'

'She's right, Gatty.' Seeing her friend off at the door, Winnie peered anxiously at the sky. 'You could go home at the weekends, an' it might . . .' she lowered her voice to an urgent whisper, 'it might take your mind off it a bit. Till you know.' She jerked her head backwards. 'She's not forever asking questions like your mam.'

'I don't know. . . .' Gatty shook her head as if she didn't know anything, and as she walked away down the street, Winnie noticed the dejected droop of her shoulders and the way Gatty veered from side to side as if she'd been drinking.

She went inside to cut three doorstops of bread, spreading them thick with margarine before sprinkling them with sugar from the blue bag in the cupboard.

'Make me a sugar butty while you're at it, love,' her mother said. 'I think I forgot to have me tea.'

When Gatty got off the bus down in the village and began the long walk up the hill, the darkness was so absolute she could almost feel it like a hand on her face. A lamp shone out from the front window of the Thomson cottage, but she hurried past with face averted.

Normally the darkness held no terrors for her. Country bred, Gatty accepted it in the same way she accepted the street lamps of the town. But as she walked up the field path, she was conscious of the beating of her heart and the soft plop of the unfrozen snow falling from branches. In the heightened state of her imagination she thought she saw the dark bulk of Pendle Hill looming ahead, advancing towards her like some dark prehistoric animal.

She began to run. A stitch stabbed at her side, but with dry mouth and pounding heart she scrabbled her way up the stony path.

When she reached the cottage at last, flinging open the door to lean against it panting, the sight of her mother sitting sewing in the lamplight brought a rush of tears to her eyes. It was all there, the security she craved, the reassurance she desired with every fibre of her being. If Polly hadn't spoken she would have rushed to her, knelt down and buried her head in Polly's lap to blurt out the fear that was squeezing the very life out of her.

'What time do you call this, young lady?' Polly asked, and the moment was gone.

For over two hours, ever since Martin had gone his usual grumbling way to bed, Polly had sat there, staring into the fire, the sewing untouched, her mind a jumble of longings she couldn't control.

In the space of one afternoon it seemed to her as if her whole world had turned topsy-turvy, leaving her vulnerable and strangely without shame. It was as if her skin from head to toe was alive with an awareness of the man called Robert Dennis. The recollection of his face as he'd drawn her towards him filled her with an elation which surprised her with its intensity. She had tried telling herself that she was a married woman – a happily married woman at that – and it hadn't worked. She had reminded herself that she wasn't a young girl any more, that at her age she ought to know better; that it was wicked, even that deep inside her she accepted that Robert was missing his wife rather than wanting her. And the joy and worry churning away inside her had blotted out rational thought.

If it had been possible she would have walked out of the cottage and gone to him. If they'd been on the telephone she would have dialled his number, just to hear his voice. She had glanced at the clock wondering what he was doing at exactly that moment, and the fact that her daughter hadn't come home from work was no more than a slight irritation on the surface of her thinking.

Her saving grace, a down-to-earth sense of humour, had deserted her completely. Was it just yesterday she had thought that this sort of thing only happened to other people? People without a decent code of honour, or the moral strength to walk away from temptation.

All she knew was that she must see him again. And soon. . . .

Gatty's sudden appearance was an intrusion, Polly's chastisement automatic. Polly looked at her daughter and saw nothing of the mute pleading in the dark eyes, felt nothing of the tension which shimmered almost tangible in the air between them.

'Have you had anything to eat?' Again, the question was purely automatic, and when Gatty lied and said she'd eaten chips with Winnie, Polly sighed. The smoked mackerel poached and keeping warm between two plates wouldn't be wasted, though.

'Dogs don't eat fish,' Martin had said more than once, but Jim did. At the rattle of his dish he surfaced from an apparently deep sleep, tail wagging and tongue lolling in anticipation of an unexpected second supper.

'I'll just make myself a slice of toast,' Gatty said, then widened her eyes in surprise as her mother merely nodded an agreement.

Gatty thought her mother was looking different somehow. Beautiful almost. For her age, of course. With the lamplight shining softly on it, her hair was like a halo round her face, much, much prettier than Winnie's mother with her dry permed hair and wrinkles showing up through pancake make-up.

Love for her mother flooded Gatty's heart. She held the toasting fork closer to the bars of the gate. What if she suddenly said: 'Oh, Mam. Help me. . . . Please listen to me and help me. I'm so frightened, an' I'm not even sure there's anything to be frightened about. I'm not clever like Martin, an' I know he's your favourite, but, oh God, just *listen* to me. Now. Please!'

'Can't you see you've set that slice of bread on fire?' Polly's voice was more weary than condemning. 'Why you couldn't eat that fish I don't know. Here, give it to me!'

In the space of a second, Gatty's mood switched from despair to anger. It was no use. Telling her mother was the last thing she could do. She gave Polly a black look from beneath the dark wings of her eyebrows, then spoke in a clear cold voice filled with adolescent loathing: 'Winnie's mother asked me to stop at her house during the week. With the snow coming, she thinks it's daft me struggling back here every night after the shop. She thinks folk who live out in the wilds are daft anyway. Catch her living in a dump like this!'

There was no way Polly could even begin to feel the arousal of anger. The strange, sweet lethargy held her still.

'Tell me why you're so unhappy, love,' she wanted to say, but the words wouldn't come. For probably the first time in her life, her thoughts were turned completely inwards on herself. What Gatty did, or wanted to do, mattered. Of course it mattered, but not all that much. Maternal feelings counted as nothing against this fever raging inside her. Pulling herself together with an effort, she said: 'I'd have to go and see Mrs Parker to arrange about paying her something. You're not sponging on her, Gatty. Your dad wouldn't like that.'

'You *want* me to go, don't you?' There was heartbreak in the question, but all Polly heard was the sullen defiance, the whining self-pity.

'Now why on earth should I want you to go?'

It was starting again – the futile wearying arguments, the total lack of anything approaching communication. Polly handed a perfectly toasted slice of bread over.

'I'd have to write to your dad first, anyway. He likes to think of us all here, just as we were when he went away. I'll want to see what he thinks about it first.'

In spite of her distress, Gatty took the toast over to the table to spread it thickly with margarine and jam. Hunger pains were gnawing at her stomach. She felt light-headed, and asked herself how on earth she had imagined she could unburden herself on her mother sitting so quietly in her chair, her hands uncharacteristically idle in her lap.

'It's got nothing to do with our dad,' she said rudely. 'What's he stopping down in London for anyroad? He can't be liking his job all that much or else why doesn't he talk about it more? He can't even be bothered to write these days.'

Polly flinched. She didn't want to get into an argument about Harry. She didn't even want to *think* about Harry. For a little while, before Gatty had burst into the cottage bringing the reality of the outside world with her, Polly had found herself deep in a fantasy where Harry *never* came back, leaving her free to be with Robert, living with him in the house with the flame-patterned curtains, and the rug with the dragon on it by the leaping fire. Her thoughts appalled her, even as they ran uncontrolled through her subconscious. And now Gatty was here, intruding on her dreams.

'We'll wait and see what your dad has to say about it,' she said. 'I'll be writing to him at the weekend.'

Gatty closed her eyes and smiled derisively. 'Well, I'm still going to stop at Winnie's.' She clapped a hand over her mouth to still the hysteria rising in her throat. Bowing her head, she finished quietly: 'I'm going to bed now. But it's best, Mam. Believe me, it would be for the best.'

'You'll go if and when I say so.' Polly spoke into thin air. Without once glancing round, Gatty had made one of her silent accusing exits, leaving her bad humour behind, expecting her mother to storm after her demanding an apology.

'I must go after her. She's not going to get away with that.'

Polly spoke the words aloud, but first she pulled her chair closer to the fire and picked up the sewing in her lap. It was a fiddly and mundane task, stitching new suspenders on to one of her narrow belts. The elastic was thick and strong and the needle had to be pushed through with a thimble.

For a moment she heard her mother's voice: 'You'll suffer for not wearing a proper corset, our Polly. By the time you're my age, you'll have a stomach fit to rest on your knees.'

Allowing the belt to drop back on her lap, Polly patted her taut flat stomach. The birth of two children had left her figure as firm as it ever was. She wasn't thin, not by a long chalk, but then she wasn't exactly fat either. Nicely rounded, Harry often said. It was a long time since she had given her shape much thought. Gatty took after her father, or her grandma, but *she* must take after her maternal grandmother who, with her wasp waist and high breasts, had been a real Edwardian beauty. Complacently Polly cupped her rounded breasts in her hands, imagining . . . imagining what?

When the door burst open she swivelled round in her chair, her expression a mixture of guilt and shame.

'Bella!' The sewing slipped to the floor as Polly stared in dismay at the small dishevelled figure standing there. 'What's wrong? Is it Jack? He's not. . . ?' Her voice tailed away.

The familiar grey shawl was slipping from Bella's head. Her pale face was pinched and mean with cold, and her eyelids blinked rapidly over her colourless eyes as she fought to regain her breath.

'He's escaped,' she managed to gasp. 'He went for an

161

orderly, battered him senseless, stole his watch and his jacket with wages in the pocket, and scarpered.' Her feverish glance darted round the room. 'They've set the police on him, Polly, but they'll never find him. I know my Jack. He knows the fells like the back of his hand.' Her voice rose surprisingly strong and harsh. 'He split the orderly's head open with a bracket he'd wrenched from the wall, an' they say he might die.'

The pink eyelids quivered so jerkily that Bella's little pinched face was contorted into a frightening mask of hysteria. Ignoring Polly's outstretched hands she groped her way to the nearest chair and sat down, burying her face in her hands.

Her voice came muffled. 'An' if he dies then my poor Jack'll be up for murder!' Bella raised her head. 'Oh, Polly! You've tried to tell me what to do afore, an' I haven't heeded a word of what you've said. But this time I'm listening. What can I do? I've allus shielded him afore, but this time I feel I can't do nothing.'

'The baby?' Polly moved to get her coat down from the row of pegs at the foot of the stairs. 'Shall I go down and get him? You can't be down there on your own. Not tonight.'

But in spite of her plea for help, Bella wasn't listening. Her head jerked towards the window. 'It's come on to snow again, and Jack is out there in the cold, running away as if he was an animal, with them after him.' Her eyes were hard and tearless. 'It wasn't his fault, Polly. Jack has to be out in the air, an' yet they shut him up in a room on his own. It was like taking a bird and shutting it up in a cage. They were supposed to be making him better, but what they've been doing to him 'as made him worse. He's not really bad, not like a lot of·folk are bad. Not many can 'old a candle to my Jack when it comes to kindness. Not when he's in a good mood.'

There was a scar on Bella's cheek that would be visible for the rest of her life. There were two teeth missing from her lower jaw, and Polly knew that her back bore raised weals that the years would never smooth. She lived on the edge of starvation in a cottage where the walls oozed damp, with a leaking roof and a door that fitted only where it touched. Yet, because Jack Thomson had smiled on her once with his green eyes, loved her and carried her in his arms across the moors, settling her in the only home she had ever known, unstinting devotion was his for ever.

'Oh, Bella . . .' Polly shook her head slowly from side to side, 'I wish I could tell you what to do.' She went to kneel by Bella's chair. 'But if Jack turns up, if he tries to come back home, you'll have to give him up. For his own sake, as well as yours. You must know that.'

With a swift movement that sent the chair rocking wildly and almost knocked Polly flat on her back, Bella leapt to her feet. Her thin little voice rose to a raucous shout.

'Oh, God, you make me sick! I might have known it was a waste of time coming to you!' She backed towards the door. 'Oh, aye. You'd split on Jack, wouldn't you? You've never had a good word for him. Never! If he came knocking on your door you'd have the police on him as fast as you could get your big feet down the hill. You've not got feelings, Polly Pilgrim. There's a great hard stone where your 'eart should be.' She wrenched the door open. 'Look out there! It's snowing like the clappers, an' unless he finds shelter my Jack'll freeze to death.' Her face was a stiff mask of pain as she clutched

163

the shawl closer round her chin. 'I hope the day comes when you don't know where to turn, an' when it does don't come to me. Jack allus said you was a heartless bitch, an' you are! Thanks for nothing, Polly Pilgrim!'

There was no point in running after her. Polly knew that once inside her cottage, Bella would bolt the door and scream abuse through its rotting timbers, just as she had done with Jack after one of their many shouting rows. For a while she stood in the doorway, imagining the small flying figure hurtling down the hill. The wind blew the snow into whirling gusts, tossing the flakes high, snatching them up again as they touched the ground. Rubbing her arms she stared out into the darkness, over to the east towards Pendle where the two lonely trees were etched like witches crouched over broomsticks, leaning into the frozen teeth of the gale.

The whole dark landscape was open, wild and bare. The air stung her nostrils with the force of ice-picks. Going inside, Polly shot the heavy bolt and went back to the fire.

But the time for dreaming was past. Somewhere out there a man crouched and waited, a man who walked soft-footed even when the ground rang hard. Jack Thomson had learnt well the art of survival out in Flanders Fields in the last war, and Polly knew he would show no mercy to anyone who refused to give him shelter.

The full horror of what he had done and what he would still do, given the chance, dawned on her. Until he was caught, they must all tread a tightrope of caution. Moving slowly from one task to another, Polly began her nightly ritual of preparation for the following day.

Gatty must be sent out of harm's way. Already it seemed as if her fear of Jack was obsessive. There must be no more lonely walking up the hill in the darkness for Gatty, at least until Jack was caught. Polly started to lay the table for the next morning's breakfast, laid a place absent-mindedly for Harry, then snatched it quickly away.

Unwilling to go upstairs to bed, she leaned against the high fireguard, staring into the dying fire. Yes, Gatty could stay with Winnie. It was what she wanted to do anyway.

The candlelight flickered on the cream-washed walls as she climbed the steep and narrow stairs at last. As she had been used to doing ever since they were tiny, Polly opened first Martin's bedroom door then Gatty's.

Martin was sleeping buried beneath the blankets, with just a tuft of fair hair showing on his pillow. He was snoring rhythmically as usual and Polly wondered briefly yet again about his tonsils and adenoids.

It was unbelievable that Gatty hadn't heard Bella shouting downstairs, and yet her face was turned towards the wall, her breathing deep and even. Polly hesitated. There was time enough in the morning to get her things together and tell her that her wish to stay with Winnie had been granted. Polly smiled, pulling the door softly to behind her. She wouldn't put it past Gatty denying that she had ever wanted to do any such thing, but she'd have to go. It was right and wise, under the circumstances.

In her own room Polly put the candlestick down on the high table by her bed. For once she was going to bed unwashed, but she'd make up for it in the morning. Tomorrow was another day.

When she snuffed out the candle the acrid smell lingered in the air. Polly squeezed her eyes tight shut, then giving into an unbearable temptation, opened them wide.

Nothing. Praise be to God, nothing up there but darkness. No wavering light warning of worse to come. For a brief moment Polly's down-to-earth commonsense asserted itself.

'Pull yourself together, Polly,' she whispered. 'You accepted that it's your own thoughts that conjure the flamin' thing up.'

She crossed her arms and settled herself for a sleep that would not come. Wide awake half an hour later, she took herself in hand once again.

'Now then, Polly Pilgrim. Less of it! That way lies madness,' she muttered. 'Ghostly lights, witches, a crazed man running for his life out there in the hills. Bella straining her ears for the sound of him stumbling to her door. Gatty wanting to leave home at fifteen. Martin with his tonsils rotting in his throat. Harry miles away, telling you nothing, wiping out seventeen years of marriage with his damn fool reticence. Money running out, and your own tiddling job in jeopardy.' She sighed heavily. 'An' you dreaming of another man's touch.'

'Stop it!' Turning over on to her side, she stretched out an arm across the empty side of the big double bed.

'Harry . . .' she murmured, but the face she saw behind closed eyelids was the face of a man with the palest eyes she had ever seen. A man with silver streaks in his thick dark hair.

— Eight —

Snow had fallen in the south of England, had landed gently on London pavements, then disappeared overnight, leaving the air sparkling clear with a high bright sky of vivid blue.

When Yvonne Frobisher called for Harry she was in a happy mood. She was wearing a fur-trimmed costume, the three-quarter jacket and calf-length skirt in tweed of a heathery shade. A small matching hat fitted close to her small head and she had pulled dark wings of shining hair forward over her cheeks. She was happy because meeting Harry had been what she called a 'novelty', and her life at the moment was without the excitement she constantly craved. It *amused* her to think how much she was looking forward to meeting him again.

He was ill at ease at first, sitting beside her in the car with his black hair straggling over the collar of his shabby, leather-patched jacket, but as they left the quiet Sunday morning streets behind them and drove west, he relaxed enough to tell her it was the first time he'd been in a car driven by a woman.

'And you're not sure you like it?'

She glanced sideways at him, her eyes teasing.

'Northern men are like that, am I right? A woman's place is in the kitchen, slaving over a hot stove. Isn't that what they say?' Her smile was warm and friendly. 'Is that your opinion of the status of women, Mr Pilgrim?'

Harry considered for a moment. 'Nay, I wouldn't say that. There's room for all sorts of women, I reckon. There's the kind what's quite happy fetching up their children and stopping at home, and slaving over a hot stove as you say.' He suddenly felt very daring. 'Then there's your sort, Miss Craven . . . I'm sorry, Mrs Frobisher, who would burn a pot of tea if they had to mek it themself.'

Her laugh was infectious, a deep-throated chuckle that set him off laughing with her.

'Have I said something funny?' he asked with mock seriousness.

She shook her head. 'Would it surprise you to know that I once went with Charles, my ex-husband, on safari, and cooked broth and dumplings in the wilds of Africa on a grotty primus stove, in a pith helmet with sweat running down my nose?'

'I thought ladies perspired gently, never sweated,' he said. 'Broth an' dumplings, did you say? You're having me on.'

'Cross my heart, darling. Charles fancied dumplings in his bloody stew, and what Charles fancied he usually got.' She turned to smile at him. 'But now I only cook when forced to or the mood takes me. My flat is round the corner from Harrods, and I have been known to send out to their marvellous Food Hall for a complete meal, or even, on one of my slimming semi-starvation days, a salad sandwich.'

'You've no need to go starving yourself,' he said

without thinking. 'You're nobbut the size of twopen-north of copper.'

He looked down and bit his lip, embarrassed at having been so personal, but she didn't seem to mind. For a while she drove without speaking, and he sat there beside her, conscious of her presence, her poise, the scent of violets coming from her, and an indefinite something about her that made him feel elated and more witty with every mile. It was *breeding*, he told himself, something a woman was born with and could never acquire. Good schools, the right foods, knowing when she was doing the right thing, and not caring overmuch when she didn't. It was a quality her brother had possessed, even as he lay unshaven and gaunt in his narrow attic bed. Nothing to do with money or possessions. Taste, he decided. Yes, that was it. Good taste. In everything.

Well out in the suburbs now, she put her foot down hard and the little car gathered speed. When they reached fairly open country, she took off her hat, tossing it behind her on to the back seat. Driving nonchalantly with one hand, she fumbled in the glove compartment and handed him a cigarette case and a gold lighter.

'Light one for me, please, darling, and take one for yourself.' She was peeling off her gloves, revealing long slender fingers topped with nails polished a deep plum shade toning exactly, he noticed, with her silk blouse.

'I don't smoke meself,' he told her, overwhelmed by the intimacy of her accepting a cigarette from his own lips. 'Not since the war.'

She immediately wound down the window, fanning the smoke away from him with her right hand. 'Oh, that awful, terrible war. It was the war that set Roger on his road to ruin. He went straight in as a captain, leading his men over the top. A case of the blind leading the

169

blind. He was mentioned twice in dispatches, then instead of going into the firm on his demob, well, he began drinking heavily, then took to the road.' She threw the unsmoked cigarette through the window. 'It was Roger's way of escaping from a life he couldn't cope with, I suppose.' Her voice was so low he had to strain to hear what she was saying. 'He was such a gentle young man before he went to France. He was a classics scholar.' She turned a corner on what Harry was sure was two wheels. 'Imagine a man like that pushed into living in a hole in the ground! He *cared* for his men, you see, and when most of them got killed and he survived, he never stopped asking himself why.' She turned and smiled brilliantly. 'The moral being, Mr Pilgrim, never ask yourself why. Do what you want to do when you want to do it. There's no such thing as retribution. Roger wouldn't have trodden on the proverbial fly, and look where that got him.'

'I loved your brother.'

Once again Harry surprised himself by his lack of reticence. It was being shut inside the car with her, he told himself. It was the easy way she had of talking as if they were lifelong friends, and not as different as chalk from cheese.

'Then that makes us friends,' she said. 'So may I call you Harry, and you must call me Yvonne. I hate the Frobisher bit, anyway.'

They drove down a long, winding road edged by tall trees, their bare winter branches making a pattern of black lace against the blue sky. 'You're not looking after yourself properly, Harry. What is your wife thinking of, letting you live down here in that frightful doss-house? Does the job you're doing make it worth while?'

Suddenly Polly's face was there before him, a tired

and apprehensive face, as she'd packed for him on that cold dark morning in the cottage. Her eyes had been ringed with deep shadows, but she'd waved him off with a smile.

'There is no job.' He scowled, drooping his head forward and twisting his cap round and round in his hands. 'I had a job at Kew, but I lost it, an' I'm having to accept that there's not much scope for jobbing gardeners, not at this time of the year.'

'Then go home, Harry.' She drove without looking at him, down a long steep lane hung over by beech trees, with glimpses of big detached houses set well back from the road.

'No!' Harry's voice was louder than he intended. 'Not till I have to crawl back, an' I'm not ready to crawl yet!'

A recent letter from Polly was tucked into his threadbare leather wallet, and he touched his pocket briefly. It was a letter like all the others, filled with optimism, telling him of the better days she was sure were just round the corner. It showed him that she was managing very well, that with her wages from the raincoat factory the money was lasting out. He scowled. Practical Polly. Always an answer for everything. Polly with never a grumble when a smile would do instead. Capable of carrying on without him. Not *needing* him, if you wanted to spell it out.

A fierce indignation took possession of him, as he tortured the cap on his knee out of shape. Suddenly, surprising him, Yvonne took a hand from the wheel and snatched the cap from him, throwing it on to the back seat.

'You look frightfully cross. And very serious. And of course you mustn't go home, not if you don't want to.' Suddenly she wound the window right down so that the wind caught her hair and lifted it away from her expressive face. 'Cheer up, Harry. It may never happen!'

'Leafy Bucks,' she said. 'Now you see why. In the summer the beech trees are glorious.' She pointed to some bedraggled hikers plodding along the grass verge, haversacks on their backs, bare knees below their shorts blue with cold. 'Silly creatures,' she said, 'especially the women. Female bottoms are better hidden. Preferably in a flurry of pleats, wouldn't you say, Harry?'

And Harry, who had never given the matter much thought, agreed at once.

'That's better.' She smiled at him. 'I like you better when you look happy. And you are happy, aren't you?'

'Do you know, I believe I am,' he said, so seriously that she burst out laughing, and as they drove down a steep hill, with a view of spreading fields in the distance, their laughter mingled like the laughter of old friends.

To Harry, the next part of their journey was like stepping back in time. The houses and shops on either side of the wide road were either half-timbered Tudor or early eighteenth century, and just before they passed the ancient town hall he saw an archway bearing the date 1624. He sat up eagerly, trying to see both sides at once, taking in the beauty of a bow-fronted inn, twisting round again to see a wooden bell turret and clock, weathered by time.

'Another five minutes or so and we're there.' Yvonne tapped his knee lightly. 'The parents might be a bit upset when you talk about Roger at first, but they have to know. It was all those years not knowing that almost broke them up.'

Nervously Harry adjusted the knot of his tie and tried to pull his sleeves down to cover the frayed shabbiness of his shirt cuffs. When they turned into a drive wide enough to take the width of two cars, his nervousness increased.

The house, of mellowed brick, was long and low, surrounded by beechwoods stretching as far as the eye could see. As if they had been just waiting for the sound of tyres on the gravel path, the big front door opened and Roger Craven's parents came out to greet them.

As Harry took the hand of the grey-haired, smiling woman in his own and looked into her eyes as gentle, wise and alive as Roger's had been, his nervousness disappeared.

'Thank you for coming, Mr Pilgrim,' she said.

'I'm glad I was able to,' Harry said, following her up the three wide steps into a large panelled hall, with bowls of flowers reflected in oval gilt-framed mirrors, and a faint but definite smell of roasting meat coming from the back of the house.

'I hope you're hungry, Mr Pilgrim,' Roger's mother whispered. 'Cook's doing beef and Yorkshire pudding, just for you.'

'Harry comes from Lancashire, not Yorkshire, Mummy.' Yvonne winked at her father. 'Yorkshire's the wrong side of the Pennines, didn't you know?'

'Oh dear.' Mrs Craven touched her husband's arm. 'I was sure you told me Yorkshire, dear.'

'Lancashire, Yorkshire · . . . what does it matter?' Harry spoke quickly to reassure the small woman with the faded blue eyes. 'Anyroad, the Wars of the Roses was over a long time ago. I won't feel like a traitor eating Yorkshire pudding, I promise.'

He sat down in the chair indicated to him and stared round the room with frank interest. Education and money, he was thinking, without the slightest trace of envy. What a difference they made. The soft muted colours of browns and cream gave the long room an air of serenity. He noticed the mop-head chrysanthemums in crystal vases, disbudded he reckoned at just the right time to bring them to such perfection, and the pots of cyclamen, under-watered as was right and proper for the time of the year. His fingers itched to check their soil for moisture.

'You've got greenhouses out at the back, Mr Craven?' Harry spoke as one gardener to another, knowing he was right when the old man's eyes lit up with enthusiasm.

'The span-roofed type. Plenty of working room. I'm having a spot of trouble with the ventilators.' He nodded at an enormous display of chrysanthemums. 'I'm pleased with those, but the tomatoes let me down this year.'

'Uneven heating maybe.' Harry coughed and apologized. 'I'm sorry. It's just that in my job I see a flower not as a flower but how it's been grown. But then my job is,' he corrected himself, 'was, never merely a job. More of a way of living, I reckon.'

'Harry's out of work at the moment.' Yvonne perched herself on the arm of her mother's chair, swinging a silken leg. 'You don't know anyone round here who needs a full-time gardener, do you, Daddy?'

Mr Craven turned from the drinks cupboard, a cut-glass decanter in his hand. 'Experience?'

'Since I was fourteen. Apart from the war. Up to the slump, I was working three houses at once. Lawns, flower-beds, vegetable gardens, hot-house cultivation.' Harry spread his hands wide. 'All gone. It's rough up north, Mr Craven. When mills close down the women cling on to their house servants, but the gardener is the first to go. I suppose it's only natural.'

'But not fair,' Mrs Craven smiled at Harry. 'You boys who came back from the war should have had everything

174

you wanted.' Accepting a glass of sherry from her husband, she set it down on the little table in front of her. 'It's all wrong that a man who fought for his country in France during those dreadful years should be begging for work.'

'An' begging's the right word,' Harry said, smiling back at her. He sat back in his winged chair, feeling that in some strange way the aura of natural good manners, the total lack of snobbishness, had spread itself to include him. Inarticulate at the best of times, their kindness had set him completely at ease. This was how he could have been, he told himself, given the chance. It was the months of enforced idleness, the shame of being out of work that had ground him down. It was Roger's sister, this beautiful young woman, who had given him back his confidence. Maybe only temporarily, but, by God, he was enjoying himself. If he never saw her again he would remember this day as a turning point in his fortunes. The feeling was as strong as if its message had been spoken out loud. When he was handed a drink, he sat there at ease, a thin shabby man, holding the stem of his glass in his rough gardener's hand.

'We can never thank you enough for what you did for our son.' Roger's mother spoke softly, her eyes dimming with tears. 'But for you he would have died all alone.' Her grey head drooped. 'Seeing to his funeral and everything. That was a kind thing to do, a sensitive and wonderful thing to do.'

'He was my friend,' Harry said simply. 'We talked for hours. He told me to go home. Almost the very last thing he did was to urge me to go home.'

'As he wished he had done. . . ?'

Harry's voice was firm. 'As he wished *he* had done, Mrs Craven.'

175

Watching him talk, seeing the proud tilt of his head and the steadiness of his dark eyes, Yvonne felt the stirring of an old familiar excitement. This one was different. God, how very different, but it was a difference she decided she liked.

When dinner was announced she preceded Harry into the dining-room, her slim hips swaying provocatively in the full pleated skirt.

'They liked you,' she told him much later, as they sat in the parked car outside Harry's lodging house in the darkness of the late afternoon. 'I hope you'll go and see them again when I'm gone.'

'Gone? Gone where?' He had talked almost non-stop on the way back, filled with the elation that was still with him, the surety that from now on everything would change. There would be no more knocking on doors like a beggar. He would search out the big horticultural firms and try his luck there; he would try the big stores in Oxford Street and Regent Street with their garden tool departments. He'd even drop his Lancashire accent to some extent. He'd dropped it today, hadn't he? He was filled with the euphoria of certain success. All in the space of one day they had given that back to him. From now on he would be calling the tune. He felt it in his very bones. 'But you can't go away,' he said foolishly, then more slowly, 'can you?'

She smiled without answering, then leaning across she kissed him, keeping her mouth closed, her lips warm and dry on his own.

'That was just practising,' she whispered. 'And yes, I am going away.' Her eyes were very wide and dark in the light from the street lamp. 'To get married. To Canada.' Slowly she traced the line of his mouth with her finger. 'To someone I knew before Charles. Someone who said he'd always be waiting for me if ever I needed him. And I *do* need him, Harry. I'm no good without a man.'

'But do you love him?' Harry pulled her to him and defiantly kissed her again. 'You're talking a language I don't understand.'

'That was better.' Snuggling close, Yvonne laid her head on his shoulder. 'You're so sweet, Harry, and of course you don't understand. But I'm not going just yet. Not for another month, not till after Christmas, so there's no need for goodbyes. Not that I ever say them. Goodbyes can be very tedious.'

Stretching across him she opened the door on his side, and feeling foolish and as though he'd been abruptly dismissed, Harry got out.

'Remember I haven't said goodbye,' Yvonne called out, as he stood irresolutely on the pavement.

'I'll think on't,' he said, and sketched her a jaunty salute, then fielded his cap neatly as she threw it out to him.

Bemused, his mood of euphoria still sending the adrenalin coursing through his blood stream, he turned towards the lodging house. His step faltered as he reached the scarred front door, the thought of his lonely bed beneath the sloping roof of his attic room checking his stride.

By the time the car had disappeared round the bend of the road, he was walking swiftly away in the opposite direction. He was a man with nowhere to go, but this time going nowhere happily. The events of the day, the wine he had drunk, the way his eyes had been opened to a way of life so far removed from his own drab and hopeless existence, had soothed and cushioned him against a reality he was in no mood to face. Not yet.

Harry didn't know how he was going to do it, but of one thing he was certain. Never again would he go cap-in-hand to anyone. No more begging for what he felt now was his by right. They had liked him, Roger's parents; talked to him as an equal and wiped out the sense of inferiority that had been threatening his very manhood.

'Remember I haven't said goodbye.' Yvonne's last words to him rang in his ears like a promise.

For the moment he was his own man again, as free as his Romany ancestors had been, walking tall across the moors and fells of his beloved countryside. That his feet were pounding pavements, that on either side he was hemmed in by shabby houses, tattered blinds drawn across their windows, didn't seem to matter.

Cramming his cap down on his head and pulling it low over his forehead, Harry walked with a purposeful stride, his shoulders back, swinging his arms as in the long ago days of his soldiering.

In the north, the snow had turned the fell grass sallow. It had frozen, thawed, then frozen again, leaving a trea-cherous film of ice over the field paths. To the east of Polly's cottage, Pendle Hill crouched beneath a sky more grey than blue, its humped-back shape softened by a thin blanket of snow pitted by dark patches like currants on an iced cake.

There was still no trace of Jack Thomson. Police stations all over the country had been alerted, but the local search parties had been called off. Rough blizzards during those first bad days had folded the snow in massive drifts on the higher slopes, and unless he had got clean away it was assumed that Jack had perished in temperatures well below freezing.

Bella had bolted herself into the tiny cottage, just as Polly had known she would. Milk and food left on her doorstep had been snatched inside. During the night, her benefactors guessed.

Twice the police had forced an entry round the back of the tumbledown cottage, coming out red-faced after an abortive search of the tiny rooms.

'By the left,' Sergeant Wilkinson had reported, 'that young lass knows more swear words than owd Nick himself. And that baby looked none too clever. I never saw none of mine lie as still as that. Even when he was asleep our Eli was all of a twitch. She wouldn't let me near that baby.'

Sergeant Wilkinson's nearly-fledged constable, a lanky young man who still read comics hidden beneath the ledger on the station counter, and during the search for Jack Thomson had fantasized himself into the role of the *Wizard*'s Lionheart Logan of the Royal Mounties, chasing his prey through the Canadian snow-covered outback, pricked up his ears.

'She couldn't have been hiding her husband behind the baby's cot, could she, Sergeant?'

'It was in a *drawer*,' Sergeant Wilkinson said, shifting the stub of a cigarette from one side of his mouth to another. 'And I wasn't born yesterday, young fella-me-lad. If our hero had been anywhere in that cottage, I'd have rumbled him. Anyroad, he'd know better than to come back and spit on his own doorstep. Crafty, his sort are. Loony but as cute as a cartload of monkeys.'

179

At exactly the same time as Harry was climbing into Yvonne Frobisher's car, Polly opened the door of the cottage to shake out the rag rug just in time to see her mother struggling up the hill, small head in the atrocious helmet-type hat bowed against the wind. For every step Edna took, she seemed to slip one back. Her body was bent like a question mark, but her usual cavernous handbag was looped over her arm, and as she drew near Polly could hear her breath rasping in her throat.

'Mam!' Throwing the rug down, Polly went to meet her mother. She took the bag from her and with a supporting hand helped her up the last icy stretch. Anxiety and concern made her voice sharper than she intended.

'For heaven's sake, Mam! I never expected you to come today. Not in this! I was going to come and see you tomorrow after I'd finished work at dinnertime. You should be by your own fireside in weather like this.'

Edna's face was pinched with cold, but her pale watery eyes shot daggers at her daughter. 'Want me to go back, then? If I'm not wanted I can allus turn round and go home. The bus'll still be there. You've only to say the word. I know when I'm not wanted.'

'Oh, Mam!' Polly gave her mother's arm a little shake. 'You know I'm glad to see you. Sunday isn't the same without you. It's just that I never expected you to even think of coming.'

'It's better than stopping in on me own.' Edna made straight for the fire, peeling off layers of coats, scarves and gloves as she went. 'They've salted the roads down the town, so it weren't so bad there. I'd forgotten how the snow sticks out here in the back of beyond. If what they said on the wireless is right, we're in for a right bad spell. So I thought I'd come and see you before you get snowed in proper.' She·looked round the room. 'Where's our Martin?'

'Out with the dog.' Polly glanced worriedly through the window. 'I told him to keep to the hill path and not go into the wood.' She handed Edna a steaming cup of tea from the freshly brewed pot in the hearth. 'We've had a bit of excitement, if you can call it that, since last week.' She held the sugar bowl out to her mother. 'Jack Thomson attacked a male orderly at the Institution then did a bunk.'

'Killed him?' Edna asked with relish, her eyes brightening over the rim of the cup.

'He's still in a coma.' Polly added two more potatoes to the four she was peeling on a newspaper spread on the table. 'They reckon there's not much hope for him.'

'Poor soul,' Edna said insincerely. 'Then Jack Thomson'll be up for murder if they catch him. Funny I never saw a word about it in the evening paper.'

Polly stopped what she was doing, the peeler held loosely in her hand. 'Bella's locked herself in.' She sighed. 'I feel so helpless. That girl's no older than Gatty, and God knows what she's doing shut away inside with her baby. He wasn't breathing right the last time I saw him. When I told Bella she ought to get the doctor she swore at me.'

Edna bent down to scratch her chilblains. 'I've told you before about interfering in other folk's lives. That lass would let you in if she wanted to. And babies are stronger than you think. I've seen babies brought up in houses no better than muck middens – aye, and thrive on a bit of neglect.' She straightened up. 'Where's Gatty? Still stopping in bed?'

'Gatty isn't here.' Polly dug furiously at an eye in the potato in her left hand. 'She's staying with Winnie for

181

the time being. I didn't like the idea of her walking home up the hill with Jack Thomson prowling about on the fells somewhere. I still feel he's alive, waiting his chance to get back into his own cottage. And Bella would hide him. I'm positive of that.' Yet again she glanced through the window. 'I wish Martin would come back.'

'Harry should be here.' Edna sniffed with appreciation as Polly drew a dish of oxtail from the fire oven, checked the meat with a fork then pushed it back, closing the door with a slam.

'You *know* why Harry isn't here, Mam.' For a moment Polly felt a surge of honest dislike for the little woman complacently rocking herself to and fro in Harry's chair. 'There's nothing for him here. He's only one of thousands moving south for a chance to better themselves.'

'It would be different,' Edna said, 'if you were in a house with neighbours on either side, so you could knock on the wall if you wanted anything. You could be lying dead up here for days and none would be the wiser. If Harry Pilgrim wanted you to live in a field, then he should've stopped to look after you. But then, it's a man's world. Always has been and always will be.'

Polly drew a basket of carrots towards her. There were only a few left and they were the last of the winter crop. The turnips and swedes she had meant to get in were buried beneath the rock-hard ground, where they could stay for weeks if the weather didn't improve.

A fox had come down from the fells in the night. She had heard the hens squawking, but he hadn't managed to worm his way into the run. Not yet. Polly nodded her head up and down twice to make her mother believe she was listening. The money was running out, and Mr Goldberg would be telling them any day now that the factory was forced to close. Polly had seen it in his face as he'd talked to them in the workshop. And she didn't even know if Harry had written in the past week, because if he had, his letter would be locked away in the cottage at the bottom of the hill with Bella.

Gatty was all right where she was. For the time being. Polly had liked Winnie's mother the day she had met her briefly in the fish market buying coley, a fish Edna always said was only fit for cats. Yes, Winnie's mother was rough and ready, but she'd keep her eye on Gatty. Mentally Polly crossed off one less worry from her mind.

'It's the gypsy blood in your Harry making him wander off like that.' Edna pursed up her thin lips, trying to make out what was eating at her daughter's heart. Leaning forward, she picked up the poker and gave the fire a good prodding. It licked the chimney back, and washed the cream walls to the colour of pink flowers. She lifted the lid of a pan in the hearth and her mouth watered at the sight of Polly's home-made soup, stiff with barley, its surface glistening with globules of goodness from its bone marrow stock.

There was no point in asking Polly straight out what was worriting at her. She knew from experience what the answer would be. 'There's nothing wrong, Mam. Why should there be?'

Edna twisted round in her chair as the door banged back almost to the plaster, letting in a rush of cold air and Martin with his face as scarlet as his jersey, his fair hair plastered into strands as if it had been combed with a rake.

'It was Jim, Mam!' he gasped, getting his say in before Polly could speak. 'I'd have been back ages ago, but he went in the woods, a long way in, barking his head off, an' when he wouldn't come out I had to go and get him.'

The little dog slunk across the floor to his basket, stump of a tail drooping, ears flat to his head.

'Just look at him, Gran. He knows when he's done wrong. But I *had* to go after him, Mam. He might've been caught in a trap.'

'Go and towel your hair, that's a good lad.' Polly pushed the pan of potatoes on its trivet over the fire. 'And kiss your gran. You haven't said hello to her properly yet.'

At the sight of her grandson, Edna's features had softened into love. Bending down to the handbag which was never far from her side she took out two white paper bags. 'Palm toffee, banana splits,' she said, holding them out, 'and aniseed balls. Which one shall it be?'

Knowing he would get the whole lot eventually, Martin pretended to choose. 'No gob-stoppers this week, Gran?' he asked cheekily, then gave her the kiss he knew she wanted, screwing up his face at the familiar smell of wintergreen embrocation which clung to her summer and winter.

At two o'clock, as soon as the last of the dinner things had been cleared away, Edna said it was time she was going. 'I dursn't wait for the later bus, not with the snow starting again.' She began to layer herself against the cold, tying a scarf round her hat and buttoning first one cardigan then another up to her chin. When her heavy tweed coat was swagged round her like a dressing-gown, she looked straight at Polly.

'For two pins I'd ask you to come back with me. The both of you. Martin could go in the spare room, and you could sleep with me.' She picked up the bulging black handbag, looping it fiercely over her arm. 'I get lonely,' she said.

The admission startled Polly so much she could only

gaze open-mouthed at her mother, but before she could say anything Martin was beside her, tugging at her sleeve, cheeks bulging with Palm toffee, eyes sparkling with excitement.

'Let *me* go, Mam! You know I'm the next to the main part in the Christmas play, an' if we get snowed in an' I can't go Ernest Boland'll get it an' he's a rotten snob. Just because his father owns a mill at Preston.' For a moment Martin stepped out of his surroundings into the role of Tom Bedwing from the *Magnet* comic, the poor but talented scholarship boy, showing his true worth at Greyfriars School. 'If I have to stop at home because the bus doesn't run and I can't get there, old snotty Boland'll get my part. Oh, please, Mam. Just till we break up for the Christmas holiday. Let me!'

As if to add its weight to his argument the snow thickened, coming down now in large feathery flakes, sticking to the frozen ground. Polly hesitated. And was lost.

'But *I'm* staying here,' she told her mother, as Martin rushed headlong up the stairs to hurl books and pyjamas into a bag. 'For one thing Harry's letters are left at Bella's cottage, and for another my place is here.'

Following her son upstairs, she added another reason under her breath. The thought of sleeping with her mother, *living* with her mother, leaving the cottage to the vagaries of the weather, couldn't be stomached.

'And besides, there's Jim,' she said, as five minutes later they started down the hill. 'He's used to running wild. He'd drive your neighbours mad with his barking.'

'One excuse would have done.' Clinging to her daughter's arm, the snow settling on her like a mantle, Edna concentrated on putting one foot in front of the other.

'Why don't you say you don't want to come and have done with it?'

Polly watched the single-decker bus drive away, with Martin bouncing up and down on a seat next to his grandmother. Turning away, she was immediately buffeted by a snow-laden wind.

At Bella's cottage she almost lost her footing on the icy ground, but regaining her balance she hammered on the unyielding door.

'Bella! It's me. Polly. Stop this daft play-acting and let me in. You can't go hiding yourself away for ever.' Hammering again she raised her voice. 'Bella! Everybody knows you're there. For the baby's sake, let me in!' Hearing a scuffle from behind the door, Polly lowered her tone to one of soft persuasion. 'You can't live off bread and milk for ever. Your baby needs broth. Good nourishing stew made with fresh vegetables. I've got some here with me,' she improvised. 'Just open the door and let me see you're all right. I'm your *friend*, Bella. Your good true friend.'

The sudden shout made Polly step back a pace. Bella was screaming at the top of her voice, the ugly raucous sound amazing Polly by its volume.

'Friend, did you say, Polly Pilgrim? You call yourself a friend? Last time I saw you, you told me you'd tell on my Jack. That's the kind of friend you are!'

'Bella?' Polly was whispering now. 'Jack's not in there with you, is he?' She cleared her throat. 'The man he attacked died last night, Bella. I've just come back from the village and they're talking about it. Bella? There's no way Jack can escape what's coming to him. Not now. So if you know where he is you have to say.'

'You bloody faggot!'

A stream of foul language hit Polly's hearing like a

blow. A four-letter word she had only seen written on walls was screamed at her with staccato emphasis, repeating itself over and over like the stutter of a machine-gun. Then, out of breath, Bella lowered her voice to its normal childish whine.

'So you can save your breath to cool your bloody broth, Polly Pilgrim! An' you can tell anybody what'll listen that my Jack isn't here.' Her voice rose again. 'But he's not dead! My Jack wouldn't die. He's lived rough afore and he'll do it again. He can live off owt, my Jack can. Berries, roots, anything. An' he'll come back to me. He's only hiding up for a while.'

The sudden blizzard had darkened the sky, and behind Polly the open fields stretching to the little wood were one great landscape of gleaming white. She had left a lamp burning in her own cottage, but here in Bella's house all was darkness, not even the glimmer of candle-light to brighten the day that was dying far too soon.

'Have you got candles?' she asked, suddenly weary. 'I can't go away and leave you in the dark, Bella. Tell me if you've got candles, and if not I'll fetch some down and leave them on the doorstep.'

'Candles and matches,' Bella answered in a singsong voice. 'Matches in a little box with the picture of a man in a striped oathing costume on it. I bet you know his name, don't you, clever-clogs Polly Pilgrim? Seeing as how you know everything.'

It was too much. Short of breaking down the door which, flimsy as it was, had a bolt the thickness of a man's wrist, Polly knew there was nothing else she could do. Tomorrow she would try again, and failing to make Bella see sense she would . . . oh, dear God, what *could* she do?

Her mother had said she had no right to interfere in

187

other people's lives. It was a fault of hers, Edna had intimated. But where did caring end and interference begin? Reluctantly Polly started the familiar walk up the hill, bowing her head against the freezing wind, feeling the snow sting her cheeks, making her eyes water and tearing at her clothes, chilling her to the bone.

At four o'clock it was as dark as it would be at midnight. Polly drew the curtains and picked up her library book. Published only that year, it was by a Lancashire author, a man called Walter Greenwood. Born at Salford, according to a review she had read of the book in the local paper, he had left school at thirteen, working in various mundane jobs and never earning more than thirty-five shillings a week. *Love on the Dole*. Polly smiled ruefully at the title. In her present mood the title struck her as a misnomer. Surely the two – love and the dole – could never be simultaneous? And yet the reviews had made it clear this book was the opposite of a hearts and flowers romance. This man, this Walter Greenwood, apparently knew what he was writing about; knew it from experience, had known at first hand the heartbreaking deprivations of the poor and destitute. Polly turned to the first chapter. 'They call this part "Hanky Park",' she read. And was lost.

The sudden knock on the door startled and stunned her into a panic as acute as if she had been suddenly shot in the back. There had been no warning. No sound of footsteps on the path outside, nothing but that immediate, startling pounding of the ancient iron knocker with an urgent beat, as if whoever stood outside demanded to be let in.

The fact that the snow would have deadened any sound, failed to register. In that moment of sheer terror, Polly imagined Jack Thomson creeping silently down from the frozen fells, hungry and unshaven, demanding shelter, not daring to approach his own cottage, knowing that she, Polly, was entirely alone.

The fire glowed in the grate with the red-hot glitter of molten láva. Leaning forward, Polly picked up the poker with its rounded brass handle, forced herself to walk the few steps to the door and, in a voice weak with fear, called out: 'Who is it?'

When she heard his voice she threw down the poker, slid back the bolts, top and bottom, and turned the key in the lock. When she opened the door wide and saw him standing there, etched against the bleak landscape, she flung herself at the tall man, winding her arms round his neck and murmuring brokenly: 'Oh, Robert! If you only knew how glad I am to see you!'

The feel of his cold face against her own, the roughness of the chin of a man who needed to shave twice a day, filled her with an overwhelming sense of joy and relief. The sense of confusion on his strong face missed her entirely as she drew him inside.

'I knew you'd come,' she told him, pulling at his snow-powdered coat and scarf with her fingers. 'I wouldn't let myself think it, but I knew you would come.'

— Nine —

Robert Dennis sat in Harry's chair, the cup of hot coffee Polly had insisted on making for him dwarfed in his right hand. Now that she had given her feelings away in the spontaneity of her greeting, she looked shy and bewildered. Frightened almost, he guessed. But of herself, certainly not of him.

The bitter drink had been made from a bottle of Camp coffee, with its picture on the front of a British officer in India sitting smugly outside his tent, with a sepoy in servile attendance. Robert stared at the label, studying it carefully, wondering what to say next.

He had gone over and over in his mind the careful little speech he was going to make if they had managed a few minutes alone. He had been sure the girl, Gatty, would be there, watching him with sullen dark eyes, and the boy, Martin, fixing his unwavering stare on Robert's empty sleeve pinned up above his left elbow.

What he hadn't bargained for was finding her alone, looking so bonny, so achingly vulnerable with her blue eyes like a morning sky. He listened gravely as she stumbled through a recital of what had happened since their last meeting when he had almost, but not quite, allowed his own feelings to get the better of him.

'Jack Thomson won't come back,' he said. 'No one could live for long in conditions like this. You mustn't be afraid, love.'

'Since Harry went away I've never stopped being afraid.' Suddenly Polly wanted to open her heart to the man who was so different from any man she'd known before. She wanted to tell him how everything seemed to be conspiring against her; even about the light on the ceiling that had foretold it all. But a lifetime's habit of keeping her innermost thoughts to herself, the superstitious side of her nature rigorously hidden, stilled her tongue.

She smiled, the husky lilt back in her voice. 'I talk to myself, you know, and I tell myself I'm letting my imagination run away with me. Nothing really hurtful has touched me.' She smiled at him sadly. 'I've lived in the country too long to be afraid of the dark. I haven't got the countryside in my blood like Harry has, but like my mother said this morning, I'd like to knock on the wall sometimes and hear a neighbour on the other side knocking back.'

'Someone like my sister-in-law, Nellie?'

'Oh, dear. . . .' She was relaxing now, letting the happy feeling his presence always gave her flood through her. In the firelight, her eyes were soft and sparkling again. 'Is she friends again yet?'

'Not yet. But she'll come round. Polly?' He leaned forward. 'About the other day. . . .'

But she wasn't listening. The relief of being with him, of feeling his strength and his wisdom flow to her through the short distance between them, soothed her like a healing balm. She was tired of the terrors clouding the normal serenity of her thinking. She wanted to forget the sound of Bella's tinny little voice screaming obscenities, the look on Gatty's face as she left the cottage carrying her shabby cardboard case. The way even Martin had jumped at the chance to get away.

'I imagined when Harry went down south,' she said slowly, 'that things would go on just the same. Well, more or less the same.' A strand of golden hair had fallen forward over her forehead, and with a childish gesture she blew it back. 'But it's worse than that, Robert. It's as though I've lost him. I can't see his face, nor remember his voice. We lived together for seventeen years, and now there's nothing.' She sighed softly. 'You are more real to me, and I hardly know you at all. How can that be?'

Robert put the cup down in the hearth. She was so honestly bewildered he wanted to reach out to her, to stroke her baby-fine hair, to pull her down on to the rug in front of the fire, unfasten her pink jumper button by button, and bury his face in the warmth of her breasts. Then make love to her, releasing the tensions of a body starved of love for far too long.

'I am fifty years old next month, Polly.' A surge of emotion made him tremble. 'Four short months ago my wife died. Our marriage, before she became really ill, was fulfilled. In every way,' he said deliberately. 'Do you understand?'

He hesitated, feeling her embarrassment in his own gut, seeing the blush rise from her throat to stain her cheeks with colour. 'And so I miss very much the feel of a woman's body against mine.' He looked away from the shock mirrored in her eyes. 'Just as you must be missing lying in your husband's arms.' His voice was a whisper now, but he forced himself to go on. 'You

192

haven't got the look of a woman, Polly, who hasn't known the joy of sexual fulfilment. When I met you that day in the park, you were golden and glowing with the beauty that kind of constant loving gives to a woman. Not like the Nellies of this world who submit to their husbands with clenched teeth, wanting him to get it over with quickly. Your marriage to Harry was never like that, was it, little love?'

The endearment almost broke her. No man had ever spoken to her like that. Not even Harry. Their loving had been good. The blush deepened in her cheeks as she remembered the last night before he'd gone away. But the frankness, the *intimacy* of Robert's conversation had touched a response in her that threatened the discipline of her rigid sense of self-control.

A tear crept down her cheek. 'I never cry,' she whispered, brushing it away with the tip of a finger. 'And I don't know why I'm crying now. Except that you make me feel that I don't know what I'm doing or why.' She smiled at him, almost sadly. 'There's only ever been one man in my life – Harry. I was seventeen when we married, and because my mother is another Nellie. . . .' She blushed. 'Well, I must have been a bit of a trial to Harry at first.'

'Tell me about him.' Robert's eyes in the lamplight were as pale and as translucent as the inside of a shell. 'Make him real for me.'

She seemed to pause for a long time. 'Harry. . . ? Well, he's smaller than you, and darker than you.'

'Younger than me.' Touching his hair, Robert grinned, but she was looking away from him.

'He hasn't your way with words. He would never have spoken to me about, well, about the things you were talking about. Not with the light on.' Polly frowned and

193

bit her lip. 'He's a man of the soil. And I mean that literally. He holds a growing seedling in his hands the way you would hold a new-born baby.' Her expression clouded. 'You'd have made a wonderful father, Robert. I saw you with Martin. Was there no way you could have had a family? Before your wife took ill?'

'It never happened.' Robert spoke gruffly. 'So if Harry hadn't gone away, been *forced* to go away,' he stressed the word, 'you would have gone on being happy. Okay?'

'I suppose so.'

'And meeting me, getting to know me, would have made me just another man, a friendly one-armed man who talked your own language. A man you might have remembered in your declining years as someone you could maybe have loved.' He spoke with slow deliberation. 'Being married doesn't necessarily mean that you are immune to physical attraction.' His smile was lopsided, making him look ten years younger. 'We'd be a couple of cold fishes if neither of us responded to another's appeal. Even your Harry won't be immune to that, believe you me.'

Her immediate indignation amused him.

'Harry must be the odd one out,' Polly said with conviction. 'How he ever found the courage to propose to me I'll never know. Oh, no. You're quite wrong about Harry.' Her blue eyes were steady. 'If he ever let me down, I'd think the world had come to an end.'

'When you say let you down, you mean looked at another woman? Made love to another woman?' Robert's gaze was as steady as her own. 'Why do you use euphemisms, Polly? Are you too puritanical to say what you really mean?'

She was as angry as he had meant her to be. 'I'm not puritanical! I'm as broad-minded as the next person.'

194

She twisted the wide gold band of her wedding ring round and round on her finger. 'You distort what I'm trying to say. You don't know me, and you certainly don't know Harry. He loves me, and he wouldn't dream of being unfaithful.' She glared at him. 'There now. You've made me say it. Does that satisfy you?'

Robert stared into the fire for a while, and as she watched him, wondering what he was going to say next, Polly marvelled at the intimacy of their friendship. She moved slightly in her chair. Was that what it was, after all? The comfortable companionship of two people who could make each other laugh one minute, and flare up the next? The lines of his strong face looked almost beautiful in the firelight. He looked like a man who knew his own mind, made unhurried decisions. A man easy to know. A man of integrity. She flinched at her own thinking. Was integrity an old-fashioned word? Was she being puritanical again?

'Robert. . . ?'

'Yes, love?'

'The other day . . . in your house. When your sister-in-law came in and . . . and. . . .'

'Caught me nearly kissing you?'

She drooped her head. 'I *wanted* you to kiss me. I've been thinking ever since how it would have been if you had kissed me. So I'm not . . . I'm not the prude you take me for. I must be going crazy. But it's just that in the midst of everything that's happening, the knowing that you are my loving friend means more to me than I can ever say.' She lifted her head. 'I'm not stupid, Robert. I know that if Harry hadn't gone away, I would never have felt like this. We would probably never have even met. I wouldn't have gone after that job and I wouldn't have been trying to read my own shorthand that day in the park. Harry would have stood between me and these kind of feelings. I'd have been *safe*.'

'And now?'

'I don't know.'

Her voice was the merest whisper as he came over to her. When he knelt down beside her and kissed her slowly, the touch of his lips was like an electric shock going through her. Her arms went round him and she held him close, straining him to her.

'I think I'm falling in love with you,' she sighed. 'It's wrong and I know it's wrong, but I can't help it. Help me, Robert. Please help me. . . .'

It was her softly breathed plea that unnerved him. He was aching with desire for her. The long years of celibacy when he had cared for and treasured his wife through her long illness had made him strong in the way nature never meant a man to be. How often had he bent over his wife's bed to kiss her goodnight with a hunger inside him like the grind of an actual physical pain? Jean, his wife, had trusted him, just as Polly was trusting him now. He closed his eyes, sensing the rising passion in her.

Gently he put her from him. Deliberately he stood up, walked over to the peg behind the door and took down his coat. Trembling, he wound the long woollen scarf round his neck and picked up his hat from the dresser.

From her chair she watched him, her blue eyes dazed with love, wide with disbelief. Going over to him, walking with that animal grace he had noticed the first time he met her, she put her hands on his shoulders, looking up into his face.

'You're the puritanical one now, aren't you, Robert?'

Groaning, he bent his head, burying it in the softness of her neck. 'Don't tease, Polly.'

Even through the thickness of his overcoat she felt the hardness of him as he drew her close. When he spoke his voice was so low she had to strain to catch what he was saying.

'More than anything in the world . . . more than you know, I want to make love to you. But you asked me to help you, little love. And because you're so dear to me that's what I'm doing.'

'I asked you to *help* me?'

She was so honestly bewildered he lifted his head and held her from him, looking deep into her eyes.

'I know you, Polly. I know you through and through. If we were to make love you would feel committed to me.' Tenderly he traced the outline of her generous mouth. 'You're not the sort of woman who could do that and not be committed.' He smiled. 'Maybe there are some women who could behave like men, taking passion as they found it, even glorying in it, sure their marriage wouldn't be hurt in any way.' He shook her gently. 'Maybe the day will come when women consider themselves to be the equal of men in that field, but not yet. And not you. Your man will come back to you, Polly my love. He'll come back to you and your children, and your life will go on. And I don't want that life cluttered with guilt, or even thoughts of me.' He kissed the tip of her nose. 'I'm an old man, Polly. Old enough to be your father if I'd started young. And I won't take advantage of your loneliness, because that's what it is. Believe me, sweetheart.'

'So you're saying goodbye?' She looked pensive for a moment. 'Are you saying you don't want to see me again?'

Stepping back from her, he put on his trilby, pulling the wavy brim down over his forehead. 'I'll be around.

Isn't that what Robert Young said in his last picture?' He opened the door, letting in a blast of freezing air. 'Soon Christmas will be here. I'll see you before then.' Pulling up his collar, he stepped outside. 'But if there's no bus down in the village, I'll be back.' The old grin was there, teasing and making him look ten years younger. 'Then the fine speeches I've been making will be just words. That's all they were, Polly. Just words. . . .'

The snow was still blowing furiously as he made his perilous way down the steep slope, but the sky had lightened imperceptibly, and already he had made up his mind to walk the five miles back to the town if necessary. And if that made him a craven coward, then so be it. If running away from love made him less than a man, then he accepted that also. But his thoughts of Harry Pilgrim, the man he had never met, were less than charitable. He reminded himself that he had never known the desolation of being without work; that in similar circumstances he might have gambled everything on making a fresh start elsewhere.

'But I'd come back home quickly, Harry Pilgrim,' he muttered. 'A man can only be a saint for a limited period.'

He moved into the shelter of the little wood where the snow lay less thickly, feeling it seep through the thin soles of his town shoes. The total silence was eerie, the beauty of the white landscape breathtaking in its splendour. But in Robert's preoccupation with his thoughts and the effort of planting one sodden foot in front of the other, it left him untouched. Turning back would have been easy. Doing the right thing in walking away made every step a conscious, almost painful, effort.

'You'd be proud of me, Nellie,' he whispered,

trudging past Bella's cottage with head lowered, almost blinded now by the snow sweeping down from the fells.

Polly sat by the fire, feeling spent physically and morally. There were a thousand things she had to do, including writing a letter to Harry, but she was too wrapped up in a bewildering state of self-questioning even to make the effort of taking the notepad from the dresser drawer and the bottle of ink from the top shelf.

It was the first time she had been entirely alone at night in the cottage since her marriage, and every slight noise seemed magnified in the silence. The clink of a cinder in the hearth made her start with fear, and when for no apparent reason the dog barked wildly, she stood up, hands folded over her breasts in an age-old gesture of comfort, staring wide-eyed at the heavily bolted door.

When she forced herself to sit down again, she found to her dismay that she was trembling, then admitted to herself that she hadn't stopped trembling since Robert Dennis had kissed her, arousing her in a way she wouldn't have dreamed possible.

All her life she had lived by rules. Unspoken rules, but as rigid as if they had been written on her very soul.

'Thou shalt not commit adultery. . . .'

How often as a child had she sat in the hard-backed pew of her mother's Methodist chapel, listening to the preacher, often an unqualified layman, shouting about the evils of the flesh and the temptations of the devil. The fires of hell lay in wait for those who trod the path of unrighteousness. Even to covet another man led to eternal damnation.

'Get thee behind me Satan!'

She remembered as if it were yesterday a little man,

a weaver from the nearby cotton mill, pounding the air with his fists as he ranted on about the weakness of the flesh. Preaching to the converted, she had thought, glancing round at the congregation, the women in their go-to-chapel hats, and the men in their stiffly starched collars. Lancashire faces, often seamed with care from a lifetime of hard work and bringing up their families on a pittance.

Polly had attended chapel every Sunday morning and evening, going to Sunday School in the afternoon to teach, from the age of fourteen, young children in the big vestry, sending them home with crayoned drawings of Jesus riding on a donkey or raising Lazarus from the dead.

She had thought she knew who she was, sure in her belief, smugly confident that the evils of the flesh were words, just words, as Robert had said.

And yet . . . and yet if he had stayed, she would have taken him by the hand and led him up the steep, winding, wooden stairs. She would have closed her eyes as he helped her to undress; she would have lain in the bed she had shared with her husband and gloried in what he was doing to her, what she would be doing to him.

As though Harry and all the years of their own loving had never been.

Long before ten o'clock, Polly gave up trying to do anything but just exist. She was so tired it was an effort to light a candle, so she picked up the lamp from the table, and started upstairs.

The ancient floorboards creaked as she walked over to the double bed. Her shadow moved and swayed on the whitewashed wall as she undressed. Her reflection in the swing mirror on her dressing-table was of a pale-faced young woman, with huge sad eyes and tousled golden hair, and the cold was so penetrating she could see her nipples stand out hard as she slipped her long flannel nightdress over her head.

In that instant she imagined Robert's head lying there, her hands stroking his thick hair as his mouth caressed her nakedness. She remembered the way his pale grey eyes had looked in the firelight, and the resolution in them as he'd put her gently away from him. He had felt all she had felt, and yet he had left her.

'I love you,' his eyes had said, and yet he had walked away.

She climbed into bed, turning the lamp out and sinking down deep into the billowing feather mattress. Outside the wind seemed to have dropped, leaving in its wake a stillness as deep as death itself. Four heavy woollen blankets gave weight, but as yet not enough warmth to prevent Polly from shivering.

How warm she would have been held close to Robert. How safe and secure she would have felt with their bodies entwined. Even the promise of a hell to come would have held no terrors for her.

I love him, she thought, and how can that be when I haven't stopped loving Harry? Turning over on to her back, willing a sleep that would not come, she opened her eyes.

And saw the light on the ceiling. As marked and definite, as wavering as if a lamp had been held in a trembling hand, the shape shifting and flowing, reminding her in its fluid-like form of an amoeba seen through the lense of a microscope in a long ago school biology lesson.

'Oh, God!' The two words were torn from her as she sat up in bed. She could feel the hairs standing up on

201

the back of her head. Terror pricked at her armpits, and a cold rivulet of sweat trickled down her spine.

Shaking with fear, Polly groped on the bedside table for the matches, fumbled to get one out of its box and dropped it; scrabbled feverishly for another and somehow managed to light the lamp.

Now the only light on the ceiling was the one from her own lamp, but she knew the other was still there. And if the room had been cold before, now it was like a tomb. She could smell the decaying scent of death. She could see the stains on the bare, wooden floorboards where once a man's life blood had seeped away.

All sense of reasoning seemed to have left her. If rational explanation existed for the light, Polly was beyond seeking it. Her heart pounded. She could feel it beating in every pulse in her body.

Tottering on legs turned to jelly, she crossed the landing into Martin's room. His bed had a young boy's smell about it, and beneath his pillow a schoolboy's annual protruded with its hard-back cover showing a boy in cricket flannels, holding aloft a bat in triumph. A brown and bruised apple core lay rotting gently on his bedside table, and a tattered copy of *The Hotspur* was open at a page showing Mr Smugg the Housemaster of Red Circle School wielding his cane.

Desperately Polly tried to conjure up a mental picture of her son running wild in the summer fields, firing imaginary bullets at anything that moved. The lamplight – the reassuring *normal* lamplight – picked out points of light on his collection of steel engravings on the walls.

Drawing her knees up to her chest, Polly tucked her feet beneath the hem of her nightdress. She lay there, waiting for a dawn that seemed an endless time in coming.

The bus wasn't in its usual place by the church when Polly got to the village at her usual time, but there were two small black saloon cars abandoned at the side of the main road, with sheets of newspaper laid over their windscreens.

To make any kind of sense, Polly knew she should collect a few things from the one shop selling everything from flour to paraffin and go home. But she wasn't making sense. Not yet.

Since five o'clock that morning she had crouched shivering with her red coat over her nightdress by the empty firegrate, telling herself it wasn't worth lighting a fire when she had to go to work in two hours' time. Her whole body was numb with shock. The emotion she had felt had drained away, leaving her sick with a creeping sense of dread. For at least an hour, she stared down at her feet in their felt slippers, a last year's Christmas present from Harry, trying to summon up enough courage to go upstairs to her room and get dressed.

Morning was a long time in coming, and when it did the sombre light was grey and heavy, as though the leaden sky outside was pressing down on the steep sloping roof of the cottage. The total silence was a cloud, folding her in, and in his basket the dog slept, twitching his ears now and again, making her start in terror and glance over her shoulder towards the door.

If she'd lived in the town the street lamps would have been lit. Even inside the houses, gas jets would be sighing in their mantles. But the oil lamp shed only a pool of light, and beyond it darkness lurked, vague with shadows, blotched with mysterious shapes.

It was no good trying to convince herself that the light on the ceiling of her room had been conjured up by her inflamed imaginings. Polly had never quite believed in the hell promised her by the Methodist lay preachers of her childhood. Hell was here, she believed, and not always of your own making. And wickedness was not enough to consign you to the fiery flames. Even wickedness came in differing shapes and sizes.

No. The light was a warning. A sure warning that something terrible was going to happen. Maybe something so awful she would die with the pain of it. Just as the hurt of what had happened in the upstairs room all those long years ago lingered still, refusing to go away.

Down in the village Polly stood irresolute, looking back up the hill, her footsteps a pattern of stepping-stones behind her. The whole landscape merged into a vista of dazzling white. Beautiful and awe-inspiring, as Polly knew her mother would have said. As long as you could watch it through a window, with a cup of tea in your hand

She hesitated, knowing she could go to Bella's cottage, and knowing equally that Bella would never let her in. Bella was waiting for Jack to come home. She had bolted herself inside till the day he came walking light-footed up the path, with his cap pulled low over his forehead, and his green eyes glittering.

He could be in there even now . . . Polly shivered and started to walk. It was four miles at least to the outer perimeter of the town, where the trams wheezed to a halt and after a while clanged their way back down the Whalley Road into the town. If the trams were running she would get to work, late of course, but she knew she had to try to get there. Even if she walked the whole way she still had to try.

The houses she passed seemed shrouded in silent meditation. Two boys pulled a milk churn along on a home-made sledge, and once a man turned out of a gate, as determined as Polly to get to work, trousers tucked into gumboots and a football scarf wound round his neck.

Polly concentrated on keeping her balance, but part of her mind was wandering free. Gatty would have to come home. Martin would have to do the same, and she would write to Harry and, in spite of all her good resolutions, *plead* with him to return.

Polly tried to 'see' Harry's face as she plodded along the road, keeping to the middle where the snow lay less thickly. Somehow they would have to try to be the way they were before he went away. Winter would end and spring would come. The lanes would be enclosed with hawthorn blossom. The air would be filled with its sweet almond smell. By the door of the cottage the rose bush would hang heavy with perfect blooms, dark red at the heart of each one, and down in the meadow by the stream, shiny celandines would twinkle like stars in the tall grass.

Robert Dennis would be – just as he had said – a nice man she used to know. A man she could have loved if her life with Harry hadn't been set on its preordained path. She would think of him sometimes, without guilt or remorse. He would slip in and out of her dreams until one day he vanished. And she forgot him.

'Robert . . . oh, Robert.' Polly whispered his name over and over, as if already he had gone from her. For ever.

At last she rounded the bend of a short steep hill and saw, with an overwhelming sense of relief, a tram with the conductor standing on its platform drinking tea from a billycan.

'Want a bit of me bacon butty?' he called out. 'Warms the cockles a bacon butty does.' His red face was split into a cheeky grin. 'You look like a proper robin redbreast in that coat, love. Stand on a corner and open your mouth and I reckon folks would post a letter in it!' He struck the bell with a flourish, closing one eye in a wink. 'Don't mind me, blondie. It's just the cold what's frozen me assets this morning, that's all.'

Polly made her way over the ribbed floor of the car to a vacant seat by the window, and as the tram clattered its way down the long straight road into town, she saw how the snow was already turning into slush, grey and dirty-looking from the traffic, and watched the people hurrying along the pavements to work.

'There'll be more than me late this morning,' Polly said to herself, willing the tram to go faster. As she got off, she smiled at the conductor, who responded by rolling his eyes up in mock ecstasy.

She covered the distance to the mill in less than fifteen minutes, turned into the yard and saw a small group of machinists staring up at a notice pinned to the office door.

Pushing her way forward, Polly read it in total disbelief.

'It is with regret that we have to announce the closing of this factory. Unemployment and insurance cards can be collected from the office at 10 a.m. Signed E. Goldberg.'

'I don't believe it!' Polly turned to a woman with a scarf tied over a grey felt hat. 'Mr Goldberg wouldn't do a thing like that!' She started to walk away from them, towards the factory door down the sloping yard. 'He'd tell us himself.'

The grey hat nodded. 'He *did* tell us, chuck. At eight o'clock this morning, clocking-on time. Right upset he were an' all. Explained it all nicely, not that I understood a word of it. Something about us being laid off permanent on account of him going bankrupt.' She glanced round at the other workers. 'We offered to stop on and finish what was on the tables, but we're not allowed to.' She pointed a hand in a woollen mitten towards the main building. 'All that good stuff in there, and going to waste as far as I can see. Bales of stuff and half-finished coats, and us wanting to get on with it, and not allowed.'

'The union,' another woman suggested. 'I keep on saying we should appeal. What's the good of paying your dues when this happens? I allus said they were out for themselves, spouting on about their members, then doing bugger all when it comes to it.'

'We're entitled,' a sharp-nosed little girl piped up, 'entitled to our rights. Who does he think we are? Just bloody nowts to be pushed around?' She spat on the ground. 'He won't be missing out, not old bloody Goldberg. Like all the rest. Out for what he can get and stuff anybody else.'

'That's not fair!' Polly spoke in a clear unswerving tone. 'There couldn't have been a fairer boss than Mr Goldberg. You saw him the other week when he tried to explain things to us. He was nearly crying.'

'Oh, aye. He was nearly crying all right. An' why? Only because his own nest wasn't being feathered the way he'd expected. I know his sort.' She jerked her head towards the empty office. 'Where is he now? Why isn't he in there, soft-soaping us?'

'Oh, shut up, Agnes!' The woman in the grey hat raised her voice. 'If you'd been on time – which you never was – you'd have heard what he had to say. Just because you can't get up of a morning. Polly's right. Mr Goldberg's a gentleman, an' it's not his fault this has happened.' Her face wrenched itself out of shape as she

207

tried to remember. 'He said that as he can't get any more stuff on tick, an' the bank won't lend him any more money, then he can't pay our wages.' Her voice rose in triumph. 'An' go on, Agnes Butterfield! Crack on you'd work for nowt! My God, that'd be the day!'

'Then where is he?' Agnes jabbed a finger at her opponent. 'Why do we have to wait till ten o'clock for us cards? Is he too much of a gentleman to hand them over himself? Frightened of muckying 'is 'ands, is he, or summat?'

'There has to be some explanation.' Polly looked round and saw Mr Goldberg's secretary coming up behind them, the neat tidy girl who had got the job she had applied for, because this efficient-looking girl had been able to type faster and understand her own shorthand. Polly looked at her and thought she'd been crying.

'I heard what you said.' The young secretary was very dignified in her navy-blue coat with brass buttons down the front, and her matching hat with its wavy brim pulled down over her pale face. A bunch of keys dangled from a gloved hand. 'And yes, there is an explanation.' She seemed to hesitate, then went on as if suddenly making up her mind. 'I may be doing wrong in telling you this.' She was very correct, very precise. 'Mr Goldberg got a telegram last night.' Her eyes, behind round tortoiseshell spectacles, filled with tears. 'His daughter over in Germany has been killed.'

'Killed?' Blank faces were turned towards her. 'Killed?'

The girl's small mouth trembled. 'There was some sort of a student protest. The wire didn't say much, but Miriam, Mr Goldberg's daughter, took part in it. Against the new – the new order out there. And in the fighting, she was killed.'

'He's gone,' she went on. 'He came into the factory this morning to tell you about the closure, when he could have gone last night.' Her pointed chin lifted. 'That's the kind of man your boss is.' Her composure wavered. 'And even if I'm lucky enough to find another job, I'll never get another boss to work for like Mr Goldberg. If you'll come with me you can have your cards. . . .'

'She couldn't have been more than eighteen, Polly.' The little woman in the grey, scarf-trimmed hat walked by Polly's side out of the yard and into the short street. 'What was she doing over there when her father was here? Families should stick together.' She tightened the knot beneath her chin. 'My daughter lives next door, and I've a son in the next street. That way I can keep both me eyes on them.'

'Some children are more rebellious than others, Mrs. . . ?' Polly tried to remember the woman's name.

'Pearl,' came the unexpected reply. 'All me mother's family are jewels. I've got a sister Emerald, and another called Ruby. Pity me married name's Higgins. It takes the sparkle out of it a bit.'

'Pearl,' Polly didn't smile, 'I think Mr Goldberg may have gone into danger, going over to Germany. They say it's a new regime out there. And Jews aren't all that popular.'

'Why ever not?' Pearl almost lost her footing on the snow-covered pavement and clutched at Polly's arm. 'Mind if we link, Polly? That's all I need, to break me leg as well as losing me job. Like you, I couldn't see much wrong with Mr Goldberg.'

'There wasn't anything wrong with him.' Polly spoke quickly. 'It's politics, Pearl.'

'Never bother with 'em.' Pearl glanced sideways at

Polly. 'I heard tell you've got a family. Who minds them for you?'

'Gatty is fifteen, and Martin is eleven.' Polly's mind was in a turmoil. 'I can't bear even to think how Mr Goldberg must be feeling. Coming on top of what's happened at the factory, I reckon his heart must be breaking.' She stopped suddenly as Pearl withdrew her arm. 'You turn down this street, then?'

'Aye. This is where I live.' The brown eyes were shrewd. 'Well, at least we know where our daughters are. There's mine now, coming back from the Co-op. She's been buying in for me since I've been working. She's a good lass.'

'And so is mine.' A twisted smile spread over Polly's face. 'I'm going to see her now. She works in a shoe shop in King Edward Street. And she's a good lass, too.'

They parted with smiles, each of them knowing it was hardly likely they would ever meet again. Pearl hurrying as quickly as she dared to take one of the heavy baskets from her daughter, and Polly trying not to think about Miriam Goldberg's dead face as she walked into the town to call in on Gatty.

— Ten —

At the side of the road, the snow was piled in mounds
of dirty grey. It was so cold that Polly's feet were no
longer feet but merely inanimate objects propelling her
along. She had forgotten to eat breakfast and hunger
pains gnawed at her stomach. Her heart ached for Mr
Goldberg in his grief, and she wondered if she would
ever see him again.

And yet, in some strange indefinable way, for all the
wrong reasons, she suddenly felt that she was in control
of her own destiny once again. Miriam Goldberg was
dead, and death was final, but Gatty was alive. Martin
was alive, and Harry was alive, and she, Polly Pilgrim,
was going to grab the future by the neck and *make* better
things happen. Robert Dennis had showed her that what
she already had was good. And by heck, she was going
to hang on to it and push the fear, the doubts and the
terror behind her.

The north of England wasn't the best place to be in
1933. The town was filled with bleak faces. It had the
reek of despair, but it was where she had been born; it
was her town, and these were her people. They might
look defeated, but Polly knew that deep in the heart of

every one of them hope lived. She would be cheating on her heritage if she gave in, and the first thing she was going to do was tell Gatty to come home. Where she belonged. Where they *all* belonged.

That night she would write to Harry. It would be a far different kind of letter than any she had written before. No hiding the truth, no letting him believe she was a whole person without him. She wasn't. She might be the stronger in many ways, but he was her man. She loved him, and she was going to ask him to come home.

'Thank you, Robert,' she whispered. 'You could have been the love of my life, but you came too late. You accepted that, and now I have to do the same.' She walked on, hurrying as fast as she could over the slippery pavement.

The shoe shop on the town's main street was empty, the rows of chairs unoccupied, the shoe boxes layered on their shelves, a shoe-horn discarded on the fawn haircord carpet.

'Can I help you?' Winnie Parker came from the back, sharp-featured, red hair tortured into a curly fringe over her wide forehead. When she saw who it was, her eyes dilated and something like fear clouded her expression. 'Oh! Mrs Pilgrim!' She glanced over her shoulder quickly, then lowered her voice. 'Your Gatty's not here.'

Polly smiled. 'You mean she's gone out for a minute?' She sat down on one of the little chairs. 'That's okay. I'll wait. You're not very busy, are you? I suppose it's the weather.'

Winnie seemed to be having difficulty finding her voice. Hoarse at the best of times, it now came out as a croak.

'Gatty was a bit off this morning, so she's stopped in bed. Me mam's there, so she's all right.' It was transpar-

212

ently obvious she was hiding something. 'Honest, Mrs Pilgrim. She's not really ill. Like I said, just a bit off.'

Polly was up on her feet in an instant. 'Tell me the number of your house! I know the street, so just tell me the number.' She was already backing towards the door, but Winnie followed, quivering, loyal, still protesting.

'She's not ill, Mrs Pilgrim!' Then she came right out on to the pavement, actually wringing her hands. 'There's no need for you to go to our house. She'll be all right by now . . . Mrs Pilgrim!'

But Polly was on her way. She skirted the market-place, and turned left past Yates Wine Lodge, up past the austere building of the schools' clinic, crossed over the road by St John's Church, and into the row of shops.

A woman who knew her mother called out from across the street, but Polly was hearing and saying nothing. Winnie's strange behaviour had worried her, and her one thought was to get to her child. She didn't even notice that the house at the top end of the narrow short street was so dirty that it stood out, the only one with unmopped flagstones. When she knocked at the door she stood back for a moment, glancing up at the filthy window. She tried the door and, finding it on the latch, walked straight in.

'Mrs Parker? It's only me. Gatty's mother. Can I come in?'

In the back room, crouched over the fire, black hair hanging in greasy strands, face more translucent than pale, was Gatty.

'Mam!' Gatty levered herself out of the chair like an old woman. 'Where have *you* come from? What are you doing here?'

It was all too much. The unbelievable sight of Polly

213

coming through the door in the familiar red coat was more than Gatty, in her overwrought state, could take.

'Oh Mam! Mam!' In a second she was in her mother's arms, held tight, wailing her distress, spilling out the agony of the past weeks, clinging and weeping, sobbing as though her heart would break.

'Now then.' Firmly Polly put Gatty from her. 'Sit down in that chair and tell me. Tell me slowly what's wrong.' Pretending a calm she was far from feeling, Polly unfastened the buttons of her coat. 'Where's Mrs Parker?'

'Out at the shops.' Gatty's dark eyes never left her mother's face. 'Oh, Mam! You don't know. You just don't know.'

The room smelled of yesterday's fish and chips, and the overriding stench of neglect. There was a newspaper on the table where a cloth should be, and a jug of milk without its cover of beaded net on the dresser. The blind at the window over the slop-stone was torn and yellowed, and the wooden draining-board looked as if it hadn't been scrubbed in years.

All this Polly saw with one corner of her mind, but none of it mattered. What mattered was breaking down the barrier between herself and Gatty.

'No. I don't know,' she said slowly. 'I don't know what's bothering you, but I'm here, waiting for you to tell me.' She took a deep breath. 'I love you very much, Gatty. Whatever it is, you can tell me.' She held out her hands, but forced herself to stay where she was. 'If you've murdered somebody, then I'll go and help you dig a hole. If you've stolen money from the shop, then I'll steal myself to put it back.' She leaned forward. 'Come on, love. If you can't tell your mam, then who can you tell?'

Tears ran down Gatty's small face. Convulsed by sobs, choking on the words, she told her terrible secret. Incoherent and jumbled, the story came out. 'An' if I'm going to have a baby, then I want to die!' she cried. 'But he *made* me, Mam. I didn't know what he was doing. I swear I didn't even know what he was doing!'

'Oh, Gatty, Gatty.' Polly came to kneel by her daughter's chair. Her heart was so full she felt her hand tremble as she raised it to lift the black hair from Gatty's swollen face. 'You are saying you went away without telling me this? You couldn't trust me enough to tell me?' She turned Gatty's face round to look into her eyes. 'What did you think I would do? Throw you out into the snow?'

For a while they rocked together, then getting to her feet Polly stood with her head bowed, trying to think clearly. Without any conscious motivation, her mind went back again to Robert.

'Why do you use euphemisms, Polly?' he'd said. 'Are you so puritanical that you daren't formulate the truth?'

So the questions she asked Gatty were direct, and without what her mother would have called proper decency.

'Had you ever been with a boy before?' she asked, and nodded at Gatty's swift and shocked denial. 'Were you torn? When you stood up did. . . ?' Her voice never wavered, and when it was finished she pulled Gatty up into her arms.

'I think you're worrying yourself for nothing,' she said softly. 'But we can't be sure. It won't be the first time a girl's got pregnant when she's never done it before.' She gave Gatty a little shake. 'Your period's only just due, and being late isn't unusual for you, so go upstairs and get your things. We're going home.' Her brow

215

furrowed at a sudden thought. 'You weren't *really* sick this morning? Not vomiting, or anything?'

'I just didn't want to get up.' Gatty started to cry again. 'It's been so awful, Mam.' Her face crumpled. 'I think it was partly him being who he was.'

Again Polly's arms went out to her, and over Gatty's head her expression was murderous. 'Rotting in hell wouldn't be bad enough for the bastard!' she said through clenched teeth, and in spite of her distress Gatty's head jerked up.

'Mam! You swore!'

'Upstairs!' Polly turned Gatty round and gave her bottom a slap. 'That's nothing, love. Wait till I get going properly. I know even worse words than that, and every one of them applies. Jack Thomson got his come-uppance, and folks can stick up for him as much as they like but I don't think he needs pitying. He's bad, through and through, and if I got my hands on him I'd kill him slowly, and watch him die. Gladly!' she ended fiercely.

While Gatty was upstairs, she found a piece of paper in her handbag and wrote a brief note to Winnie's mother. Propping it up on the mantelpiece, she shook her head at the film of dust on the chipped ornaments. Something inside her that was all her mother itched to take them down and give them a good wash.

Her mind was clear and cool. One part of her was convinced that Gatty's fear was more a product of shock than anything else. But the other part told her that fear was sometimes rooted in reality, and if that were true, God help them all.

Jack Thomson's baby. . . . Her mind crawled with the implications. Gatty, fifteen years old, bearing the child of a man like that. . . .

Sitting down, listening to Gatty's footsteps above her, Polly's face was a mask of tight control, but inside she was dying a little. Gatty, her little girl. Missing her scholarship and not caring. Treating her mother's love of books with lofty disdain. Scorning discipline, secretive, stubborn, going her own way, and shouting defiance when questioned about her comings and goings, as if determined to be different, determined to live a life of her own.

Gatty as a tiny child. Like quicksilver in all her movements, active from morning till night. Needing little sleep. Getting up on her own to run out of the cottage in the early mornings, nightdress trailing in the long grass. Climbing trees when her brother sat beneath them reading. Snatching his book away, and screaming at him, then appearing suddenly at the cottage door, a bunch of wild flowers in her hands. Pleased as Punch when Polly put them in jam jars on the window sill, and dashing out for more. Dandelions, bread and butter, harebells, buttercups.

'Hold your chin up, Mammy. Let me see if you like butter.'

And now. . . .

Polly turned round as Gatty came down the stairs wearing her coat and carrying the brown cardboard case.

'Right,' she said. 'Let's go home.'

They caught a tram out to the terminus, but the rest of the way they had to walk. Gatty looked frail and ill, but Polly hardened her heart.

'Let's see how quickly we can walk,' she said. 'Come on, love. Don't look at me like that! What's five miles when you say it quick? See how deep the snow is by the

217

hedges where it's drifted.' She smiled without glancing at Gatty. 'Come on. One two, one two! Remember how your dad used to urge you and Martin on when we went for walks? How he'd make you swing your arms like soldiers? And how mad at him you used to get?' Polly knew what she was doing. To her eternal shame she knew full well what she was doing. 'Walk, Gatty!' Her mind was screaming silently. 'Walk till you drop, then get up and walk again.' On and on. Horrified at her motivation, but insisting just the same.

Leaving the houses behind, they found the going harder down country lanes where no cars had been. Taking the case from Gatty without checking her stride, Polly stopped suddenly when Gatty stopped, to pull the woebegone little figure into her arms.

'It's going to be all right, love. Look at me! I promise. I won't let anything bad happen. It'll be all right. You'll see.'

Feeling shaken, Polly took Gatty's arm and urged her on. Hot baths, gin, something called Penny Royal, snippets of conversations overheard from women in Mrs Bebson's post office, whispering together over by the herbalist corner. No! The hot bath, maybe. That could do no harm. But medication, *suspect* medication, that wasn't for her daughter. Enough harm had been done.

Polly was so engrossed in her thoughts that they passed Bella's cottage without a glance. The whale-shaped mass of Pendle Hill was majestic in its stark whiteness, but what was it after all but just a hill? Pendle would be there when they were gone, when all this trouble was no more than a few pinpricks in the continuing pattern of life.

'Almost there, love. Nearly home.'

In less than half an hour Polly had lit the fire, using

two fire-lighters piled on sticks, and built a pyramid of coal until the flames roared up the chimney-back. The kettle had boiled and Gatty had drunk a pot of tea down thirstily, sitting in her father's chair, watching Polly work. Silently watching and saying nothing.

The zinc bath was brought in from its nail on the wall, filled to a depth of six inches then topped up from the kettle and an enormous pan, pushed almost into the heart of the fire in Polly's determination. At last she was satisfied that the bath was ready, too hot for comfort but she knew what she was doing. 'Oh, dear God,' she prayed. 'Let it work.'

As though Gatty was a child again, Polly helped her to undress, and the sight of the tiny pink-tipped breasts made her want to weep. But there wasn't time for weeping, or sentimentality. With sleeves rolled up and face flushed from the heat of the fire, Polly helped Gatty into the bath. More hot water ladled in. A towel to wipe the sweat from Gatty's brow.

'Sit there, darling. Be good. Just for once, don't argue. Just sit.'

When Gatty whimpered twenty minutes later and said she could stand it no longer, Polly helped her out, lowered a long flannel nightdress over her head and followed her upstairs.

Blankets from Martin's bed were carried through and piled on top of Gatty's flower-sprigged quilt. Flushed and sleepy, Gatty lay down, her hair all rumpled and her dark eyes glazed with fatigue.

'I'm so tired, Mam,' she whispered, sighing with the relief of being in her own bed again. 'Winnie kicked in her sleep.' The dark eyes opened with an effort. 'She doesn't have a nightdress, Mam. She just sleeps in her knickers and vest.'

'But she's your own true friend,' Polly said. 'You'd told Winnie, hadn't you?'

Polly knew by Gatty's face that she had, and a small hurt pierced her heart as she went back downstairs.

It was dark outside before Gatty woke up. She had slept for five hours, worn out with the terror of the last few weeks, and the long, endless nights lying beside Winnie, with blanket fluff like grey dandelion clocks on the bare floor beneath the narrow bed.

For a while she lay still, wondering where she was. The fear hadn't gone away, but she was warm, she was safe. She was a little girl again, and her mother was downstairs listening to the wireless. She could hear the sound of a dance band on the wireless. Henry Hall maybe, playing his signature tune, 'Here's to the Next Time'. Yes, that was it. And the bed was so warm. She was warmer than she'd been for ages. The sheet and the blankets smelled clean, of Acdo and the bleach her mother cheated with at times. Not fusty and sour like Winnie's sheets. Winnie, her good true friend. Gatty snuggled her face into the pillow. There was a faint niggling, dragging pain in the small of her back, but she was so tired, so very, very tired. In another minute she was fast asleep again.

When she stumbled down the stairs another two hours later, Polly knew at once that the nightmare was over.

'Oh, Mam. . . .' Gatty came straight into Polly's arms, and for a minute or so they cried together.

'Thank you, God. If there wasn't anything really to thank you for, thank you just the same.' Polly held Gatty away from her, and spoke quietly and slowly, measuring every word.

'You were never what you imagined you were, love.' There, she was doing it again. 'You were never *pregnant*, love. You have to believe me. But the long walk through the snow and the hot bath just gave nature a bit of a nudge. It would have come anyway, but maybe not yet, with all that worry and guilt. And now we have to forget it. It's our secret for ever. Yours and mine, and Winnie's. We will never mention it any more. It was just one of the bad times that everyone has, but this one has a happy ending. You've to wipe it clean out of your mind. One day you'll meet a boy you love, and you'll marry him, and it won't be like that. It'll be right and good, because you love him. And next time you're worried, you tell *me*. Okay?'

Gatty stiffened, her eyes wide. 'Next time? Oh, Mam! I'll never ever be so silly. You can't think. . . ?'

'I didn't mean that, sweetheart. Nobody could be that stupid!'

They laughed together, holding each other and rocking, till suddenly Polly lifted her head and sniffed. 'Fancy shepherd's pie, love? Not much meat, but plenty of crisp potato topping? Carrots and turnips, and Mrs Pilgrim's special rice pudding to follow?'

'Oh, Mam.' Gatty's eyes filled with weak tears again. 'You're so good. I'll never grow to be as good as you.'

Polly's shout of a laugh startled them both. 'Don't put me on a pedestal, love. I'm only human.' For a moment she saw Robert Dennis's face as he'd held her still for his kiss. 'More human than you know.'

There was a calm, lilting happiness to the rest of the evening. Shut away from the world in the isolated cottage, mother and daughter reached for each other, found the response they both needed, and sat together round the fire, Polly with her knitting and Gatty sitting quietly, letting the fear go gently.

When she went yawning to bed, Polly began a long letter to Harry. She told him about losing her job, about Mr Goldberg's Miriam lying on a mortuary slab in far off Berlin. About Bella and the baby bolted in their cottage, and how everyone believed that Jack Thomson was dead. It wasn't easy to write his name, but she did it. Some day she might tell Harry, but not, certainly not for a long time. Maybe not for ever.

'I miss you,' she wrote. 'I'm lonely without you, and next week it's Christmas.' Her pen ran dry and she dipped it into the bottle of blue-black ink. 'You can't be working at Christmas,' she went on, 'and with Christmas Day falling on a Monday that means you can come home. Even just for the weekend.'

She took out her bank book, looked at the credit balance and sighed. There were four pound notes in the biscuit barrel on the dresser, and making up her mind quickly she took two of them out and put them in the envelope with the letter. The time for saving pride was gone. If Harry didn't need them then he could give them back to her. But she wasn't going to miss seeing him because he was short of money. They had to talk. For too long now she'd been in a dark tunnel, but somehow, now, there was a glimmer of light at the end of it. And she was reaching out to that light with everything she had.

That night she slept in her own bed, without once glancing up at the ceiling. Things were going to turn out all right. It wasn't going to be easy. Gatty wasn't going to turn into a plaster saint overnight, and Harry wasn't going to be easy to live with if he came home without having found what he'd gone looking for.

But the future was theirs; they were a family, a close-knit loving family, just as Robert had known them to be.

And they were going to be happy, maybe in a way they'd never been before.

In the morning, when she went out to the earth closet, the snow which had fallen so silently through the night was piled in drifts like white sand dunes stretching away as far as the eye could see. The pile of logs by the back door was frozen hard and covered in snow, and when she managed to prise some loose and took them inside, they thawed in the heat from the fire-lighter, forming grey puddles on the raised stone hearth.

Gatty was still sleeping, and Polly decided to leave her alone. There was no way Gatty could walk the miles to the tram that day, even if they were still running. There was food enough for a few days. Living in the country had taught Polly always to have a stock of the basics, but there was milk to fetch, and there was Harry's letter to post in the box down in the village. If he didn't get it tomorrow, it could be too late for him to make his arrangements to come home for Christmas.

Christmas . . . Polly thought about Christmas as she tidied the room and drew the porridge in its double burner pan away from the fire. She took the tea caddy down from the mantelpiece, and stood with it in her hands, staring out of the window and dreaming. The caddy had once been her grandmother's, and there was a picture of an old lady in a white shawl on the front, gloating at the cup of steaming Mazawattee tea in her hand. Polly stroked the tin and put it back. If the tap froze she would have to shovel clean snow into the big iron pan to make the breakfast cocoa and porridge, the way they'd had to do two winters ago, and she would have to take her iron-tipped clogs from the cupboard and wear a pair of Harry's socks over her stockings.

Without Harry there'd be no Christmas tree carried up the hill on his back from the grounds of one of the big houses, no walking down to the Christmas Eve service in the church, with Harry trying not to look supercilious as they recited the Lord's Prayer, and joined in the singing of 'Away in a Manger' and 'While Shepherds Watched their Flocks by Night'.

Polly's mind drifted back, remembering the orange and shiny penny in the toes of the children's socks, Martin's long-coveted *Hotspur* annual, and one year, when Gatty was twelve, a string of red beads which she wore uncomfortably to bed, refusing to take them off. She also recalled Harry's face when the minister one year had exhorted his congregation to be saved by standing up for Jesus, thereby making sure they went straight to heaven, and Harry refusing to sign the pledge, a sacred binding oath against drinking, swearing and gambling, and Martin crying and telling his dad that by his refusal he was asking for eternal damnation where he would burn up in the terrible Lake of Fire. Afterwards they had linked hands round the Christmas tree in the Sunday School hall, singing 'Auld Lang Syne', then walking home up the snow-covered hill, still singing.

'Oh, Mam! I wish every day could be Christmas,' Martin had said fervently, and in a moment of unusual sentimentality Polly had said it could be, if they made it so in their hearts.

Out here, in the country, everything outside would be still and quiet. But down in the town there'd be brightly lit shops, people jostling each other cheerfully on the pavements, their arms laden with gaily wrapped presents. Even in spite of the shortage of money, everyone managed something for Christmas.

Especially a Christmas like the one this promised to be. Snow and Christmas went together, Polly decided, glancing at the letter on the mantelpiece, and making up her mind. Snow, and Christmas, and *Harry* went together, and she'd post that letter if it was the last thing she did.

With Polly, to think was to act, and within five minutes she had written a note to Gatty in case she woke up, put the guard round the fire, found the clogs and wrapped her head and shoulders in a white shawl, tying it round the front of her red coat.

But when she stepped outside, the force of the snow-laden wind took her by surprise. It had sprung up since she went out earlier, and now the drifts seemed to be shifting, their surfaces rippled, as the tearing wind caught the snow and whirled it around with a wild and furious strength.

There was no need for her to go out. There were eggs and potatoes in the house, and they'd managed without milk before, but the letter was in her pocket, burning a hole, asking to be posted. And she was strong. Hadn't her beloved father teased her long ago when she grew taller and bigger than anyone else in her class – including the boys – that she'd turn out to be a lady blacksmith one day?

The blood in her veins was still singing from the euphoria she'd felt the day before. Gatty was safe. Nothing terrible was going to happen to her. Polly felt she could have turned east and climbed Pendle Hill without catching her breath. She was young. Well, a long way from being old anyway, and Harry *must* get her letter.

Somehow, they were all going to be together for Christmas. It had to be. She was going to *make* it be.

Within a few yards of the cottage she was covered in snow. It stung her eyelids and pricked at her face, and with head bowed she struggled on and found herself in a waist-high drift. Fighting her way out of it, she forced her way on to what she thought was the middle of the familiar rocky road down the steep hill, but it was no longer familiar. Even the dry-stone wall was covered, level with the path. She could no longer see, and it seemed as if the starkly white landscape had taken her and made her a part of it, without landmarks to guide her on her way.

Above her the sky was brooding, dark and heavy with the promise of yet more snow to come. Polly wished she had left a lamp lit for Gatty, and began to worry about leaving her alone in the cottage. A few stumbling steps on and her commonsense asserted itself. She had locked the door behind her and, besides, Jack Thomson was dead. He had to be dead. Not even Jack, with his inborn sense of survival, could have existed for long in conditions like these.

Sliding, gasping for breath, moving forward by instinct, she reached the little wood and here, partly sheltered by the trees, the snow was less deep. Polly's breath was a hurting pain in her chest. Opening her mouth for air it was immediately filled with stinging snow, as if directed at her by the fierceness of a jet. She coughed, spluttered, then grabbed at the shawl as the force of the wind tore it from her head.

Coming nearer to Bella's cottage, Polly felt a sense of such loneliness it was as though she'd been cut off from life itself. The loneliness of being on her own in the cottage had been a self-inflicted, full of practical worrying, frustrated kind of feeling. It even had an irrevocability about it. But this was something quite different. She stopped, panting, feeling a trickle of sweat down her back from her exertions, and stared at the ramshackle cottage.

Snow had changed its shabbiness into a thing of beauty. It was like a pretty little cottage on a Christmas card, all sloping roof and white frosted eaves. There should have been carol singers with lanterns held high in mittened hands, singing their hearts out, in a semi-circle. There should have been lamplight shining from the tiny windows, and a robin on the post at the gate.

The emptiness of the tiny cottage struck Polly's senses like a blow. The door was open, swinging on its hinges, buffeted by the wind. Snow had drifted inside, piling up in an obscene drift across the stone-flagged floor.

Stepping through it, calling out, although she knew there would be no answer, Polly walked slowly into the tiny living-room. The grate was black and empty, grey ashes of a spent fire scattered over the hearth. Caught in the tearing wind, the rocking-chair moved of its own volition. The once white American cloth on the table in the centre of the room was grey with dust, and on the shelves of the cupboard to the window side of the fireplace the few plates and cups left intact after Jack Thomson's last brainstorm stood huddled together in a pathetic display.

'Bella?' Polly's voice quavered in her throat. 'Bella? Where are you?'

Walking slowly towards the foot of the stairs, Polly called out again: 'Bella? Are you up there, love? Bella? It's me, Polly.'

Her heart was beating with dull, hard thumps. As she climbed the stairs her iron-rimmed clogs shattered the total silence. There was no handrail, only the flaking plaster on the walls at each side to hold on to as she stumbled. Downstairs in the living-room, the freezing cold air had swept the smell of neglect clean, but up here, at the top of the stairs, there was a strange sweet smell that made Polly wrinkle her nose.

Inside the bedroom it got worse. Holding her breath, Polly tiptoed over to the far wall where the blanket-lined drawer in which Bella's baby slept stood on an oak settle.

And he was in there, swaddled in blankets, covered up like a bundle of washing, only the shape telling what lay underneath.

It was a terrible thing to do, but Polly did it. The horror was there, in her mind, but she had to see for herself before she could accept it.

'Dear God,' she murmured, as her fingers tore at the coverings. 'Bella never did anything wrong to You. Why did You have to do this to her?'

There was the baby, his little tuft of ginger hair sticking up on top of his pointed head, the way it always did when Bella forgot to slick it down with water. Polly lifted a tiny hand, but it was hard and stiff, and the fingers didn't curl round her own as they always had. He was very pale, but the blue tinge had gone from round his mouth. Polly lifted him and held him, but his little body didn't bend into her own. Her tears fell on him as she gently laid him back, and she wiped them from his face with the hem of his flannelette nightie. She covered him up again and stood back from the makeshift cot, sobbing quietly, the white shawl slipping from her head and a lock of yellow hair falling over her forehead.

Where was Bella? Still crying, Polly turned and left the room.

The clatter of her clogs on the uncarpeted stairs seemed an affront to the dead. The white silence outside was more in keeping. Walking through the open door, Polly stood in the windswept, neglected garden, its neglect hidden by the all-enveloping carpet of thick snow.

'Bella?' Her voice was a scream tossed away by the wind, then something, an instinct barely acknowledged, told her to go round to the back of the cottage to where the old barn, its ancient timbers rotted, crouched against the dark skyline.

Polly pushed her way onwards, her feet sinking deep, the hem of her coat wet and sodden against her legs. And saw Bella. . . .

She was lying face downwards in a deep drift, just outside the old barn, her head on her spread arms as if she'd found it a comfortable way to sleep.

At first Polly thought she was alive, but when she turned her over gently she recoiled in horror. Bella's face, that thin peaked face of deprivation, had been chiselled by the frost into a mask of such ugliness that Polly turned her head, feeling the bile rise in her throat.

Bella's little hands were clenched into solid paws, as if she had just laid down defeated by her anguish, her waiting for Jack to return. Polly touched the rock hardness of them, kneeling down in the snow, leaning over the still form as if she would will warmth into it from her own body.

There had been no warmth in Bella's drab life. She had spent long days waiting and hoping, trying to bear the creeping suspicion that Jack was dead. She had seen her baby die, and she had crept out into the blizzard to die herself. Was that the way it had been?

'Oh, God! Dear God!'

Had Bella been lying there yesterday when Polly was urging Gatty up the hill, too obsessed by her own anxiety even to glance towards the cottage? Had she not cared enough? Tears flooded Polly's eyes, and she made no attempt to brush them away. Was Harry right? Was there no God looking down in His mercy on the Bellas of this world? Yet, wasn't He supposed to care even about the fall of a sparrow?

Polly knelt there, the sadness gradually erupting into a wild unreasoning anger. 'Hadn't Bella suffered enough? Did You have to take her baby from her?' she shouted to the empty, leaden sky.

With her baby dead, what was there left for Bella? She'd loved her home, that derelict shell of a home, with its sticks of furniture and her pots on the cupboard shelves. And she'd loved her husband. Right or wrong, she'd never wavered in her love for him. Polly went on kneeling there in the freezing cold, naked, raw and bleeding with the torment of her thinking.

In those moments she was Bella's mother, not her friend. All her maternal feelings, her compassion, her longing to protect, to guide those she loved rose to the surface of her emotions.

The sky was turning black. There was going to be another heavy fall. Tenderly, Polly leaned to wipe the snow from Bella's face, then stood up, swaying with grief.

And saw, through the open-ended back of the barn, Jack Thomson hanging from a beam, as frozen as washing put to dry on a line, tongue lolling, green eyes staring in a last awful grimace, staring at the ground from a head sunk forward on to his chest.

Polly screamed, and screamed again, and it was a terrible sound in all that white frozen wilderness, with no one near enough to hear.

— Eleven —

When the letter came addressed to Harry Pilgrim, Maureen, the maid-of-all-work at Mrs Cook's lodging house in Acton, picked it up from the mat inside the front door, held it to her nose and sniffed.

'April Violets, honest to God,' she told herself. What in the name of heaven was a quiet-spoken man like Mr Pilgrim doing getting a letter like that? It wasn't from a man, that much was sure, an' it wasn't from his wife back in Lancashire either. This letter had a London postmark, and the writing was different: slanting backwards and small with twirls on the g's and the y's. Maureen pressed it to her nose again, before taking it down to the basement kitchen.

Mrs Cook, having a bit of a rest now the early morning rush was over, turned the letter over and held it up to the light, narrowing her eyes into suspicious slits.

Maureen tried to be helpful. 'You'll not be seeing nothing through that envelope, Mrs Cook. The paper's as thick as me little finger. Shall we be giving it a whiff of steam from the kettle?'

'What an idea!'

There'd been nothing remotely interesting in the

232

letters from Lancashire. It hadn't been worth the bother of steaming them open. Besides, this one could probably be got at with a pencil, the paper being so thick. Mrs Cook got up from her chair, rose on to her toes, leaving her down-at-heel slippers behind, and propped the letter up in front of the clock on the mantelpiece.

'Mr Pilgrim can have it when he comes in; when he *condescends* to come in.' Sitting down in her chair once again, she folded her hands over the greasy apron stretched taut over her ample stomach. 'Mighty pleased with himself is our Mr Pilgrim at the moment. Ever since Norma Shearer called to ask after him last week.'

'She wasn't like Norma Shearer!' Maureen looked mortally wounded. 'Norma Shearer's eyes are much closer together. She was more like . . . more like Vivien Leigh.'

' 'An who's she when she's at 'ome?' Mrs Cook was in one of her rare good moods, and Maureen was eager to make the most of it.

'Mr Pilgrim winked at me last night. Honest to God, he did.' Over by the sink, she stared up through the basement window with as rapt an expression as if she was drinking in the beauty of a sunset. 'He's got lovely eyes. Dark brown and sad. Like Herbert Marshall's.' She turned round, clasping her apron up into a point in both hands. 'I saw Herbert Marshall at the second house pictures on Saturday night. In 'I Was a Spy', with Madeleine Carroll and Conrad Veidt.' All the passionate yearnings of Maureen's young dreams were in her voice. 'It was such a beautiful film, honest to God it was. It was about this Belgian nurse who, because she couldn't turn her back on the sick and suffering, felt she had to serve in a German hospital. Caring for *Germans*.' She opened

233

her eyes wide to emphasize the point. 'But she's a spy, and when they trap her . . . well, Herbert Marshall. . . .'

'Don't like 'im.' Mrs Cook jerked her head with its slipping bun towards the stairs. 'Smarms 'is hair back, an' smarmy hair means smarmy everything else, an' if you don't get up them stairs quick an' do what I pay you good money to do, there'll be no pictures for you this next Saturday, gel!'

Maureen took the stairs two at a time. She thought Mrs Cook could be right about Herbert Marshall's hair. Honest to God she hadn't thought about it like that before, but slicked back hair wasn't romantic. Not at all . . . Clark Gable was a real he-man, but even he had a little lock of black hair fallin' down over his forehead. An' Leslie Howard . . . but then his hair was fair an' it was the dark ones she liked best. Like Mr Pilgrim. . . .

Maureen started to trundle the carpet-sweeper over the threadbare carpet. He was a good looker all right with his jet-black hair tumbling over his forehead. Pity he hadn't more of a posh accent. He might've got taken on as a film star himself. He'd go well with Janet Gaynor, with her being so small and him not being all that big. The carpet-sweeper's brushes were caught in the frayed edge of the carpet. Bending down, Maureen struggled to release them. She was quite unaware of what she was doing. Her mind and her spirit had soared away from the drab monotony of her daily existence. She was there on the silver screen, luscious lips parted in ecstasy, as Mr Pilgrim, transformed into the Red Shadow, swept her up into his arms and carried her across the sand dunes into his tent, his black hair falling in neglected abandon over his tanned forehead.

'There's something rather attractive about a man who has a tan in winter. Sets him out from the herd.'

Yvonne held on to Harry's hand for longer than was necessary as she let him into her flat in the afternoon of the next day.

He had come in answer to her letter, arriving far too early and having to pass the time mingling with late-night shoppers in the crowded street. Standing in the doorway of a big store, he watched them pushing and jostling, carrying overtired toddlers and loaded down with parcels, women anxiously clutching lists, men over by the perfume counter having the stuff sprayed on their wrists by the counter assistants.

Harry shook his head from side to side. They just didn't grow girls like that back where he came from. Not girls with so much stuff on their faces it must have taken them an hour to put it on. Why, if a girl made up like that walked down the village street, people would think she was a prostitute! All that crayon drawing round the eyes, and rouge and lipstick. Not to mention the dyed hair. Harry moved closer to a counter to get a better view. As the girl leaned forward he could see the roots of her white-gold hair, as dark as the soot on a chimney-back.

'Can I help you, sir?' She was smiling at him, holding out a tiny scent bottle with a silver-meshed rubber bulb fastened to it. Before Harry could stop her, she had picked up his hand and squirted the stuff all over it. He recoiled as if he'd been stung by a bumble-bee, and wiped his hand down his trouser leg.

'How about buying a bottle for your wife? It's only ten and sixpence, sir.'

He gawped at her as if she'd suddenly come out with

a mouthful of swear words. 'Ten shillings and sixpence? For *that*? For that little drop in that little bottle?'

Shaking his head as he walked away, he thought about women back home who had to feed entire families on that much. Women down the market of a Wednesday or a Saturday, opening worn purses and weighing up in their minds whether they could run to a pound of oranges for the children, or a half pound of tomatoes to sprinkle with sugar for a Sunday teatime treat. He felt he'd been made a fool of, and thrust the scented hand deep into his pocket.

Five minutes later he was inside Yvonne's flat, seeing her smile at him with that trick she had of holding her head on one side, looking at him from beneath those incredibly long eyelashes.

'Nay. I'm more weather-beaten than tanned,' he told her seriously. 'When I die they'll be able to make a handbag out of the skin on my face.' He withdrew his hand from hers. 'And don't go getting the wrong idea about the way I smell, either. A young woman on the make-up counter in the store round the corner has just squirted me with the stuff.'

She was wearing something loose and floating in a delicate shade of blue. Harry couldn't make up his mind whether it was a dress or some sort of flimsy dressing-gown. Outside in the street the people were muffled up in scarves and top coats, but here in the flat the atmosphere was as warm as a hot-house, though the white marbled fireplace was filled not with leaping coals but a massive display of bronze and gold mop-head chrysanthemums.

'You said you had some news for me?' He sat down where she told him to, on a wide chesterfield covered in cream material, the cushions bound in the same soft

236

brown as the deep-pile carpet. 'My landlady had obviously opened your letter, so she'll be wondering what it is as well.'

Her dark uptilted eyes held the same affectionate amusement he remembered from their last meeting. He'd never considered himself to be much of a caution before, but Roger Craven's sister obviously found him as good as a music-hall turn. Harry felt his spirits rise. He couldn't get enough of watching her laugh. It made him feel ten feet tall. If she'd wanted him to, he would have stood on his head on the white fluffy rug at his feet and wiggled his toes.

'A drink, Harry?' She was holding up a jug so that the light from a standard lamp caught the crystal and set it winking. 'It's much too early of course, but we have a toast to drink.'

She came towards him with two glasses, handing one over, then sitting down beside him. The neck of whatever it was she was wearing was cut so low he could see the sweet hollow between her high, small breasts. He looked away, his face burning.

'Now I want you to listen, Harry. But first drink up and tell me if you like it.'

Leaning forward, she touched his glass with her own. Copying her, Harry drank deeply from the glass. 'Put some lead in me pencil, that will.'

Horrified at what he'd just said, Harry clapped a hand over his mouth. That was the sort of remark guaranteed to make Polly laugh. Man to wife sort of banter. And yet here he was behaving as naturally with this beautiful, sloe-eyed young woman as if he'd known her for a lifetime, gone to the same schools, and knowing nothing but the ease of money and the privileges that stemmed from a similar environment. It was because, he realized again, she had no silly snobbishness about her. She was like her brother had been. Totally at ease. With both the high and the low, as his mother used to say.

'Our Harry can mix with anybody. Both the high and the low. Comes of his Romany ancestry. There's never been a prouder man on this earth than a real true Romany.'

Yvonne was over by the drinks table again. 'In that case,' she was saying, 'you must have another one, Harry.' She wasn't offended, or shocked, and the knowledge that she found him witty stimulated him once more, till he felt equal to anything.

This time he sipped the drink slowly, savouring the smooth feel of it on his tongue and the pleasant burning sensation as it slid down his throat. 'Gin based?' he asked, and she nodded. 'Guaranteed to strip the bark off a tree, Harry.'

She took a cigarette from a silver box on the low table beside them, and at once he picked up the lighter standing next to it and flicked the flame into action.

'The good news,' she said, blowing out a stream of smoke, then remembering to waft it away from his face. 'I told you my parents had taken to you last Sunday. My father especially. You were with him a long time walking round the gardens and shut away in the greenhouses. Did it never occur to you to wonder why he was asking you so many questions?'

The drink was doing its work. 'He just needed putting right on one or two things. It's one thing being a keen gardener; it's another thing knowing the job inside out.'

'As you do, Harry?'

'As I do.' He put the glass down on the low table, frowning at it as if surprised to see it was half empty. He held out his hands, palms upwards. 'See these hands?' He touched his forehead. 'See this brain-box? Well, what I've got up here in me noddle is an untutored intelligence. That means that what I know hasn't come from studying textbooks and taking exams.' He grinned. 'Oh, I've read books on the subject. Dozens of 'em. But growing things is instinctive, lass. It's in the blood, like being able to write books or paint pictures is just something a person is born with or he isn't. An' I was born knowing how to garden. How to take a barren piece of land and make things grow on it.'

Suddenly he lifted the glass and drained it. 'An' they took that away from me! My mother-in-law wanted me to take on a job in a factory, if I was lucky enough to be offered one, but I couldn't, and I wouldn't. That's why I came down here, and here's where I'm going to stop till I get what I want!'

Leaning forward, so that the soft blue stuff of the robe she was wearing fell away again, Yvonne got up and went to refill his glass. Her eyes were very kind, black almost, in the softly shaded room.

'You're very sweet, Harry. I can see why Roger liked you so much.' She sighed and shook her head. 'He had the same proud dedication as you once.' Her voice was as warm as an embrace. 'And because you were his friend, and because he had you at the end, my parents feel they owe you a debt of gratitude. They want to pay you back, Harry.'

'I don't want no paying! Being with your brother at the end was all pain and sorrow, but it was *life*. He gave me far more than I gave him. He never lost his dignity, you know. Right to the end, when he was down as low as he could go, he was still a gentleman.' Harry nodded. 'In both senses of the word. A gentleman, and a gentle man.'

'Harry, listen.'

Stubbing out her cigarette, Yvonne looked deep into his eyes. They were very close together on the wide cushioned sofa, and he could see the faint down on her cheeks by her small ears, exactly like the bloom on a sun-kissed peach.

He started to tell her this, but she laid a hand gently over his mouth. '*Listen*, Harry. Will you listen to me, for Christ's sake!'

The blasphemy didn't shock him. Nothing she said or did in that moment could have shocked him. He smiled and felt his smile wobble at the edges.

'My father has a friend living a mile away. Lord Carson. The furniture people. You know?' Yvonne shook her head. 'Well, of course you don't know. How could you? But Jimmy Carson lives in a house set in acres and acres of ground. Part of it is landscaped, part of it kitchen garden, as well as miles of parkland, and all of it is neglected. The house itself is beautiful. Georgian red brick. I want you to *see* it, Harry. So take that silly grin off your face, close your eyes and bloody listen! There's a marble fountain in the middle of the lawn, and a row of monkey puzzle trees over to the far side. The Carsons had six daughters, all married now, but when they were little Roger and I used to go over and play with them, running wild in the gardens. They adored Roger. He was such a funny little tadpole of a boy when he was small.'

She gave Harry's arm a shake. 'You haven't gone to sleep? Right. Here comes the best part. The Carsons have a gardener, an old, old man, as ancient as Noah. He lived with his wife in a cottage on the edge of the estate, and last year she died. Since then the old man has deteriorated to the extent where he can no longer even trundle a barrow. Jimmy Carson couldn't turn the old chap out, he's not that sort, but recently they have persuaded him to go – at their expense – into a home. A good private home, Harry, where he can sit out the rest of his life in the sun, talking to his buddies. He was in the Boer War and his only son was killed on the Somme. He's like you'll be some day, when you're old and grey. You'll like him, Harry.'

'*I'll* like him?'

Opening his eyes, Harry looked at her for a long moment, doubtful, the dawning of something he daren't believe clouding his dark eyes. 'Am I going to meet him, then?'

'I hope so.' Her voice was very low and husky. 'You're to go and see them, Harry. Soon. Tomorrow. My father has convinced Lord Carson that you're the man he needs to pull that garden into shape. Hard work, Harry. Bloody hard work, and most of it on your own, because the house eats up most of the money. But there's the cottage for you and your family. All mod. cons with a bathroom upstairs. The old man never wanted the bathroom, but it's there. Waiting, Harry. All you have to do is go and see them, and if you talk to them like you talk to me, then the job's yours.'

He continued to stare at her for an endless moment. There was no sudden whoop of joy, no shout of triumph. Instead his eyes filled with tears, and in them she saw reflected all the anguish of the last months, the disappointments, the insults, the fearing that hope was gone. In his dark eyes was the picture of the man he was, the man who could grow seeds from lumps of granite, a man who had only asked to work at the job he had been born to do.

'It's true, Harry.' She kissed him gently. 'Miracles
241

don't happen, but this one has. And now you must love me. Because I need you. You must come with me now, and you must hold me close. Because I'm scared, Harry. I go away soon and I'm scared, and you were Roger's friend, so that makes it all right.'

When he stood up his head swam, but he allowed her to take him by the hand. The bedroom was all white and pink, and the sheets smelled of roses. Harry's clothes seemed to fall away from him, and she knew no shyness as she stood before him, small and perfectly formed, the light from a street lamp outside in the street silvering her skin.

As they lay close together in the wide bed, he felt the joy of what she had just told him sing through his veins. The feel of her smooth skin was almost more than he could bear. But it was she who guided him into their loving, until with a sigh he forgot everything as their bodies merged and became one.

'Be happy, Harry,' she whispered, as they lay spent of passion at long last. 'You're a lovely, lovely man, and the nicest thing about you – *one* of the nicest things about you – is that you don't know it.' Raising herself on an elbow, she stared down into his troubled face. 'There. You're regretting it already, aren't you, darling?'

'I am not!'

She smiled into his troubled eyes. 'I know you, Harry Pilgrim.' Her voice was teasing. 'You haven't exactly been in the habit of doing this in the late afternoon, have you? Not with someone you hardly know.'

'I feel I've known you for ever and a day,' he whispered, but she saw the shadow on his face.

'Nothing is spoilt, Harry. Nothing. I'm not a marriage breaker, for all my faults, and God knows there are plenty.' She sighed. 'This is our secret, yours and mine.

242

I needed to be loved, and I think I'm right in saying that you needed me just as much.'

She slid out of bed, not bothering to take the sheet with her, picking up the blue silk robe and trailing it behind her. 'I'm going to take a bath. Want to join me?'

'Later,' he said, and she turned and saw the colour flood his face.

When she'd left the white and pink room he lay still. As he closed his eyes, he had a sudden fleeting vision of Polly, toiling up the hill in her red coat, loaded with shopping, a scarf covering the glory of her yellow-gold hair.

Polly found the letter she had written to Harry deep in the pocket of her scarlet coat, creased and forgotten, where it had lain for two days.

'Would you like me to take it down to the post office, Mam?' Gatty spoke quickly, as she saw the look of desolation on her mother's face. 'I can easily go down to the village and back now the worst of the snow has melted. They've had the snow ploughs out, and dad might just get it before Christmas. They always tell you to post early to make people write their cards in time.'

'It's too late.'

Polly was downstairs for the first time in three days. The only other times she had taken to her bed had been when her children were born, and even then she'd rebelled against the two weeks' lying-in time thought necessary after childbirth.

The chill she'd caught after her struggle through the snowdrifts, culminating in the discovery of the horrors down at Bella's cottage, had left her weak and lethargic.

It had faded the fresh colour in her cheeks and dulled the bright blue of her eyes.

'All right, then, take it if you want to,' she said. 'It'll do you good to get out for a while.' Polly looked at her daughter, her chin quivering. 'Thank you, love, for looking after me. If the buses are running, go into town if you like. Go to the shop and see Winnie. She must be worried sick about you. Go and see your grandma and tell her I'm expecting her on Sunday. With Martin.'

'Sunday's Christmas Eve, Mammy.'

Gatty used the childish name without thinking. It had seemed to her, as her mother lay feverish in her bed, staring endlessly at the ceiling, that the events of the past few days had turned her mind. Refusing to eat, only drinking when Gatty held the cup to her lips, Polly had looked at her through pain-dazed eyes, shivering one minute and throwing the blankets off the next. Once or twice, during the night, she had cried out in terror, and Gatty had crept into bed beside her, holding her mother's burning body in her arms, their roles reversed, as she took on herself the position of protector.

'Is there any money?' she asked now.

Polly nodded listlessly at the biscuit barrel on the mantelpiece, and Gatty took out the two pound notes and tried to speak briskly.

'I'll get some shopping, Mam. I know what to get.' She lifted the blanket on the settee drawn up to the fire. 'Have a nice lie-down. I'll be back at dinnertime. Try and sleep. You'll feel better if you have a nice sleep.'

Polly nodded, and did as she was told. Before Gatty had closed the door of the cottage behind her, she was asleep, as suddenly and completely as a new-born baby.

She was struggling through the steep snow. She was holding Bella's dead baby in her arms, all stiff and cold. He was looking up at her with staring green eyes, but they weren't his eyes. They were Jack Thomson's eyes, bulging from their sockets. He was coming towards her with his slow, swaying plod, walking on the balls of his feet, and round his thick neck the mark of a rope stood out clearly.

Bella was there too, pointing an accusing finger, her features rock solid and unmoving in the grotesque mask of her frozen face.

Now Polly could see them advancing against a backdrop of trees, and a sky lost in a whirling flurry of snowflakes. Suddenly it was no longer Bella, but Gatty, and the baby Polly was holding in her arms looked like Harry. So where was Bella? And if that was Gatty, why was her face as hard and cold as marble when her mother reached out to touch it?

From behind Polly a huge white branch came cracking down from a tree, and she screamed and screamed . . . and screamed. . . .

There was a loud knocking in her ears. Polly opened her eyes, stretched them wide and saw a log burning in the hearth where it had dropped from the fire. Pushing the blanket aside she stood up, then steadied herself on the end of the sofa as the floor seemed to rise up and smack her between the eyes.

The screaming in her ears had stopped, but the knocking was still there, loud and persistent. A heavy sob broke from her as she dragged herself to the door, drew back the catch of the lock and opened it wide.

He was there, Robert, standing outside, etched against the grey and windless morning, with a pale sun behind him hanging sombrely over the larch and rowan trees in the far distance.

Stepping inside, he reached for her. 'I'm here, little love. Shush. . . shush. . . shush. . . .' Over her shoulder he saw the pillow and the blanket on the sofa. His face was very close to hers, watching her carefully, willing her to calmness. 'You were dreaming, sweetheart. I heard you call out. But it's all right now. I'm here, and there's nothing to be afraid of.'

Gently but firmly he rocked her backwards and forwards, soothing, whispering words of comfort, and only when she stopped trembling did he lead her back to the sofa, tucking the blanket round her, trying to hide his dismay at the sight of her white, pinched face.

'I'm sorry,' she kept repeating. 'Sorry . . . sorry . . . sorry. . . .'

At last the tears came, the first tears she had shed since her terrible discovery three days before. He sat down beside her, smoothing the hair back from her forehead. He gave her his handkerchief, told her to blow, then watched without speaking as her eyelids drooped over tired blue eyes and she sank into a sleep so much needed, he guessed, it was more like a small dying.

Outside all was silence, the weak sunshine dappling the great oak tree. Robert sat without moving as one hour passed, then another. He relived the minute when he had opened last night's paper and seen the shouting black headlines: 'Triple tragedy in lonely cottage.' His heart had palpitated madly as he'd read further. 'The bodies were found by a Mrs Pilgrim, a thirty-three-year-old married woman, who had struggled through waist-high snowdrifts in the long shadow of Pendle Hill to report her findings to the village police sergeant.'

Only his commonsense had prevented him setting off

there and then to walk the miles in the dark to her. He had gone into the office, tried to work, found it impossible and had walked out, leaving his colleagues staring after him in amazement.

She woke at noon, blinking up at him like a child, trying to smile, her frayed nervous system reaching for some sort of normality. He let her talk, listened to her account of how it had been, watching her all the time with his pale grey eyes.

There was a pan of soup on the hob, and he pushed the trivet over the coals, lifted the lid and stirred it round. He ladled some into a bowl and made her drink it, seeing the colour come back to her cheeks and the blue marks round her mouth fade away.

He made up the fire, went outside for logs, let the dog out, bathed her face, helped her across the cinder path to the privy and waited for her to come out before guiding her gently back into the cottage. There was no embarrassment in what he was doing for her, no revulsion on his part. When her stomach rejected the soup, he held her head, wiped the sweat from her brow, brought water and bathed her face. Some of the vomit had gone down the front of her nightdress, so he went upstairs, rummaged in a drawer for a clean one, lifted the soiled one over her head, sponged her body, lowered the clean linen over her head, buttoned the row of tiny pearl buttons, then took her brush and tidied her hair.

For yet another hour Polly slept, and this time when she awoke Robert knew she was much better.

'What a time to get 'flu,' she whispered. 'Just before Christmas.'

He didn't ask her any questions about Harry. The time for questions wasn't yet.

'It won't always be dark at three,' she told him. The

247

light was there in her blue eyes again, and he knew she would survive.

'I'm going now to meet Gatty from the bus,' he told her, 'and if she's loaded with shopping I'll help her up the hill. If not, I'll go home and come again tomorrow. You're not going to get rid of me as easily as that.'

'Oh, Robert. . . .' She held out her hand and he took it, and as before she felt his strength flow between them. 'You're a good man,' she whispered.

'I wouldn't bank on that. I've been on my best behaviour today!' He grinned, raised his hand and was gone, closing the door behind him with a soft click of the lock.

Although the snow had partly thawed, it still lay in patches as far as the eye could see across the bleak and undulating moorland to the east. The wind came from the east too, whistling with an icy touch down from the great hill of Pendle. Shivering, Robert turned up his collar awkwardly with his one hand as he slid down the rocky steep path to the village.

His ears were freezing, his nose dripped, and his eyes watered with the cold, but there in the little main street a red telephone box afforded him shelter as he waited for the bus to come up from the town.

Acting as nursemaid to Polly during the long quiet hours of the winter's day had lifted a curtain on his memories. Just as he had sat with Polly, so he had sat with his wife Jean towards the end of her life. Patiently he had sat there, waiting for the moment when she would open her eyes in her brief moments of wakefulness. He recalled how she'd smiled at him before drifting away from him, and he remembered how the world outside had almost ceased to exist during that last week.

Could it be that he was still feeling bereft without the

feeling of responsibility? Had Polly filled that need? He knew for certain that her dependence on him was a temporary thing. She had guts, and courage, and once her weakness had passed she would be her own self again, ready to challenge the world, and fight it if need be.

Polly Pilgrim wasn't his. And another thing – did he really want her to be?

His sister-in-law Nellie was 'speaking' to him again. Her olive branch had taken the form of a batch of her light-as-a-feather scones, and although she would never apologize for her rudeness to Polly, Robert knew she regretted her behaviour.

The closed-in atmosphere of the telephone booth was stifling. In his concern for Polly, he hadn't eaten all day. He had to get out into the air, but even as he pushed at the heavy door to open it, he saw the bus from the town trundling round the corner.

There were only three people getting off it. A woman festooned with parcels who hurried away in the opposite direction, Gatty, and a man of average height, hatless in spite of the cold, dressed in a brown jacket and carrying a suitcase.

Robert guessed who he was immediately, even before he saw the way Gatty clung to his arm, laughing and talking nineteen to the dozen. Father and daughter, flesh of the same flesh, so much alike they might have been brother and sister.

Stepping back instinctively into the telephone booth, Robert pulled the brim of his trilby lower over his forehead, turning his back as they came towards him.

There was no need to hide. Lost to everything but each other, they walked by, on past the grey stone cottages and the tiny general store, turning eager faces towards the hill, and home.

Robert waited until they'd walked out of sight before leaving his shelter, then he ran on his long, grasshopper legs to where the bus had already turned, ready for its journey back into town.

He was happy for Polly, and at the same time sorry for himself. His feelings were contradictory and alien to his normal habit of straightforward thinking.

'A single all the way,' he said, sitting down on the seat by the door, a man who had thought he was in charge of his own destiny, and now wasn't too sure.

As soon as Robert had gone, Polly did what she called 'pulling herself together'. The long day of sleeping had left her refreshed, and although her legs felt like rubber, she told herself she was better, much better.

A product of her mother's strict upbringing, she felt out of place and uneasy downstairs in her nightdress. Only soppy women slopped about like this. Either you were in bed ill, or you were up and doing. On your two feet. There was no in between.

Christmas was almost here. There were a thousand and one things to do. Gatty had been marvellous, but now Polly was at the helm again. Taking her time, she dragged herself wearily upstairs and started to dress.

Harry would get the letter in time. She felt it in her bones. And if he didn't come home, she would take the last of the money out of the savings bank after Christmas was over, leave Martin with her mother, Gatty with Winnie, and the dog . . . well, Mrs Bebson at the post office would have him, once Polly convinced her that

Jim would be more scared of her cat than the other way round.

If Harry was ill, or if he was in any kind of trouble, then she would see for herself. Enough was enough. Living like this was no good.

But without Harry, what sort of a Christmas was it going to be?

Slowly, holding on to the banister, Polly went downstairs again. It would have to be eggs again for tea, and she'd eat one even if it choked her. Strength was what she was going to need in the next few days. Strength, determination and hope. All three.

The floor was undulating beneath her feet, but she told it to be still. She was in charge once again, and that was all that mattered. Holding on to the table for support, whimpering with weakness, she reached up to the dresser shelf for a blue bowl and began to crack three brown-speckled eggs into it.

'You go on, Dad,' Gatty drew back as they passed Bella's cottage, averting her gaze from the bracken-grey of it, trying not to see the way it seemed to have sunk even lower into the frost-trimmed long grasses. 'I'm not frightened. There's nothing to be afraid of now. You go on, and I'll follow slowly.' Her small face was serious and intense. 'I want you to tell mam yourself. I want the two of you to be together. Just for a little while.'

'You're sure, love?' Harry hesitated, but nodding her head Gatty urged him on.

'Go on, Dad. Hurry! Please. . . .'

So, striding forward, Harry Pilgrim made his way home. In front of him, the great mass of Pendle Hill no longer green as on the September morning he had seen it last, merged into the swiftly falling darkness. The trees at its foot were as black as pitch, its gullies were clothed in purple, as the fading light crept over the snowy slopes. His heart beat wildly as he began to run, his feet slipping on the stones, shiny from the ice beneath the hard-packed snow.

Long before he reached the cottage his key was in his hand, and when he stepped inside he saw her spreading the cloth over the table in the way he remembered so well. In the next minute, the dog was leaping up to greet him and she was in his arms.

She was thinner than before, but her eyes were still as blue, her smile as warm. He kissed her, then held her from him, suddenly uncertain, the past months of their mutual frustrations and agonies coming between them.

He told her quickly, the words tumbling from him as he pressed his cold face against hers.

'There's a cottage, love. Only three up and two down, but with a bathroom built on the back.' His voice rose in a shout of triumph. 'Hot water, love! At the turn of a tap, with a back-boiler behind the fire. A good grammar school for Martin not far away, and a good train service into London for Gatty if she wants to work in Oxford Street.' He shook her gently, as if forcing her to believe him. 'It's true, love! Don't cry. I know it's a miracle, but they do happen sometimes, and one's happened for us.'

'It's a long story, Polly, but this one has a happy ending. I told you about the man, the friend I made in my lodgings?'

'You told me hardly anything.' Polly traced the outline of his mouth, running her fingers over his face as if she could hardly believe it was real.

'I've never been much of a letter writer.' He led her

over to the settee, and they sat down, arms around each other, smiling into each other's eyes. 'It's all on account of him. On account of his family.' For a moment a shadow crossed his lean dark face, then was gone so swiftly Polly thought she must have imagined it.

'Oxford Street?' Polly whispered. 'Our Gatty working in Oxford Street? She'll be over the moon.'

'She's changed, love. We met at the bus stop, and she never stopped talking.'

'We've all changed, Harry.' Polly looked at him soberly. 'You've changed, too.'

'In what way?' Suddenly he was on the defensive.

'You've got your confidence back.' Her blue eyes teased. 'You talk like a southerner already. Like you've got a hot potato in your mouth.'

'I never.'

'I like it.' She laid her head on his shoulder. 'Tell me what it's like, love. Paint a picture for me.'

'Well . . .' he thought for a moment, 'well, for a start, it's warmer. The snow's all gone, and when it came it was no more than a thin coating on the ground. Folks don't look as *tossed*, Polly, love. Not where we're going to live. It's right out in the country, but the trees are softer somehow. Beech trees mainly, and the way things grow!' He held out his hands. 'Work. Oh, but there'll be plenty of that. Yon garden's in a right mess. He's a lord, Polly, the man I'll be working for. All white whiskers and a clipped way of talking. He wondered if you'd give his wife a hand up at the house?'

'I had it in mind to be a secretary,' Polly smiled, 'but I might consider. Till something better comes along.'

They kissed again, then rocked together, smiling, excited, as happy as children.

253

'Your mother?' he asked her. 'How do you think she'll take us going away?'

'Badly.' Polly was honest. 'But she'll be happy for us.' She contradicted herself. 'Well, she won't be happy, but she'll make the best of it. You know mam.'

'She can come and see us.'

Polly smiled. 'Oh, she'll like that. Having a son-in-law working for a lord, and living down south. She might even come to terms with you.'

'Oh, Polly. . . .' Harry stared into the fire, his eyes suddenly serious. 'It was like coming back into another world, coming back up here. Seeing the groups of unemployed men on the Boulevard when I got off the train.' He sighed. 'Oh, there's a depression down there, but not like up here. They've no idea, Polly. They see the figures in the papers, but they don't understand. We've been given another chance, love. We're the lucky ones. But up here they have to go on, day after day searching for work, even when all hope is gone. We mustn't ever forget them. Or ever forget that this is where our roots lie. We're Lancastrians, Polly, and will be till the day we die.'

For a quiet, inarticulate man, he wasn't doing too badly. Polly's blue eyes were gentled with laughter as she saw the change finding the right kind of work had wrought in him. And there was something else . . . something she couldn't put her finger on.

There was a lot more to be said. But there were secrets that would remain secrets for ever. Creating not a rift between them, but a better understanding. She knew that and accepted it. All that mattered was that they were together again.

Bringing the cold wind in with her, Gatty burst into the cottage, saw the two heads close together, one so fair and the other so dark. Pretending disdain, she humped the shopping-bag on to the table.

'Well,' she said, 'if nobody else looks like shaping up, then I suppose Mrs Muggins'll have to make the tea!'

Stretching his legs contentedly over his own hearthstone, Harry beamed on them both. 'Now I *know* I'm home,' he grinned. 'Get the kettle on, our Gatty. Your old dad's spittin' feathers!'

A Selection of Arrow Bestsellers

ARROW BOOKS, BOOKSERVICE BY POST, PO BOX 29, DOUGLAS, ISLE OF MAN, BRITISH ISLES

NAME ....

ADDRESS ....

....

....

Please enclose a cheque or postal order made out to Arrow Books Ltd. for the amount due and allow the following for postage and packing.

U.K. CUSTOMERS: Please allow 22p per book to a maximum of £3.00.

B.F.P.O. & EIRE: Please allow 22p per book to a maximum of £3.00.

OVERSEAS CUSTOMERS: Please allow 22p per book.

Whilst every effort is made to keep prices low it is sometimes necessary to increase cover prices at short notice. Arrow Books reserve the right to show new retail prices on covers which may differ from those previously advertised in the text or elsewhere.